BLACK
THE
TIDES

K. A. WIGGINS

SNOWMELT
& STUMPS

FOR THE ONES WHO KEEP RIGHT ON TRYING.

LILY

I'M STUCK IN a loop, trying not to look at the ghost of a girl with golden curls and hazel eyes.

I've been here before. I know what's coming next.

Shadows skitter across her face, darken and split the skin. Her childish features contort in a scream. Darkness wells in the corners of her milky eyes and spills down her cheeks in a continuous inky stream.

She smiles, slow and empty.

"We're coming."

Then the nightmare repeats.

I'VE SPENT MOST of my life (at least the parts of it I remember) believing I was haunted.

It turns out I was—by my past self. Cadence is the remnant of everything I once was, before the loss of our parents and reprogramming by the not-so-benevolent Towers of Refuge stripped me of knowledge, identity, and purpose.

But as far as disembodied spirits go, she's pretty tame. At least her pestering ways never gave me screaming nightmares.

"Again, Cole?" Ange stands beside my cot, knuckling sleep out of her eyes. I'm still not used to seeing her face so bare—down here, there's no need for extravagant makeup nor the shielding illusion of protection provided by masks.

Her long-lost twin peeks around her shoulder, terrified the dream-eating Mara are going to descend at any moment. Amy still hasn't gotten used to the idea they can't venture this far below the surface. The depths belong to other monsters. And good old-fashioned nightmares, evidently.

I summon up my best "protector-of-the-people" smile. She doesn't look reassured.

My hair is matted with sweat, my sheets twisted too tight here, trailing off the cot there. Blood darkens the bandages where I've reopened at least one of far too many gashes. They're not healing well. Wading through viscera after being torn by jagged bone and crumbled tile turns out to be less than ideal, but no one said I had to *look* heroic.

Ange sighs and heads for her supply shelf, Amy scurrying in her wake. They were separated for like a decade, or so I've heard, and I'm sure there's a story there, but Ash and Cadence have been so busy catching up it's hard for anyone else to get a word in edgewise.

Speaking of which—"Did you see it that time?"

"Nope," Cadence says. "Yet again, nightmareless. What a shame. Feeling so left out. Boo."

Pest. "Shouldn't you have?"

"Dunno. Probably. Ask Ash when he wakes up."

I consider reaching over to the next cot to thump him with a pillow. He'd be fine with it—to him, I'm an old childhood friend—and Cadence would only laugh. But, despite their best efforts, I just can't let myself give in and fall into their pace.

Besides, he needs his sleep. He seems to be healing faster than I am, but he was pretty beat up to begin with. Getting tortured by a monster will do that. The sooner he recovers, the sooner we can make sure nothing like that ever happens again, to anyone.

The three of us—if you count Cadence and me separately—are all that stands between humanity and the bottomless hunger of the Mara. There are thousands of people living in Refuge alone, and Ange says there are hundreds more hidden in the tunnels down here, too. Not to mention who knows how many outcasts who somehow cling to survival outside, despite flooding, toxic fog, Refuge raids, and, of course, the dream-eating Mara.

Ash groans and rolls over. He blinks. A slow smile takes over his face.

I hate it. He's always so happy to see me.

Except when he looks at me, he sees her. Cadence. *His Cady.*

They were kids together. He came to save her. Instead, he found me.

Whatever. It's fine. He and Cadence can chat in the dreamscape all they want. The important thing is we all get back in fighting shape and save the city before it's too late.

The memory of the nightmare's whispered warning—*We're coming*—sends a chill up my spine.

Ash stifles a yawn to peer up at me. "What's wrong?"

"She had another nightmare," Cadence says. "She wants to know if you saw it, too. I didn't. I had a lovely dream about marshmallows. When was the last time you roasted marshmallows?"

"Man, it's been ages! First thing when we get back, we'll have to get everyone together for a roast. Rei started this challenge where we see how many we can stack in one bite, not that he needs the sugar, and then Hatif—"

And they're off. Again. I roll my eyes and swing my legs out over the cold concrete floor. They keep darting off on tangents about things I don't understand and people I don't remember. To be fair, Cadence did try to share the memories once they started coming back to her. They just didn't take, I guess. They're like stories someone has told me, faint shadows in comparison to the vividness and depth of real things. Or, at least real-to-me things, I guess.

Like that nightmare . . .

Anyway, I'm more interested in the here and now. I've got better things to do than reminisce. There's another whole layer of civilization down here in Under, people building and creating and, well, perhaps not thriving, but doing so much more than just clinging to life in these dark tunnels.

Ange has been bringing in her artisans to show us their creations. They craft wonders from repurposed materials scavenged from the ruins above ground and destined for Refuge's secretive upper echelon of Superiors or the pleasure of Freedom's hedonistic denizens.

Engineers bring hand sized models of machines they claim to have built to harness the waves and create light and warmth, not only for the comfort of those living down in these tunnels, but to fuel subterranean growing rooms and produce the odd, colourless food they seem to prefer to nutrient fluid. Considering Refuge has been drugging their own people's food supply, I can't fault Under's people for avoiding anything that even bears a passing resemblance to Noosh.

At first, I watch this parade of odd performances without comment, not sure what to do with all the information these strangers offer up so eagerly. Is this Under's version of Refuge's training floor? Do they expect me to pick a new job or something?

Not much use for a surveillance technician down here, sure, but now that I can fight the Mara, shouldn't protecting them keep me busy enough for the foreseeable future? Just how much does Ange expect of me?

While I stew in resentful silence, Ash comes up with seemingly endless thoughtful questions and insightful observations. Apparently, Nine Peaks—where he and Cadence are from—is a hotbed of agricultural, artisanal, and engineering innovation, based on the reactions of Ange's people. Though he keeps them talking longer than I'd like, I find much of it interesting despite myself. So many things I'd never considered or imagined.

When I can manage to sit up for more than five minutes without my head spinning, Ange even has some of her people help take me on tours of the workshops and growing rooms and dwellings tucked into small offshoots of the main tunnels. But it takes Cadence's "they're trying to impress you, stupid," to figure out why she's going to the trouble of educating me.

She's putting me on display, and at the earliest opportunity, sending me out on parade.

Everywhere I go Ange's people drop what they're doing to follow and stare openly. But it's a good kind of staring, even if it is uncomfortable. They're warm, friendly, interested and interesting. They believe I'm going to usher in a new era, destroying their enemies and lifting these people out of hiding to rejoin a transformed, united Refuge.

They're absolutely right. I've got to get back to fighting form. I finally know what I'm meant to do and who I'm meant to be. There's no time for hanging around feeling sorry for myself.

I wallow my way off the bed, ignoring the sharp protests of too many cuts and bruises. I manage a couple of staggering steps before the room goes wavy. I snatch at the curtain dividing the cots from Ange's workspace, tipping dangerously before I snag enough fabric to keep me upright.

"I don't think so." Ange snakes an arm around my waist. She hauls me back to bed and plants her forearm across me, pinning me down when I protest. "Did I say you could get up?"

"'You're not the boss of me, lady.' C'mon, say it." Cadence laughs.

Ash just looks worried. He's up on one elbow as if to come after me, but he's gone pasty under the silvery sheen that constantly swirls over his skin, and his lips are set against the pain. The light of his magic gutters in his eyes, a bare flicker of what it should be.

I ought to apologize—to him, to Ange, to all the people waiting for me to get back on my feet and save them. I settle for staring at a stain on the ragged curtain cordoning off our cots while Ange roughly changes the dressings I've gone and made a mess of.

"There's someone here to meet you. Behave yourself." She gives the bandages a thwack to signal she's finished. Or maybe as punishment—I never really know with her.

She has good reason to be angry, even to hate me. It's my fault her partner, Cass, got killed. And, it turns out it was also my fault her sister was nearly tortured like Ash. I first encountered Amy as Morristu in Refuge, when I hid like a coward and let her take the fall for me.

It seemed like the only thing to do at the time, but I can pretty much say that about everything that's happened over the last few months. Doesn't make any of it right. So whatever Ange wants from me, whatever she needs me to do here, it's hers to ask.

Amy sidles into the makeshift infirmary.

"We've met," Cadence says drily.

Ash nods. Ange glances at him, caught off guard. She can't hear Cadence. Neither can Amy, who seems to take his gesture as encouragement. She beckons to someone on the far side of the curtain.

A small girl darts into the room and lunges at Ash. I cry out at the sight of my nightmare come to life. He catches the child, groaning a little at the pain.

"You're hurt," she says in a piping, unfamiliar voice.

Her curls are wilder and several shades darker than the girl in my nightmares, her irises the same hazel, but set in a delicate face with light brown skin. Amy rushes forward, but the child just twitches free of her pawing and nuzzles Ash before peeking over his shoulder at me.

"Auntie Ange said you saved my Ash and I should say thank you but I won't—it was your fault he came here in the first place—so instead I'll say 'nice to meet you' because daddy says you should greet people like that for the first time, and I've never met you before and it all cancels out so I won't say thank you." She pauses for a dramatically ragged gasp before continuing, "So, nice to meet you, Cady."

"*Daddy?*" Amy says.

"Lily!" Ange says.

"Um," I say.

Cadence just laughs.

"Oh, right. I'm Lily," the child says, reaching over Ash to extend a tiny hand in my direction. "Ash's partner."

"Lily, get down!" Ange clamps a hand around the child's neck and tugs.

Lily fastens herself tighter to Ash. He looks decidedly gray under the onslaught of careless knees and elbows.

"Just shake the kid's hand already!" Cadence sputters.

I grab Lily's outstretched hand and yank her off Ash. He slumps back onto the pillows, his mouth twisted in a grimace of pain, or maybe suppressed laughter. It's hard to tell. I focus on the child instead.

"Call me Cole. And maybe go easy on Ash, he's still recovering."

Lily shakes my hand with great concentration. Then she grins. "He'll be fine. He's magic! He said you're magic, too. Real strong magic."

"I like her," Cadence says. "Reminds me of me."

I glance at Ash over Lily's head. Tears roll down his cheeks; his shoulders shake, lips pinched to hold back the laughter. Ange has one hand over her eyes. Amy stares longingly at the child, oblivious to all else.

"So, can you save daddy now, too?" Lily asks.

The room goes silent, the air heavy, pressing down on me with the welcome weight of purpose.

I slide out of bed, still holding Lily's hand, ignoring Ange's sound of protest. "That's what I'm here for."

POWERLESS

I'D FORGOTTEN HOW lonely Freedom could be in the daytime.

Shattered tiles and fallen-in ceilings clutter barren, shadowy halls. Ange says it still comes alive at night, the club-goers' desperation to escape the grinding dullness of their lives for a few hours enough to bring them creeping back to risk a very final escape at the rending talons of the Mara.

If they were here now, this place would be lit up with spinning lights and shaking with throbbing beats, the air alive with the threads of the dancers' every dream and desire, their desperate longings beacon and bait to the ravenous nightmares.

But soon the Mara won't be the only hunters stalking these halls. I'll be waiting for them—maybe even as early as tonight.

I hope.

"I won't tell, if that's what you're worried about," Cadence says. She's just as eager as I am to get back to the fight. Eager enough to sneak out at the earliest opportunity.

We left Ash sleeping, with Lily dozing at his side and Amy nodding off in a nearby chair. Ange was out for the day, busy running the hidden collective and silent resistance that occupies a portion of the tunnels miraculously spared from the floods.

Ange thinks I need more time to heal, but it's not like I fight with my feet. My hands are working just fine. I should be able to seize the threads of desire and longing that unwittingly call to the monsters and weave the Mara's mortal prey to safety without any trouble.

Ash wants me to wait until he's back in fighting form, but it wasn't him that beat back the Mara in the first place. I can do this with or without him—and it's past time I stop waiting for other people to take care of the hard stuff.

I can make my own decisions now, and choose a path for myself. Though, to be honest, I could use more practice at it. One of the worst things Refuge did to me—and it messed with me plenty over the years—was insisting on unquestioning obedience. Turns out, shutting off your brain and learning to suppress everything you need or want is only good for the people who want to control you.

I'm done being controlled.

"Took you long enough," Cadence says, without a hint of sarcasm.

She never used to be able to listen in on every thought. Or, at least she never let on she could. Lately, she's been busy enough chattering away with Ash to leave me in peace. But out here, there's no one to entertain her but me.

Lucky me.

"You don't have to be rude about it. Besides, it's not like I want to be stuck with you, either."

I trace patterns in the dirt to avoid dwelling on our warped reality. It was a shock to discover we're the same person. Except, we're obviously not. We don't think, or act, or talk alike at all—

"And thank goodness for that," Cadence says. "You're so boring, even when you're not."

—So we basically went back to normal. I pretend she's a ghost and she pretends not to be mad I exist—

"I'm not mad. I just think I'd have done a better job if I were the one walking around."

"You'd have got us killed in the first week."

"Like you did so much better. 'Ooh, I'm so obsessed with corpses, look at me all angsty and conflicted.'"

"It was a confusing time! And you weren't exactly helping."

"I helped plenty. Without me, you'd never have held on to your sanity. You'd either be a mindless drone, or Mara-chow."

"I almost was because of you!"

"Whatever."

I pick up my pace as if I can outrun her. It's chilly and damp down here without a roomful of sweating bodies warming the place up. The air smells sour. I'm worried Ange will smell Freedom on my clothes, until I remember there'll be no hiding it from her anyway. Not when I show up with Lily's dad in tow.

"You're gonna be in trouble," Cadence singsongs.

My feet hurt. I shouldn't stomp, but rage helps keep me warm and moving. All those lives lost to the Mara, both in these halls and in all the floors layered above them . . .

The girl in my nightmares—Suzannah Bell—wasn't the first Mara-taken I've ever seen, but she was the first I've encountered in the dreamscape. I met her there after she'd died, which shouldn't have been possible. Maybe that's why I keep reliving her final moments. Or maybe it's that she was so young—at least, the dream-version of her was.

Just the thought of kids getting hurt makes me choke up like nothing else. I had to fight not to cry in front of Lily when she asked me to save her dad. Which I will do—

"We'll do," Cadence says.

—Just as soon as *we* can. And then, after we save him, we'll save everyone else.

Despite the dank atmosphere, it feels so good having a plan. Tonight, after a quick-and-easy rescue mission to retrieve Lily's dad, will be step one: chase the Mara from Freedom once and for all. Step two: clear them out of Refuge. Step three: save the rest of the city.

"You know they won't just wait nicely for you to come end them, right? They can go through walls."

"We have to start somewhere." Plus, apparently there are other monsters outside. Turns out, the Mara aren't the only thing that haunts this city.

"Just saying, your strategy sucks."

"You want to go back, have a little planning session with Ash and Ange?" I can practically hear Cadence pouting. "Didn't think so. So maybe keep that snark to yourself."

———— ※ ————

GETTING TO THE exits isn't the hard part. I used to be a surveillance technician. I've seen the maps.

But I've never actually gone outside, not unless you count that time I climbed up to Refuge's roof. Or the time I got sucked into the dreamscape and walked the desperate streets living the miserable life of one of those clinging to life outside through her own eyes. I'm more than a little curious to see what it feels like to experience the rest of the city in my own skin, especially now that I know how to protect myself.

However, despite all the dreary hours I spent as a drone in Refuge staring at floor plans on a screen, I get turned around more than once. Turns out, when you're just one of the little dots running around a maze, it's harder to keep the shape of the whole thing fixed in your mind. And easier to forget all those tiny signals represent real people. In this case, Refuge Force, patrolling the exits.

The tromp of their boots emerges so gradually from the distant murmur of wind swirling through fog, the surf lapping at the shoreless rubble, the far-off cries of circling seabirds, that I nearly stumble out of a side corridor into the enforcers' path. As it is, one of the two uniformed agents of Refuge falters, his blank goggle-and-mask-covered face swivelling in my direction.

My breath catches. I glue myself to the wall, pulse roaring, and hope to disappear into the shadows.

The second enforcer continues on for several paces, passing safely beyond the opening. I hear him grumble, words muffled behind the filter of his mask. The first raises a hand, still peering in my direction, and waves the other on. When he turns to catch up to his partner, the light catches the ID printed across his back: 09-Hayne-05.

I swallow a gasp. Haynfyv. He's back on duty so soon? I nearly sacrificed him in my quest to take out Serovate. Keeping him in one piece hadn't been my main priority at the time, but I must've done a better job protecting him from harm than I'd realized . . .

Is he letting me go out of gratitude? Unlikely. He must not have been able to see me in the shadowy side corridor. There's no way one of the mayor's special commissioned enforcers would just let me go, even if we didn't have a history.

Which reminds me—I never did figure out what Maryam Ajera wanted with me. Assuming her "summons" wasn't just another one of the monster-possessed enforcer Serovate's schemes all along.

"Does it matter?" Cadence says. "Hurry up—before they come back!"

Wary, I creep to the rusty double doors as fast and as quietly as my burning feet can carry me and spare no more than one heart-pounding-dry-mouthed-wide-eyed breath before pushing through to the open street.

Cadence snorts at my awe and laughs all the harder when I immediately choke on the dense, toxic fog that eddies in the wake of the just-closed door.

The brilliant sunlight that had so astonished me from the rooftop of Refuge barely filters down to this level. I stumble up a dank heap of rubble that might once have been steps and into a shifting, muddy-yellowish landscape.

I can't see more than a dozen steps ahead, not for any length of time, though the swirling fog offers fleeting glimpses of dark water and looming walls. I set off in as straight a line as I can manage, suddenly conscious that I've stepped beyond the edges of my maps without any idea how to return.

"Dramatic much? No worries—I'll get you home safe." Cadence says, with more condescension than reassurance.

It's too late to turn back, anyway. I keep walking, ankles rolling on slimy bits of crumbling concrete and rusted steel, trying not to make more noise than necessary. My clothes grow damp, then drenched, chafing over suddenly sensitive skin. My eyes water. My nose and throat burn.

How does anyone survive out here? And, more to the point: how long can I?

"Such a whiner," Cadence sighs. "Don't worry princess. I got you. We'll be in and out in no time—or, more like 'out and in,' I guess."

I shake my head and blink streaming eyes clear. Maybe I should've put a little more thought into this. Lily had made it sound so simple, but to save her dad, first I'll have to find him. Her directions—head straight until you run out of street, then climb—seem less helpful with every step. Especially as those steps stop clinking and crunching and start squelching and splashing.

"You do remember the part about the city being flooded, right?" Cadence says. "Relax. I know where we're going. Tide's just a little high is all."

Reassuring—if something hadn't just broken the surface of the water in front of me.

STABBITY

"STAB IT! STAB! Stab!" Cadence shrieks.

"With what?" I scramble backwards without taking my eyes off of the thing rising from the waves.

"Anything! Whatever you've got!"

I claw at my sides as if a blade will magically appear. "Um."

Cadence groans. "Seriously? You just thought we could go monster fighting unarmed?"

The monster in question is a smoky darkness amidst the roiling sick fog, smooth headed, long-necked, and razor fanged. Unless that wasn't all neck . . .

I trip, bloody my knee, and dig in to brace myself instead of pushing back up. I need my hands free.

"Yeah, no, put your hands down. This is the part where you run," Cadence says.

"But what about—"

"Does that look like Mara? Do you see threads, Weaver? Are you armed? Ready for combat? No? So run."

I shake my outstretched fingers as if magic will spontaneously crackle to life between them. Nothing happens. Nothing but a hair-raising, ear-bleeding shriek from the creature rearing in front of me.

I run, clattering over loose debris and splashing through puddles and bouncing off crumbling walls, until my chest burns and I'm hopelessly lost.

"We're not lost," Cadence says. "And you're fine. Out of shape, sure, but fine."

"What was that?" I scrabble higher up a pile of rubble, flinching at every splash. "Why couldn't I fight it?"

Cadence does one of her insubstantial shrugs. "Some kind of water monster. You're not up on your lore enough for naming it to make any difference. Not the kind of thing you fight with threads, not unless you know what you're doing. Which you don't. You'd have been better off grabbing one of Ash's blades before you snuck out. But this is good, actually. We're almost there. Just keep climbing."

She could've told me I needed a weapon. Not that I knew how to handle one. I'd just assumed dreamweaving worked against everything. And how many different kinds of monsters were there, anyway?

"Not the time," Cadence says, rudely. "Climb."

This particular pile of rubble turns out to continue up a seemingly endless slope. The fog starts to thin, revealing the mouth of an enormous structure. The jagged surface underfoot evens out into soggy, decayed carpet and pitted concrete.

I skirt gaping holes, shuddering at the thought of falling into the inky, brine-reeking shadows below. The ceiling is distant, serrated with greyish blocks of wood and oxidized metal. Shards of glass bite into the open space between slim, weathered columns. It's not a tower—the space is too high, and wide, and long, opening out in unexpected directions. I can't imagine what it would have been used for in the time before—the scale seems far too large for mere humans.

I test each footstep; terrified the floor will give way at any moment. But the fog has thinned to a bare throat-scratching mist and the space ahead is increasingly bright and well kept. Light shines through grimy but now largely intact windows. The heavy decay of the city gives way to fresh salt and . . . smoke?

"Nearly there," says Cadence. "You should probably let him approach first."

"Lily!"

The shout is mingled terror and fury, and relief so vast it catches at something high in my chest. A figure darts out around a low structure further down the massive corridor and stumbles to a halt, evidently realizing his mistake.

He's dark, no taller than I am, and not much broader. His shoulders hunch, arms raised in a defensive posture. "Who are you? What are you doing here?"

I throw up my hands, palm outward, and back up quickly. "Lily sent me."

It's not a lie. Not the whole truth, either, but it stops his threatening advance.

"Lily? Where is she? What've you done to her?"

IT'S EASY TO forget about monsters when everything's going your way.

Sam—Lily's dad—turns into my new best friend the moment I introduce myself. Ash had been staying with them while searching for me, as he explains, and Sam's unabashedly delighted to hear both Ash and his young daughter are safe. And the look on his face when I mentioned Lily's mom is with them—I wander to the surprisingly good view out the windows to give him a moment, focusing on sparkling sea and distant mountains only barely clouded by fog here at the edge of the barrier, instead of the almost-stranger's sudden upwelling of emotion.

There has to be a story there. I'm not about to ask, even if Cadence spends most of the walk home speculating.

Between Cadence's startling navigational abilities and Sam's familiarity with the city streets, we make good time, arriving not long after dark. Nothing bars our way. Not Mara, unidentified water monster, nor Refuge Force. We slip back into the labyrinth below Refuge without a ripple.

I practically skip through the corridors, eager to make my triumphant return. Several twists and turns in, Sam tugs my sleeve and points. We're skirting the edge of Freedom and the club is in full swing, bass shaking the floor.

I shrug and change course. He'll probably get a kick out of seeing it—and I'm keen to scope out my battleground. The next time I face the Mara will not be like the last. Now that I know how to take the nightmares down, their reign of terror is so very nearly at an end it makes my fingers itch.

But the first glimpse of Freedom since my momentous battle with the Mara is a little disappointing if I'm honest. The lights seem erratic, the crowd sluggish, the music fuzzy. The shine has worn off—lacking newness, or maybe intoxication. The stunned awe on Sam's face nudges something inside me, though, with a flicker of that first overwhelming astonishment I felt when I first saw it. I can't resist pulling him through to the next hall, and the next, laughing at his wonder and, more to the point, glowing at the subtle attention of the crowd.

It's different than before. Back then, I was little more than another ornament to accent Ravel's extravagance. Now, the eyes of the dancers flicker to me and away, startled, grateful, unsure. They know me not as a decorative extension of their leader but as defeater of the Mara, rescuer and hero.

I don't fully realize what I'm seeing at first, but after the first few halls, the trend is clear: the styles of Freedom have shifted. The dancers' styles are mimicking things I wore— the costumes, yes, the gold and white, the feathers and chains, lace and delicate traceries Ravel put me in—but it's more than that. Their outfits are artfully torn, their feet bare. They toy with colourful cords and delicate chains that hang loose from cuffs and bracelets to trail over their hands—held up more than once in salute. There are mimicries and interpretations of the cloak Ange had given me, too, the one I cast off to fight and beat back the Mara.

So I keep walking long after I meant to turn back, pretending to show off each new aspect of the club to the gawking tourist while basking in some well-earned glory.

All this, after one successful battle. Imagine how they'll look at me when I free them for good. First the Mara, then Refuge, and maybe I can even do something about the sea monsters outside, after, once I've made the tower safe for the first time in living memory.

And then we turn that last corner and he's waiting for me.

Ravel, wounds painted over, back taut with pain, eyes dark and hollow and burning.

"Flame," he rasps, that liquid voice raw.

I turn away, tugging Sam along with me.

This wasn't a good idea. I didn't think, didn't meant to run into him, didn't want—

And, between one struggling gasp and the next, they're here.

RUIN

CADENCE YELLS MY name, shocking me out of stasis. I reach for the threads of dreams and get ready to slice me some Mara.

But my hands flail through empty air without snagging on anything. Strange, in this crowd, where hope and desperation are usually thick as incense, but it's fine—I can use my own threads.

The hand I swipe across my chest comes up empty. I try again, scrabbling at the front of my shirt for the moonlight glow of all that I am, and want, and need to be.

Nothing catches under my fingers but ordinary, useless cloth. I stare at my horrifyingly empty hands and then up at the shadowy forms of the Mara circling.

"Oh, crap," says Cadence. "I have no idea—"

I shoulder in front of Sam as the circle tightens.

If it were just me, maybe I could run. Maybe. But with Sam here, there's no choice.

My first swing seems to blow right through the murky fog of monsters. They flee from my fist—A cheer snags in my throat.

The shreds of fog swirl and coalesce, forming sneering mouths. The amorphous mass of the Mara darts in, luring me to strike, then pulls back, leaving me teetering off balance, committed to a blow that has no hope of landing.

A cry rings out behind me. I spin in time to see Sam's knees crunch into the floor. Three long tears down his back well with blood. I reach for him. A ribbon of pain lashes across my side. The Mara lick my blood off one dagger-sharp claw and roll far too many eyes with taunting pleasure.

"Watch out—" Cadence cries.

There's a blur of motion. I know even as I turn I'm too late, too slow, too weak—why am I so weak?—but I strike out at it anyway.

Better to go down fighting.

This time, the nightmares form claws, catching my fists. Their grip tightens, slowly, so I have long, excruciating moments to realize just how much more force they have at their disposal.

The small bones in my hands grind together. The monsters' claws dig in—first pinpricks, then burning spikes drilling through my flesh. Something snaps.

The pain is blinding, paralyzing. There's screaming, not all of it my own. Strange faces, wracked with anguish, flicker behind my eyes. Tormented voices fill the space inside my head, battering at its edges.

I don't know what will kill me first—the monsters' powerful, if ephemeral claws, taking my body apart by inches, or the unseen onslaught.

And then the voices go silent. The faces fade, and the crushing grip slackens. I stagger in its absence. I can barely see, barely focus through the pain as the diseased fog of the Mara disintegrates—swept into nothingness by silver light.

Ash seems to fall out of thin air. He collapses to his knees beside me, then slumps to the floor. He rolls over onto his back, panting. "Don't do that. Ever. Again."

"Yeah, way to go, Cole," Cadence says unfairly. "You just about got us killed."

"You just . . . " I slide to the ground. Ash's shoulder is warm against my knee. Too warm. Feverish. "W-where did you come from? What happened?"

His lashes flutter. He goes limp, head lolling. I nudge him, panic rising at touch of his unresponsive weight.

"Ange is on her way," Cadence says, seemingly unconcerned. Which makes no sense, so it's probably an act. Or a distraction technique. "You better come up with a good explanation for this before she gets here."

"What happened to 'we'?"

"Wasn't *my* powers that failed to show up for the fight."

My head spins. I think I'm going to be sick.

The floor beside Ash looks cool and inviting. I don't know what just happened, and I'm not sure I want to know.

Except I do. The old me would have given up and waited for someone else to solve her problems. The new me is here to fight and win. I can't let a little near-death trauma stop me now.

"Look, just tell me what happened. Why didn't it work?" I sweep my hands through the air to illustrate its emptiness. "No threads. I can't see theirs, or mine. What changed? Cadence? Hey!"

"I don't know, okay? It's not my fault."

"Well, it's not like I did anything differently."

She doesn't answer.

Sam crawls over, his face tight with pain. I'd forgotten about him. He shakes Ash's shoulder, then looks at me reproachfully. "You said it was safe here."

I stare past him at Ravel, standing on the edge of the crowd. Why are they all still here? They should have run when it became clear I was losing.

"Go away." My voice is stronger than I expected. Yay me.

Ravel's lips part, ashen and haggard under layers of streaked paint and glitter. He spreads his hands in helpless appeal, nails chipped and ragged.

I close my eyes and wait for him to leave. When I open them, he has.

Good. At least one of us is learning.

I stare numbly out across the crowd. I'm still sitting, so the view is mostly ripped stockings and short skirts and navel piercings. Some of the dancers are doing what they do best: ignoring the rest of the world. Sinking into self-absorbed fantasies. But more than a few pause at the spectacle we present.

I don't need to know what their expressions look like, rigid with shock, horror, or numb disbelief under those bright, lying masks. Which is why my first sight of her is a pair of sturdy boots striding purposefully in our direction.

"I can't carry both of you, you know," Ange yells over the music, hands on her hips. "I can't even carry one of you. What were you thinking? And what did you do to your *hands*?"

Ravel stands beside her, shifting his weight and twitching in his attempts to avoid my glare. I close my eyes. Open them. Think about closing them again.

"Did you at least win?" Ange demands.

Ravel winces.

Cadence snorts. "One of us did. I mean, do you see any bodies?"

I jut my chin at Ash's prone form.

"He'll be fine," Cadence says, still trying for matter-of-fact. But a softer note creeps in.

I shake my head. No. We did not win.

"Great," Ange huffs. "Well, come on, get up. You'll have to help me haul him. Again."

She has to pull me to my feet, grasping my forearm when she sees what's become of my hands. Sam scrambles up to join us.

Ange eyes him suspiciously. "Who's this?"

I look at him. Open my mouth. Think better of it. Shrug, and then wince as my latest wounds shriek louder than the lingering aches of the last crop. At least I actually won the battle I earned those in. "He's coming with us."

Ange's lips thin.

"I'm Sam." He peers at her. "You—you must be Amy's sister?"

Ange gives me one piercing look before turning her back on the both of us. She pries Ash up off the floor, batting away Sam and my efforts to help, but lets Ravel direct two strangers to her side to help with the burden.

By the time we're near the end of his territory and what I've come to think of as the beginning of Ange's, Ash is semiconscious and can more or less keep himself upright with just Ange's help. The strangers from Freedom peel off at a nod from Ravel. He seems to think he can follow us all the way back to Ange's headquarters. That is, until she turns the full force of her formidable glare on him.

"Ange," he whines. Then he turns to me, foolishly hopeful. "Flame . . ."

But I slump against the wall, hang my head, and ignore him until she sends him away.

Ange steers all of us back to her infirmary and our beds, grumbling all the way. She makes Amy take Lily out of the room first.

I won't get to see their grand reunion with Sam. Kind of unfair, since I'm the reason he's here—but since I nearly got him killed, it's not like I'm in any position to complain.

This is not how I saw tonight ending.

The last thing I do before I pass out is promise myself I'll do whatever it takes to get my magic back.

REJECTION

T TAKES SEVEN days to fall from saviour of the city to exile:

Day one: Ange's fury won't appeased, despite a stomach-churningly adorable reunion between Sam, Lily, and a perpetually overwhelmed Amy that takes place in the infirmary after all, Sam's injuries sentencing him to cot alongside Ash and I.

My eyes are only damp from the pain that shrieks at me every time I move. Nothing more. Cute family, though.

Day two: Ash overexerted himself coming to our rescue, but since he didn't acquire any new wounds, when he finally wakes up, his condition is surprisingly good. Of course, that's aside from the way he appears to be torn between anger, concern, and disappointment in me from any one minute to the next . . .

Oh, and Cadence isn't talking to me for some reason. She makes Ash relay anything she wants to say, which isn't much—or, at least, isn't anything I want to hear. I don't know why she thinks she can blame me for everything all the time. I don't remember her arguing we should stay safe in bed. Unfair how she acts all helpless whenever it's convenient, even though most of the time she's the one getting me in trouble in the first place.

Day three: Lily, now that she's coming down from the excitement of Sam's arrival, bounces around pestering us all day. She seems aware that something is wrong—and irate no one will tell her what it is.

I feel her pain. And also my own—my hands are wrecked worse than my feet ever were. I don't even want to think about how long they're going to take to heal.

But it gets worse, because—

Day four: Ash and Ange finally decide we need to talk.

I don't know when they got around to scheming without me, seeing as how we basically spend all our time in exactly the same place, but they've clearly come to an agreement. All that's left is to break the news: since I've lost my powers, the only way they can think of to get them back is for me to leave the city and return to Nine Peaks with Ash.

Obviously, it's a stupid plan.

I don't even remember that place—it's certainly no home of mine. And apparently it's far away. Really far. It could take us days, maybe even weeks of travel through monster-infested wastelands to get there. Plus, there's no guarantee anyone there can even help me if (Ash says when) we reach it.

Besides, I can't just leave. First of all, it's not like we can just walk out of the city on a whim. If it were that easy, why would any of us still be here? The barrier surrounding us is supposed to be impenetrable—though that does raise some interesting questions about how Ash arrived.

But more importantly, I'm the only one who can keep the Mara from killing everyone.

Day five: Except, of course, I'm not. Ash can—and obviously has—fought the nightmares and won. Given the sudden and inexplicable loss of my abilities, I don't think it's wrong to rely on him a little. It's not like I want to run away from the responsibility or anything. Even if I can't stay and fight, he should. We can't just abandon everyone.

Why can't they see that?

I'll wear them down eventually. I have to. I fall asleep scheming—

Day six: —and wake with new arguments to try each morning. Anything to move us forward. Anything to feel like I can still make a difference. To feel like we have a chance.

Until this morning, day seven: I wake up in a new world.

It's like something out of Cadence's memories, all green and blue and open. Very, very open. Can't-find-the-ceiling open.

"W—where . . . ?" My tongue is thick, my head fuzzy.

"Deer Lake."

Ash stands between some huge brown things, green stuff up to his knees. When I scramble to my feet, there's a winking gray-green surface just behind him.

"Trees," says Cadence with a sigh. "Bushes, grasses, I don't know, assorted plants? And maybe a pond? I definitely wouldn't call that a lake. Come on. I've shown you this stuff before. Don't act stupid."

The memories Cadence shared hadn't prepared me for how overwhelming nature would be. It's everywhere; huge, and kind of damp, and surprisingly smelly. I sneeze.

"What—how—this—?" I'm babbling. I know I'm babbling, but the last thing I remember is the dingy ceiling in Ange's makeshift infirmary. In the tunnels under Refuge. In a flooded, monster-overrun city *sealed by an impenetrable barrier.*

And now I'm . . . somewhere else. "Deer . . . ?"

"Deer Lake," Ash says." It's one of the safer places to camp near the city, and my bike needed to charge up before we could go much further anyway."

I just stare.

He shifts his weight. "Um, so—wow. This conversation seemed a lot easier in my head . . ."

"She doesn't know what you're talking about." Cadence makes it clear she thinks that's somehow my fault.

Ash spreads his arms and waves at the general green-and-blue-and-brownness surrounding us. "Ta-da. We made it."

I keep staring.

"Uh . . . you should maybe sit down."

I take another look at the lake-pond-thing and sink down onto a damp bit of trampled, weed-covered earth. It's wet, and kind of smelly, and I'd stand up again except I'm not sure my knees will hold me.

Ash settles a few feet away. "So, uh, where should I start?"

He's found a change of clothes somewhere along the way, and the dark, tough, close-fitting outfit reminds me of the first time I saw him in the dreamscape. His magic has built back to something like its former strength, too. It's a continuous shimmering over the surface of his skin and hair, a silver-bright glimmering in his eyes not unlike the sun rippling on the wind-stirred surface of the water behind him.

Awe wars with anger. Anger wins. He's no longer a mysterious stranger, or the longed-for hero I first made him out to be, when he walked only at the edges of nightmares. He's just Ash. And he's been keeping secrets from me.

"We decided to get you out of the city," Cadence says. "There were too many things you didn't want to hear. Your fixation on fighting the Mara was only going to get us all killed. So Ange slipped you something to keep you unconscious long enough for Ash to get us out. We're going home, where they can help us get back normal. Or, at least, you know. Back to being, uh . . . us."

I glare at Ash. "You had no right to do that."

His jaw tightens. "It was the best we could do. Letting you get someone killed wasn't an option. Neither was leaving you behind. Cadence agrees."

"*Cadence* doesn't get to make decisions for me." I roll to my knees and shove him.

He barely sways. I shriek, partly in frustration, partly because whatever Ange gave me to knock me out had been holding the pain in my hands at bay—until I messed that up for myself, too.

I stalk off into the plants. Except the stupid things are so tall it's more like wading. Less than ten steps in, my feet snag on something and I go sprawling, plunging both wrecked hands wrist-deep in mud.

Ash hauls me back to my feet. "Better not go near the water."

I turn a wordless growl of pain and fury on him that he's meant to interpret as something along the lines of: "Why not? Why should I listen to anything you say? In fact, I'm done. I'm out of here."

He backs up, eyes widening. I turn and quick-wade in the opposite direction, pretending I'm holding my arms out to wipe the mud off on the tall grasses instead of for balance.

"Cole? Cole, that's not a good idea . . . "

The grasses swish behind me. I slog faster toward an opening where it looks like the ground might be drier.

"Let her blow off some steam. It's not like she'll make it far anyway," Cadence says.

Mud squelches between my fingers as they ball into fists. Fire under my skin reminds me why that's not a good idea, and I wish yet again for the ability to take a swing at her. Between my most recent batch of injuries and her incorporeal existence, it's not a wish that's likely ever to be granted.

But Cadence and Ash have seen to it that I'm no longer trapped within Refuge's walls. For the moment, I've left everything I know behind—and that includes both the immediate threat of the Mara, and the repressive regulations drilled into me by the tower-state. I can wish for whatever I want, including the ability to punch a ghost.

The thought lifts my spirits—and my gaze. It's not only astonishingly bright, but also uncomfortably warm here. Wherever *here* is. My feet stay cooler than my head, well sheltered by the high ground cover and a liberal coating of mud over my shoes, but the ground underfoot rolls and dips. I skid on loose stones and snag on roots and twigs as I wallow my way through the unfamiliar landscape.

Everywhere I look, there's something new. The detail is astonishing—and it's all moving all the time. Grasses bend and leaves flutter moments before the breeze brushes my cheek. A gentle rustling rises and falls with the wind. Layers of shadows and patches of sunlight shift and sway in a constantly turning kaleidoscope that tricks the eye.

It's beautiful—and terrifying.

I don't know where I am. I don't know what's out here. And I don't have any way of fighting it off when it sneaks up on me.

I find a fallen branch and sling it over my shoulder for protection, balancing it in the crook of my arm. Nasty little bits of bark or something worse skitter down my back but, as I've so recently learned, it's better not to head into unfamiliar terrain unarmed.

The ground levels out and the wall of green to either side grows even more solid. It's not just made of trees—bushes and vines and other assorted and unidentifiable growing things have nearly swallowed bulky heaps that look decidedly man-made under their organic coverings—a tumble of bricks, a splinter of boards, a slide of shingles. It must once have been a relatively straight row of buildings, but on a much smaller scale than the Towers of Refuge and the other structures I'm familiar with back home in the city. The trees loom high over what remains of these walls.

I keep to the clearest part of the path, scuffing through musty-smelling heaps of decaying leaves under a near tunnel of green, branches tangling overhead in many places.

But the way ahead is barred. I could turn right or left, though there's only more of the same everywhere I look. Instead, I grip my branch more firmly and edge up to the barrier.

It comes up past my shoulders, but not by much. Bushes bristle against rotted wood, all of it propped against something that rattles when I nudge it, making leaves tremble in a wave out to either side.

Metal. There's metal under all the plants. I elbow my way through the greenery, exposing thick, interlaced wire. It's a chain-link fence.

Metal means people. I can't stay out in all this green forever, and I'm certainly not going back to Ash. Maybe whoever built this fence can help me?

I let my stick fall and hook my arms over the top of the sagging obstruction. It's easy to kick the rotted wood aside and wedge a foot in the open links, but precarious when I put my weight on it. The fence sways and rattles. I heave and kick and somehow manage to haul myself up high enough to swing one leg over the top. But, disappointingly, even from this higher vantage point there seems to be little more ahead than yet more trees, all linked by endless undergrowth over the sad remains of small—most likely wood—buildings. A breeze ruffles the outer layer of leaves, carrying with it a low noise—and not the kind, I suspect, that comes from trees and bushes.

Someone's out there. I shake off the instinct to hide. Strangers are by definition an unknown. They could be dangerous—but somehow, despite how alien this landscape looks, it feels—not familiar, not safe, exactly, but . . .

I can't quite put it into words. There's—there's a sort of rightness about this place, or—no, that's not it, either. It's as if I'm spying on a place where I'm not welcome—but neither am I in danger of attack. The air isn't thick, it's *full*—occupied, but not hostile.

And though I feel like an intruder, I don't leave. I need to know more—need to pry my way into this place's secrets and understand—

"Death wish, much?" Cadence interrupts, shattering the alien atmosphere that very nearly had hooked its claws into me. "What did you think was out here? Bunny rabbits and bluebirds?"

That low noise swells again from just up ahead, still calling to me. A chill ices down my spine. The trees are closer here, and seem nearly as tall as Refuge itself, rustling skyscrapers blocking out the sun. It's cool and shadowy, and it would be peaceful—except there's that low, trailing sound again.

The breeze makes the shadows under the trees bob and creep in a way that looks almost . . .

I lean, peer into the undergrowth, try to piece together the edges and curves of half-seen shapes that seem alive. Almost, but not quite, human.

The fence bounces and swoops beneath me, first groaning, and then shrieking as my weight taxes the ancient metal. My foot slips at the same moment a thorn pricks my finger. I scrabble for handholds and remember too late the state of my hands. I start to slide—and a pair of hands grabs ahold of my waist.

"You don't want to go in there," Ash says.

"You don't get to decide what I want." I kick at him, then scramble for balance on the unsteady fence. He pulls harder. The links dig in painfully.

I will not let go. He can't make me.

"Oh, stop pouting already," Cadence says. As if she's one to talk. "He's just trying to warn you. Refuge isn't the only place you have to worry about monsters."

I take one frantic final glance at the shadows under the trees and let go of the fence. I go flying back into Ash, knocking the air out of him. He curls over, gasping.

"Now look what you did," Cadence says. "Such a troublemaker."

"I think I liked it better when you weren't talking to me."

"I think I liked it better when I didn't have a you to get in my way in the first place."

Oof.

I mean, I'd kind of known it was coming ever since she remembered who we really were, but still.

"Oh, don't even," she snaps. "It's bad enough having to watch you making a mess of things. I shouldn't have to listen to your self-pity on top of it."

"So maybe don't listen? Why are you even still here? I don't need you. It's not like you can do anything anyway. Just leave me alone."

"Fine, maybe I will."

"Good!"

"Okay!"

"Enough," Ash wheezes, finally catching his breath. "We're wasting time. Cady, you're being a pest. Cole, I know this is all new to you and I'm sorry, but we need to keep moving. We have to make it across the river before nightfall. I'll explain more tonight. For now, you'll just have to trust me."

"The last guy who wanted me to trust him tried to sacrifice me to the Mara."

Ash just gives me a look.

I can't hold his gaze. I know he'd never hurt me. And, to be fair, Ravel wasn't really trying to sacrifice me so much as use me to build his own power.

Ash isn't telling me everything, but at least he always seems to be trying to do the right thing. That's more than I can say for most people I've met.

So I follow him further from my city, even though it cries out for me with every step.

6
FIRELIGHT

ASH CALLS THIS fresh misery "camping." The best part about it is it comes at the end of a long day of "travel" and takes place in "nature"—which it turns out I also hate.

I collapse on a thin mat that does little to shield me from the lumpy, cold ground because after hours of perching on Ash's two-wheeled nightmare contraption, sitting is no longer an option. I can't decide which is worse: my numb tailbone, my bruised and rubbed-raw shoulders, my aching arms, or my much-abused hands.

That's an exaggeration—it's still the hands.

Ash is busy cheerfully rustling around in the huge pack he made me wear all day and pretending everything is fine. I practice clear communication and asserting my desires every time he gives me an opening.

"Comfortable?"

"I want to go home."

"You look cold. Why don't you scoot over and sit by the fire for a bit?"

"Take me home."

He unfastens the top of his jacket and tugs at the fabric below, unspooling a surprising length of fine woven fabric in rich, deep hues. Once the whole scarf is detached from his person, he shakes it out and makes as if to drape it around me. I back out of range, arms raised defensively.

He shrugs and tucks the scarf back under his jacket, then goes back to rummaging in his pack. "You must be hungry. Here, try some of this."

I ignore the spicy-smelling thing. "I'm going back with or without you."

"Yeah? How?" Cadence says. "Do you even know which direction Refuge's in?"

I hook my thumb at the gravel track we rode in on. Ash leans over and adjusts my aim until I'm pointing at a dense clump of prickly-looking trees.

"That way. It'd take maybe a week walking if you don't count the forests, ravines, mountains, starvation, monster-infested ruins—oh, and there's the river."

I grimace. We had spent most of the afternoon skirting the river's banks, and had crossed it twice. Four times for Ash, really. He'd insisted on walking me across the skeletal bridges and going back to wheel his bike across in a separate trip each time for safety.

Fun fact: it turns out my city was far from the only place overrun by monsters when the old world ended. Nearly every once-settlement or body of water seems to hide a threat. So, not only do we have crumbling and washed-out bridges to contend with, but also a remarkable assortment of monsters lurking below the surface, eager to lunge up and snag unsuspecting passers-by.

"Feel free to head on out," Cadence says. "Not like I can stop you anyway."

"Cady, enough," Ash says. "Cole, just hang in there until we get you home. The council can sort you two out."

I perk up despite myself at the word "home." But the place he means is strange to me; so far away up in the mountains it seems almost make-believe.

Something tickles my arm.

I swat. It splats. The resulting smear makes me gag and reel away from my mat.

Ash jumps up to follow. I wave him off.

"Come sit closer to the fire." He pats a patch of trampled grass. "The bugs will leave you alone."

"Nah, you'll just be able to see them coming," Cadence says.

Something buzzes past my head. I stomp back to the pool of flickering light. Ash reaches for my arm. I jerk away, but he's only wiping leftover bug guts off with his sleeve.

Note to self: avoid Ash's sleeve. And Cadence is right; it's worse near the fire. Black flecks zip around, making me all the more conscious of the infested, buzzing shadows outside our little circle. I bat at everything that comes within reach, trying to chase the little beasts off, but they just keep coming back for more.

Ash watches me flail in silence for a bit. Then he sighs and that silvery light of his stirs. It radiates from his skin until there's a misty halo standing out a few inches all around him. He holds out an arm and waves it to show me how the bugs bounce off.

"Human insect repellent," Cadence says. "That's a new one. Did you come up with it on your own?"

"This really cool girl I used to know discovered it." His tone is light, teasing.

"Can't've been—what did you say you call her now? Mogwai?—and no chance it was Banshee, nor her sisters, not likely . . . Aleya, then? Not Qareen! No? Oh, come on. I know all your friends, don't I?"

Her agitation surprises me.

"It's you. You're the friend." Ash's grin fades. His voice drops to a whisper. "You—you're serious? You don't remember?"

The fire pops. Some of the wood collapses, sending up a spray of sparks. I flail at yet more bugs, irritated by both my missing abilities and Cadence's history with Ash. A history I'm not a part of.

I know we're technically the same person—at least, we definitely *were*—but it sure doesn't feel that way. I also know I'm supposed to be over their shared past.

Apparently, that hard-earned clarity is yet another thing I've lost.

"Gotcha!" says Cadence. Her laughter sounds forced. "Come on, did you really think I'd forget? Just, um, keeping you honest."

"Uh, right. Good one . . . "

But he relaxes, picking up a bit of wood and tossing it in the fire. The wind shifts, blowing smoke in my face. I cough, eyes watering against the bitter onslaught.

"C'mere." Ash reaches out and pulls me closer, keeping one arm slung over my shoulders.

I elbow him away. He gasps, curling a little before he catches himself and shakes it off. Oops—clearly he still hasn't fully recovered from his injuries.

He also kidnapped me and dragged me out here in the first place.

I still feel bad, but now I'm angry too.

"Just let me—" Ash reaches around me again with exaggerated caution and waves his arms in demonstration. "See? It'll keep the bugs off and filter the smoke."

I pull my knees up and wrap my arms around them in a painfully rigid posture, but I don't move away. Ash keeps one arm across my shoulder and prods at the fire with the other. He hums a little, a low, oddly familiar tune. Maybe I've heard Cadence sing it before.

"You must have a lot of questions." His voice is quiet, his gaze fixed on the crackling embers.

I follow suit, relaxing a bit now insects aren't dive-bombing my head.

"I don't know why your memories aren't coming back properly. Or why you can't hold onto them when Cadence and I try to share. And I don't know why your magic disappeared. It could have something to do with, uh . . . Well. There *are* two of you. That's kinda unmarked territory."

Cadence snorts. I feel Ash's shrug more than see it.

"Yeah, I get it," he continues. "Huge mess all 'round. I know you didn't want to leave, but I didn't see much else we could do. Neither of us is in great condition to fight, and to be honest, are limits to what I can manage by myself, even in top form. A city full of monsters isn't exactly a one-man job. Plus, I was expected home weeks ago."

I shift in place, partly still sore from spending hours on the hard seat of his bike, mostly because I don't know what to do with the idea that Ash couldn't have taken on the Mara singlehanded. Could I have been that much stronger than him? Or simply that deluded?

"Duh," says Cadence. "That's not exactly news. But how did you get her out of the city in the first place?"

Cadence knew Ash couldn't save us all along? That's definitely not what she'd told me—

"Same way you got in? Don't tell me you forgot that too." Ash shakes his head. "Those tunnels, though—yikes. Between the bodies and whatever that was in the water, I wasn't sure we'd make it."

Wait, what?

He swipes his stick at the fire. Sparks bounce off the shield of his power. "To be honest, I cheated just a bit on the way in. But since you can't dreamwalk right now, it was a real chore to get you out, especially unconscious."

I twist to look back over my shoulder at him. He's not much taller than me, and with his power extended as a barrier around us, he just looks human. Dark curls stick to his skin in the heat of the fire. The smudged hollows beneath his eyes betray exhaustion, his lashes seeming longer than ever without that silver coating. He blinks back at me.

"If there's a way out, why doesn't everyone just leave?" I ask.

"Don't be stupid," Cadence says. "Since when do people do the smart thing?"

"It's not that easy," Ash says over her. "We had records of a tunnel that leads out past the barrier, but it's still partially flooded—and it very obviously wasn't empty when the sea invaded. You have to dive and swim a good distance through the, uh, obstructions, and either hope the water monsters don't notice you, or be able to fend them off. On top of that, the barrier's weaker below ground, but it's still there. Regular humans can't just stroll past it. Even for me, it took a lot to push through. It's a rough crossing."

"But you got me across."

If he could take me out of the city, even without my powers, couldn't he take others? Ange? Lily, and Amy, and Sam? Even if lots of people wouldn't cooperate, like Cadence said, we could save the ones who were willing . . .

"Not the worst idea, actually," she says. "Could be worth exploring."

"No one's doing any exploring," Ash says. "We're heading home. The elders will know what to do. Anyway, our first priority has to be getting you back to normal."

Normal.

"I'm going to bed." I shove away from Ash's arms and stand up.

I've seen what he thinks my normal should be. Playful. Strong. Laughing. *Cadence.*

That's what he means. That's what he wants.

"Duh," Cadence says.

"Guys? What am I missing?" He rolls to one knee, leaning to get a look at my face.

"She's just pouting," Cadence snarks.

Unfair. Always so unfair. "Am not!"

"Are too!"

"Am n—"

"Hey!" Ash grabs my arm, careful to avoid my hand, and tugs me back down. "I don't know what's going on with you two, or your abilities, or what to do about that city, but I do know there are a lot of people back home who are going to be super excited to see you. Let's just focus on getting you there. You can worry about the rest later."

We sit in silence so long I droop with exhaustion. Cadence must be sulking and Ash probably fell asleep sitting up. Is that a thing people can do? I don't want to get caught looking to check. Besides, it is nice and warm and peacefully insect-free over here by him.

The fire, I mean. It's nice by the fire.

"I promise, you'll like it there," Ash says quietly.

Huh. Still awake.

"You don't remember what you're missing, but everyone loved you. I could barely keep Hatif—Liam, you'd remember him Cadence—from coming after you with me. You were so talented, so smart, so good at absolutely everything." He's so close I can feel his quiet laughter. "You were a brat, too. Always up to something. And I was right there with you. But no one could stay mad at you long.

"I cried the day they told me you were going on a mission with your parents. Not because I was scared for you—I wanted to go too. It wasn't fair; the rest of us buzzing around within a day's march of home on glorified camping trips, wasting time studying maps and planting trees and foraging while you got to fight real monsters.

"Your dad gave me my first set of blades and told me if I practiced every day, he'd take me. Next time."

He lays a long knife sheathed in thick leather across my lap. The grip is pitted and worn, but when I slide the blade out a few inches its edges glitter with honed menace.

When he lays his hand over mine, it lights up in silver. "I practiced every day. For years."

Cadence makes a soft sound. My eyes well up, not for the loss of the father I don't remember, but for that small boy, waiting and longing for a day that would never come. He touches a finger to my cheek, the silver light of his power making the teardrop shimmer.

"This is a happy story," he says. "I found you again. I just wish it could have been sooner."

MOUNTAINS

STALL AS long as I can. There's no way I want to get back on the bike.

I stall as long as I can. There's no way I want to get back on the bike.

One of Cadence's distraction techniques ought to do the trick—and I have more than enough questions to keep him busy for days. "What was on the other side of that fence?"

"What fence?" Ash fastens his pack and holds it out to me.

Yeah, I don't think so. Not happening. "Yesterday. Before you made me get on that thing."

"The bike? Cady used to love biking. We had these cute little miniature bikes to practice on. Spent more time repairing and recharging them than riding, but still."

I cross my arms, still ignoring the outstretched pack.

He plops it down and throws up his hands in mock surrender. "Okay, okay. You're talking about the haunted village."

Cadence snorts. "It wasn't haunted."

He shrugs. "Sure, no one lived there, but that's the point. Monsters still took it, even though there's hardly any water and it wasn't a real settlement."

"What, it was a fake settlement?"

"Exactly—there's a whole little village inside, all fake. There's a sign on the other side, facing the old highway.

At some point, they collected all these really old buildings and made a pretend town in there to show how people used to live a long time ago. There's something like it up past Nine Peaks, but bigger. So, even though it wasn't a real human settlement, I guess it was haunted by the past enough that it drew monsters anyway."

A fake village. I can't wrap my mind around it. How could people move whole buildings? And why go to all the effort? And—had what I'd felt really been monsters?

I chew my lip, considering. The voices, those shadowy presences, they hadn't felt like the Mara. But maybe different kinds of monsters have different ways of hunting. I'll have to be more alert next time . . .

Ash wrestles me into the pack while I'm distracted and swings his leg over the bike.

"He's better at this game than you. Give up and get on already," Cadence says.

Ash grins and pats the rock-hard seat behind him invitingly. I groan and ease onto the stupid thing.

He revs the engine and takes off so fast I have to wrap my arms around him just to stay on. I slit my eyes against the rushing wind and endless stream of insects hurtling by.

From a distance and blurred by tears, nature isn't so bad. It's even better when we break free of the dark trees. The mountains seem nearer today, like prickly towers jutting up against the sky, gray and reassuringly solid.

I almost miss the dirty yellow miasma of my poisoned city. The sky is so blue and the air is both clean and not. At the speed we're moving, it becomes horrifyingly clear just how much crap is floating around out here. At least Ash shelters me from the worst of it. Most of the bugs and bits seem to splat on him before they can reach me, as long as I keep myself tucked behind him.

Today's route seems more direct. There are fewer spots where we have to get down and walk over or around craters and heaps of debris, or thick mud, or shallow water. And I don't hate the sparsely covered rock of the canyons as we weave high above the dangerous river nearly as much as I did yesterday's dense, dark forests. When we reach a stretch of road that runs through a vista of rolling hills and craggy ridges beyond, that's interesting too. The hills are bumpy with amusing dusty blotches like old fabric that's been washed too many times when we stop in a hot, arid spot mid-day to recharge the bike.

Ash folds panels out of the sides of the hated contraption to catch the light while we eat. I stagger in circles trying to regain feeling in one half of my body while doing my best to ignore the pain in the other. In addition to pre-existing damage, now my fingers are chapped, my mouth is dry and my lips blistered. My skin is prickly, itchy, and getting redder all the time, and my hair is stiff with grit.

I lean over and scrub my forearms against it, dislodging a filthy rain that patters into the dirt. I try not to look too close at the results. Apparently Ash hadn't sheltered me from as much of the airborne yuck as I'd thought.

"That stream should be shallow enough if you want to wash up a bit." He points to a ditch at the side of the road. "Just keep an eye out, and if you hear something rattling, don't move."

I eye the vegetation-choked trickle. Cadence cackles. A whole section of the weeds start thrashing.

There's something alive in there.

I stumble back, yelling for Ash. The bike falls with a crash. He sprints over, twin blades flashing silver.

After yesterday's river monsters, I'll happily let him take the lead. The Mara might be deadly, but they aren't nearly so disgusting.

He dives over the edge. Weeds fly. Foul-smelling mud splashes in great, greenish-brown globs.

Stillness.

"Ash?" Rubbing my arms against crawling revulsion, I peer into the ditch.

He's knee-deep in brackish water and crumpled reeds, shaking. His head is bent, and he seems to be trying to get up, but he slips further into the muck with every movement.

I edge closer, in danger of sliding in myself.

I really don't want to go in after him, but if he can't get up . . . "Ash? You okay?"

He makes a choking sound and finally looks up. His face is painted with mud, teeth bared. He kind of wheezes in my direction.

"This." He lifts an unidentifiable mottled clump. "Your monster."

He waggles it, first gasping, and then howling with laughter. The thing in his hand is roundish. Stubby, wiggling bits poke out around the edges.

"That—you—*gah*—" Cadence joins in, speechless with giggles.

They're laughing at a water monster. Granted, it's a lot smaller than the river monsters we ran into yesterday.

A lot smaller. Call it a ditch monster? But I bet it could drown you just the same. It's certainly not funny.

Ash shouts and flings the thing away. It glops back into the mud.

"It bit me!" He snatches his hand to his mouth, gets a good look at the mud covering it, and starts chortling again as he scrambles up the slippery bank.

"What if it's poison?" I back up to give him space. If he passes out, I'd rather it happen up here where I might have some chance of helping him and not in the bottom of a monster-infested ditch.

"Poison," Cadence chortles. "It's gonna get you, Ash. Eat you right up. Just stand still for a few months and you'll be sorry!"

"Don't be rude. I'd take at least a year to digest, and you know it. Besides, I'd have to be the one eating it to get poisoned." He shakes his hand, spattering mud everywhere. "Ouch, I think it drew blood."

Then he looks past me. His smile drains away in an instant. Ditch water spatters the dust. "My bike!"

He races past, monster bite forgotten. I check the bank for signs of pursuit.

Ash hauls his evil, two-wheeled contraption upright easily enough. Unfortunately, one of the charging panels stays behind. In pieces.

A lot of pieces.

"Ouch is right," says Cadence.

Ash scrubs his face, smearing mud, and jerks his hand away with a hiss.

Not sure how a little more mud in the monster bite could hurt at this point, but what do I know?

I nudge the shards of the bike's charging panel with my toe. "Maybe we can fix it?"

"Sure. I'll just carve some moulds, melt it down over a campfire, and rewire it with plant fibres."

"Oh. Really?"

"Not in a million years. No, don't kick it. We'll take the pieces back for scrap. Someone will be able to do, uh . . . Well, something. Can't leave it here or the turtles might really turn into monsters."

"Turtles?"

He raises an eyebrow. "You don't remember them either? Of course not."

"They bite," Cadence sputters, clearly still overcome. "*Turtle*-monsters. Venomous snapping turtles . . ." She dissolves into giggles.

"You know we don't get those. Probably just a little love bite from a Northwestern Pond or Western Painted. Must've given the poor little guy a good scare." Ash looks at his bike and sighs. "This'll slow us down, though. Give me a few minutes to change before we hit the road. And—maybe just stick close. The turtles won't do you any harm, but there could be rattlers around."

I nod intelligently and wait until he's out of earshot. "Not a monster?"

"Not even close. Just an animal. They have those out here."

"But it hurt him."

"Wild animal. They'll do that."

"Are there many?"

Cadence makes a sound I can't interpret. "Once. Maybe again, one day."

"What's that supposed to mean?"

The wind rustles the roadside plants. Dirt skips across my shoes and patters against my legs.

"They'll fill you in when we get home."

"You mean when we get to Ash's home."

" . . . whatever."

— ※ —

I FALL ASLEEP almost as soon as Ash lets me stop walking.

The connection to the charging unit on the other side of the bike turns out to have been damaged as well. That, along with a cloudy—and, more than once, rainy—afternoon, means we won't be able to ride again for another day at the earliest. At least Ash strapped the stupid pack to the back of the bike while he pushed it. I got hot enough just carrying myself all day.

I've been learning a lot of new things: there are wild animals outside the city—yet another bit of nature I'm not too keen on. They can hurt you, but that doesn't make them monsters, and there used to be lots of them, and might be again one day. I hope "one day" isn't anytime soon . . .

Also: if you're hungry enough, you'll eat anything. The spicy stuff Ash carries, isn't all that bad, actually: kind of savoury, and chewy. Though I sort of miss Noosh—Refuge's bland, ground-bug-based liquid diet. Cadence says it's because I was indoctrinated and lost all sense of taste.

I fold another piece of smoke-preserved dried something-or-other into my mouth to prove her wrong.

Another thing I never really wanted to know: ditch water smells even worse after a few hours in the sun.

Sweat is also unpleasant. There's something called "chafing" and also, similar but evidently worse because it's on your feet, "blisters."

Morning comes with a whole new crop of small hurts to add to the too-slowly healing old ones. I let out a yelp when try to I stand. Ash hurries over to help. Cadence won't stop laughing.

"Should've let Hatif come along after all, huh?" Ash says cryptically, if sympathetically.

"Liam, right? I don't see what good hauling him along would do," Cadence says.

"Mm? Oh, right. You were gone by then. Hatif can dream-weave too, now. He's not as strong as you . . . were. But he's the best healer on our squad. Qareen—Orisa, you'd remember her as—can do a little weaving, too, but she likes fighting a little too much to really master it."

Dreamweavers can *heal*? Why did no one tell me this before I lost my magic?

"Didn't seem important at the time," Cadence says unrepentantly. "I never really trained as a healer anyway. Boring stuff. All chores and no fun."

Ash gives me a strange look. I flinch at its intensity, and discover a sudden need to inspect my fingers. It's obviously *her* he's really trying to see.

"I didn't know you felt that way," he says quietly.

"Sounds like things turned out for you, anyway," Cadence says, louder, brasher, as if to make up for his careful tone. "Two healer-gifted on your squad? Impressive. They'd come in handy right about now."

It's Ash's turn to flinch. "Not their fault. They'd have wanted to come, if they'd known there was a chance you'd survived. We were told you'd died, but I *knew* you had to still be alive."

He trails off—giving me time to wonder just what would have happened if he hadn't stubbornly clung to belief in my survival. Most likely, I would have proved him wrong sooner rather than later.

"It's just . . ." He takes an uneven breath, lets it out again. "Mogwai is captain now. You know her—or, Cadence, *you* remember Zoe. She's great. She just doesn't really know it yet. It wouldn't have been fair to her if I'd hijacked our first solo mission."

"So you thought you'd, what, sneak off on your own and make sure I was really dead?" she says.

"You're not dead, Cady."

"No? Then what am I?" She sounds more exasperated than angry.

I don't buy it. But I'm more curious about something Ash said. "Did you?"

He blinks at the sudden change in topic. "Did I what?"

"Sneak away to come find us. Won't that get you into trouble?"

Ash's injured bike seems to summon him—he turns to it without answering. He takes his time inspecting the remaining charging panel in the morning light and brushing dirt from the grimy spokes.

"We should get going," he calls over his shoulder. "I'd hoped to reach home today, but the power's only up to five percent. Could take us another two, three days if we have to walk most of the way."

Having some skill in redirecting uncomfortable conversations myself, I know a diversion when I hear one. I also know what it means—it had cost Ash something to come for us.

Just how much, I have no way of knowing, but judging by Cadence's conspicuous silence, it could be a lot. Or maybe she has no idea either and she's just being mysterious to mess with my head. The smothered snicker she lets out at that thought doesn't clear matters up.

I do what I can to help Ash get us packed and moving again. Just walking hurts at first, until I loosen up enough to take in my surroundings. We've moved away from the river, and the mountains, though I can see higher bits of land in the distance, when I can see anything at all.

As far as I can tell, nature consists of tall, dark, spiky trees that cut off the sun, lower, fluffier trees and bushes that make it hard to see where you're going, not to mention nearly impossible to actually get where you think you're going, and dry flat bits where there's mostly dust and low-growing stuff like grasses and little patchy bushes that snag your toes and scratch your calves and trip you up when you least expect it.

Then the whole thing repeats—big trees, little trees, flattish, dryish bit, more trees—oh, and also the other kind of flattish bits that are very, very wet. And extra-bug-infested.

Between the boggy patches of our route and the intermittent cloudbursts Ash insists on marching straight through, I'm not sure my clothes ever fully dry out. We're getting low on food, we're completely out of clean clothes, and both sitting and standing are now equally miserable, which is making me bizarrely jealous of Cadence's smug incorporeality.

So, of course, she can't help rub it in at every opportunity.

To keep us from bickering, or maybe just to distract me, Ash tells stories about his home. Some are about us as kids. Cadence likes those ones because they're all about her. Even when they're about her getting in trouble, or more frequently, her getting Ash and everyone around her in trouble, I can tell she loves it. But there are other stories, stories about what it's like in Nine Peaks now, and what it'll be like for me when I get there.

I know these aren't real stories the same way I knew Cadence's tall tales couldn't be real even back when I was trying to be a good, mindless drone in Refuge. They're too bright, too warm, too perfect. Things aren't like that in real life. And every time he tells me how much everyone is going to love me, and how great it's going to be, and how happy I'll be once we get to Nine Peaks, all I can think about is how they're really all waiting for Cadence. How disappointed they'll be when I show up instead.

But three things keep me going past the dread and the bugs and the blisters and the chafing and the itchy, sweaty, too-many-days-without-a-wash grossness of it all.

There's Ash. He's just so happy about all of it, even the miserable bits. And also, utterly relentless. Part of me hates to disappoint him.

There's Refuge, and Freedom, and Ange, and Under. They're counting on me. If Ash's home is where I can get help and regain my powers, the sooner I get there, the sooner I can get back to defeating the Mara.

And then there's that stupid, hopeful part of me that keeps getting me into trouble. That guilty, childish wish for someone to take all my troubles and make them all better.

What if I get to Nine Peaks and everyone is just as happy to see me as Ash says they'll be? What if it's like coming home—for real?

I know better than to believe it'll be as great as he says. But I can hope.

8

CLOUDBURST

A NEW CROP of blisters later, I've been unwillingly introduced to rattlers (reportedly dangerous, obviously horrifying, avoid in future), not to mention squirrels (less dangerous, actually kind of cute), spiders (only sometimes dangerous, but extra next-level horrifying), and an alarming number of *very*-dangerous-looking creatures with spikes sticking out of their heads that both Cadence and Ash insisted were not only animals and therefore *not* monsters, but generally harmless. I'm pretty sure they were joking.

Decidedly *not* harmless are the assorted water monsters we have encountered inhabiting everything from a marshy patch on the flats to a stagnant, overgrown pond, to a barely-there trickle of creek and a small but bridgeless river. That last time, we barely managed to drag the bike through without further damage or loss of life. So far, speed, caution, and Ash's blades have carried us through safely, but I'd hate to be out here without him.

Ash has also taken to singing a marching song called "Sunny Sunshine Coast" every time it rains, which happens at least once a day. Feels more like once an hour. Cadence joins in with excessively creative harmonies whenever she feels like it—which seems to be most of the time, despite the fact that she's not doing any of the actual marching.

I didn't notice at exactly what point they drifted into making up their own lyrics, having tuned them out for the sake of my sanity—Cadence drops a few beats to cackle at that—but I just caught them rhyming "Mara-taken" with "eggs-and-bacon" and now I can't stop listening.

I think I might've been humming the tune in my dreams last night.

Okay, maybe not just in my dreams. It's catchy, even if I refuse to learn the lyrics. Or make any up. Though I do think they could've come up with a better rhyme for "taken" than "bacon."

"Cole thinks we're bad songwriters," Cadence says. "She thinks she can do better."

"A lyrical battle the likes of which the world has never known," Ash chants to the rhythm of the song, which by no coincidence whatsoever is also the rhythm of our steps. "As we march through the mountains hmm-somethin'r-other alone."

"Weak," Cadence says, at the same time that I look pointedly over my shoulder and say, "I thought the mountains were back there?"

"Something-something-something-and-genius-all-un-shown," he continues sadly, but with a glint in his eye.

I snort, and then he snickers, and suddenly all three of us are howling ourselves to tears in the pouring rain.

I lean on the bike to keep upright, my stomach aching with laughter. The frame shifts under my arms, nearly dumping me to the wet ground. Ash grabs my shoulders and pulls me away, shouting the song's lyrics again from the start over the sound of rain and our laughter as he gallops in circles with me in tow, spinning us in dizzying whirls up and down the road. Between the singing and the laughing and his prancing antics, it takes me until the end of the sixth verse to realize we're *dancing*.

I jerk away with a gasp and stand swaying, the rain suddenly sharp against my skin.

"Cole? What is it?" Ash comes a little too close.

I take a quick step backward, hit a slippery patch, and go down hard.

"Don't," Cadence says when he reaches for me again. "She just needs a minute. We're fine."

So he just stands there in the middle of the road, shoulders bowed, looking lost and suddenly, terribly tired. His hair is slicked down with rain and his power is sleepy, barely a shimmer in the depths of his eyes.

And I sit in a puddle and watch him, wondering about what could have been.

What we could have had, if I hadn't lost who I was and become who I am in a world where you weren't supposed to look, never mind touch. If I hadn't learned that dancing was all about desperation and power and control instead of the natural outpouring of joy and freedom and fun that Ash had made of it, if only for a few careless moments. If I had become someone who had learned to heal, instead of someone who only knows how to hurt and be hurt.

Ash sits down beside me, apparently without regard for the wet ground soaking through his pants like it has mine. Not too close, and not angled in. Not watching me, just . . . there.

"Sorry," I say, small and so quiet I'm not sure he'll hear over the drumming of the rain.

"Don't you dare," he says without turning his head. "Don't you apologize for how you feel or what you need. Not to me. Not to anyone."

My face gets hot and my eyes sting, and I'm glad he's not looking at me. I feel . . . miserable.

It would have been better if he'd yelled, or hit me, or ignored me altogether. Now I feel like he's done all of those things and more, and I can't even blame him for it because, as far as I can tell, he was trying to *help*.

But instead, it's like he's just put one more expectation on me that I have no idea how to live up to. One more way that I can't be who and what I should be. And I hate it. I hate feeling this way and I hate thinking these thoughts and

I hate that the one thing I thought I was meant to do was ripped away from me almost as soon as I found it.

And I hate the cold fear that whispers all day and all night that Cadence is right, and she would have done better.

"You're right," Ash says, as if, like Cadence, he's taken up permanent residence in my head and is listening in on every thought. "I came back for Cady. Finding—finding what I did was . . . It was a shock, sure. There's never been anything like this before, not that I know of. How could I have prepared for—for you? But, Cole—"

He reaches a hand close to mine, not quite touching, but near enough for me to reach out and take it if I wanted to. He's watching me now, watching with an intensity that makes the hair on the back of my neck rise, though I refuse to look back at him. "Finding you was not a disappointment. Just because you were unexpected does not make you a mistake."

I shake my head, moving both hands to my lap and drawing my knees up. Ash's hand curls, and then relaxes, and remains. Waiting.

But he looks away, giving me space to breathe again. "My grandfather is on the council. He had high hopes for me. After my parents . . . left, he sent me to the dorms. He said he wanted me to learn people. He meant for me to learn to lead them.

"No, that's not quite right. More like: how to work them, to make them do what I wanted.

"So I learned. I studied and I tested and I discovered how to give people what they needed to make them like me, to make them want to follow me. And then, when the time came to step forward and lead them, I said no.

"My grandfather is not a bad person, Cole. He wants what all the elders on the council want: to protect our people. To grow our strength. To restore our world. But he cares more about the outcome than the path, than the cost along the way. He's willing to sacrifice anything, anyone, to get there. Including my parents. Including my team. Including me."

Now he's the one avoiding my gaze, his arm tense, as if he wants to pull back, to curl into himself protectively as I have.

I'm not sure what to expect. He seems hurt, which means he's likely to lash out. That's what Ravel had done, the moment he realized I had glimpsed his vulnerability. And right now, I can't even retreat into the dreamscape if Ash decides to turn on me.

"I want to think there's a better way," Ash continues, before I can decide whether it's safer to stay where I am or back away slowly. "I want us to do better. To save everyone and make each other and the world around us better without tearing ourselves apart along the way.

"I almost became the leader he wanted me to be, just so I could prove I could do it better my way. But I'm so afraid I'm just as bad as him, because when it comes to what I want, when it came down to achieving my goal, I was willing to sacrifice anything, or very nearly, to reach it."

I stiffen, ready to dart out of his way. The hurt in his voice doesn't bode well for what will come next.

"I'm so sorry, Cole—and Cady, you too. Sorry I didn't come for you sooner. Sorry I couldn't make everyone safe. Sorry I made you leave. But I promise you—I haven't given up on your friends. On your city. No matter what happens when we get to Nine Peaks, I will do everything in my power to help them."

He lifts his hand from the mud, tense but open, palm up. Invitation, not rejection. Not accusation. Not lashing out.

I'd give a lot to be able to reach out for it. But that is a stretch too far for me to make.

So, instead, I uncurl, just a little, and move my hand from its sheltered spot next to my body to place it, palm up, where his had been only a moment ago. The earth is still warm.

Ash tilts his head, considering, and finishes what I can't, taking my still-healing hand in his own with the smallest of sighs.

"You shouldn't have kidnapped me." I measure my words, holding very still in case they run away on me. "You shouldn't have made that decision for me. But—but I think I'm starting to understand." My face and neck seem to catch fire. "You keep helping me. I don't deserve it."

"Okay, we get it," Cadence interrupts. Our hands spring apart. I stumble to my feet, flushed heat notching up a level higher. I'd forgotten about her. "Everyone forgives everyone else for making their life impossible. One big happy family. Can we get going already? We're losing daylight."

She launches into an unusually dirty new verse of the marching song at top volume. Ash shrugs, and lifts his knees comically as he marches back to the bike. He leans into it to get it rolling out of the mire.

Feeling left out, Cadence?

Instead of responding, she just gets louder and further off tune inside my head.

It's fine. We need to keep moving, anyway.

Maybe it's because we haven't made much progress today but, somehow, despite the unrelenting downpour and the caked on layers of mud, my feet feel lighter.

9

HOMECOMING

B Y DAY SIX on the road, I've stopped believing Ash's home even exists.

I'm also not entirely sure clean clothes and food that didn't start the day fuzzy and breathing aren't a figment of my imagination. In particular, I would very much rather not have had a front row seat to where Ash was sourcing dinner, but then it turns out travel is mostly a chain of unpleasantness spaced unevenly between where you started and where you intended to finish.

And then our poor, battered, sporadically powered bike grinds up one last hill and dies, and this time it doesn't matter because a glittering mirage rises in the distance. Only it turns out to be real. Our journey is at an end.

"Welcome to Nine Peaks." Ash twists to watch me, probably hoping for a spark of recognition.

I try. I really do. But any warmth I feel isn't from long-lost memories of a childhood home.

Six days in the wilderness with Ash, and only Ash has changed things. He's no longer a phantom from a dream, as I first knew of him, or the impervious hero I imagined him to be when I wanted someone to solve all my problems for me, or even the heartless, unyielding kidnapper who dragged me away from my home and my purpose.

He's Ash: strong and determined, funny—at times, even silly—and competent, careful to give me space but relentless in never, ever letting me run away, and so infuriatingly calm when I'm not that it drives me crazy. I notice everything about him without meaning to, the same way I can tell what Cadence is thinking just from the feeling in the air.

Well, maybe not quite the same way.

But he believes everything I need is on the other side of these walls, so I can't help a tiny shiver of excitement as he rolls the much-abused bike toward a massive ring of what looks like packed earth under a serrated crown of wood and weathered metal.

Not having the words is far from a new experience for me. But this—this is on a completely different scale.

I crane my neck so far I nearly topple over backward. Whatever that is on the other side is tall. I know trees. It feels like I've seen nothing but trees for days. These, whatever they are, are much, much more.

"Not bad, huh?" His voice is hushed with awe and pride.

I nod in mute amazement. I count nine structures spearing the sky. Some actually do seem to be gigantic trees, airy ornamentation spiraling around the trunks and draped between massive, sprawling branches.

But then the impossible size of it all clicks into focus. Those carved and painted things are swaying bridges linking open platforms and an assortment of partially-and-fully enclosed man-made things. It's like a whole building— dozens of buildings, even—has been taken apart and scattered throughout the treetops.

The other structures are more like the kind of towers I'm familiar with, but smothered in growing things. Amidst all that greenery is the glitter of glass in the sunlight. The outer skin of the tall columns is lacy with the perforations and ridges of balconies and windows and gardens and what seem like purely decorative features channeling light and shadow into a shifting, organic display.

It's awe-inspiring from the ground. I can't even being to imagine how stunning the view must be from one of the upper levels.

The crumbling road grows smooth under my feet as we near a broad ramp. It climbs to a pair of heavy gates, and beyond—

He stops. "Maybe you should wait here."

It's the only warning I get before the gates swing open and a crowd spills out in a roaring, many-headed surge.

Ash slings an arm around my shoulders and drags me forward to meet the mob, accurately predicting my first instinct, which was to run for cover in the opposite direction. The strangers engulf us in an onslaught of questions, demands, complaints, and orders.

"Where have you been?"

"You've been missing for weeks!"

"Who's that?"

"You've got a lot of explaining to do."

"Your unit came back without you. We thought you were dead."

"We had to tie Banshee down to keep her from going after you. Rei too."

"You're in so much trouble!"

"What did you do to your bike?"

"Did you fight lots of monsters?"

"Get back inside!" The order comes from a hard-faced woman with deep scars, deeper eyes, and a sleeveless tunic showcasing arms that look as if she could strangle a sea monster.

The crowd certainly seems to take her seriously, stampeding through the gates and sweeping us along in their midst.

I stay glued to Ash's side, though it's more than a little embarrassing. He obligingly turns out his elbows, holding back the tide to give me space to take it all in.

I don't know what I expected, but it wasn't this. A massive, rolling meadow fills much of the land between the walls. Pathways weave amongst the low hills. Some lead to what seem to be doors set into sides of the raised earth. Flowers compete with tall grasses and clusters of small trees overshadow orderly rows of plantings. Around the perimeter are the gigantic columns of the towers, though they're not like any towers I know.

Inside the city walls, I can see the roots of the exotic towers—not the heavy blocks of crumbling concrete and steel I'm familiar with, but light, airy forms that seem to float above the earth, draped with vegetation and perforated to show glimpses of the sky and mountains beyond. And, of course, some of the giant structures really are trees, rooted and spreading and glittering with elegant structures, as if a tower has been carved into dozens of pieces and strung between the branches and trunks. Tidy lower buildings cluster around their feet in heavy piles of warm honey-toned or silvered-grey wood.

But all that's nothing compared to the diversity of the people milling about.

After the visual excesses of Freedom, perhaps I shouldn't find it so surprising. But here, the bright and varied forms of dress aren't the only things that stand out. Not a single person has the bony, grey-hued look of a Refuge drone. Some seem to have hair so long it hangs all the way down their backs—real hair, not ribbons or feathers! There are not only a vast array of hair shades and styles, but also more skin textures and hues, bodies, and ages than I've ever seen. The smallest child barely comes up to my knees. The elderly are marvels to see—how is it possible for them to survive so long out here? I've never seen so many women in one place before, either.

I don't know where to look first. People crowd in, curious, peppering Ash with question after question. He smiles, and shrugs, and jostles them back when they get too close, all the while steering us through the winding pathways toward a long, dark structure made of massive, weathered boards. The doors that nearly span the width of its end are at least four times wider than any of us, and a good few feet taller than I am. They're also painted to look like a staring face with gaping maw.

I shiver—it looks like it's slavering to swallow us whole. The scarred woman from the gate follows us into the dark, cool interior, and for the first time, I realize she's driving

Ash in front of her like a Refuge enforcer marching a disobedient drone to Corrections.

Are we in trouble? I feel like someone probably should have told me if we'd been captured—

Ash catches me before I flatten my nose against a painted barrier. I hadn't been paying close attention, and in the sudden darkness as we passed through the doors and out of reach of the bright outdoor light I'd just assumed the way would be clear. He nudges me to one side, and we step around the false wall and into an enormous open space, smelling of earth and shadows.

Sunlight filters down from narrow openings in the ceiling, emphasizing the darkness rather than illuminating the interior. Nine chairs at the far end hold eight figures. Beneath the softly glowing silver mists of a dreamwalker's power, more than one head is bent under white or grey strands.

The scarred woman takes the last empty seat on the left. We're left standing in the middle of the dimly lit hall.

"You're late." The speaker's deep wrinkles and ropey silver hair are framed between a wide-brimmed hat and layers of scarves.

"Not just a little late. Weeks late. We thought you were dead." A white-haired woman sewn into a whole garden's worth of elaborate floral embroidery and beading adds.

"We were worried—" A tall woman, grey threaded through her dark braids, draped in heavy-looking woven fabric. Her brow furrows as her gaze flickers between Ash and I.

"We expect a full report," the woman who met us at the gate interrupts, sharp-voiced and straight-backed. "Why did you abandon your squad? Where have you been? And who is *that*?"

There others rustle in mingled approval and discomfort, a ripple of searching glances, nervous fingers plucking, lips flattened in disapproval or parted in question. No two look alike—or seem to think alike.

I shift my weight. Blisters burn and itch, my hands aching only slightly more than everything else at this point. I rub one foot against the back of my other leg, dislodging a hail of grime. There's a general tut of disapproval.

"Old farts," snorts Cadence, not without warmth.

Their gasps shiver the air.

"What?" Cadence says. "I'm back, fogeys. Didn't you miss me?"

The tall woman with the braids and blanket-cloak jolts like she's been jabbed with a pin. She rustles over to peer into my face.

I flinch, but Ash is right behind me. There's no escaping.

"Hi, gran," says Cadence.

The woman's hands are as soft as a breath. They flutter across my cheeks, sending more flecks of mud pattering to the floor.

"Cady . . ." Her fingertips tremble against my skin. She steps back, blinking fast over shining eyes.

I stare over her head, breathing almost as fast. *Gran?* I didn't think—I mean, I know my parents had died in Refuge, so I just never expected—Ash never said there would be—

"It can't be." The first man to speak tips his head to glower more effectively under his hat's brim, not at me, but at Ash. There's something to the shape of his face under the wrinkles that makes me wonder. Those scarves, not unlike the one Ash keeps tucked under the collar of his jacket—Ash did say his grandfather was on the council . . . "You're mistaken. That child died years ago."

The woman—our grandmother?—brushes a finger along my left cheekbone, tracing dark stains that won't wipe off with the mud. Birthmarks. Her hands knot at her sides.

She turns to face the seated council. "There's no mistake. Cadence has returned to us."

Ash makes a low, humming noise behind me.

I twist away to stand on my own. "Cole. It's—it's just Cole, actually. Or, kind of."

They look at me, then, infuriatingly, past me.

"And how does "kind-of Cole" come to be with us today, Ash?" This from the scarred woman.

"Here it comes," Cadence says.

"I found her." He speaks in a soldier's voice. Or a drone's. Neutral. Expressionless. It makes my hair stand on end.

"Where?" The woman barks.

"Where do you think?" Cadence says. "Where you abandoned me, that's where."

They all look at me. I blink, stepping back until I bump into Ash.

"She's had a long journey," Ash says. "A lot has happened—"

Cadence snorts.

"Perhaps it would be better to offer the child a few moments to recover? Ghost will remain to make his report in full." The "*and in private*" remains unspoken by the humourless elder—my top pick for Ash's grandfather—but implicit at the end of his order.

For it is undoubtedly an order. *Ghost* must be Ash's code name, like Banshee and Rei. They're treating him like a soldier, and not one they're particularly pleased with, either.

"No fear—the fogies know better than to let me out of their sight," Cadence says. But there's a hint of uncertainty in her sarcastic voice when she replies to them, "Is that really a good idea?"

There's no way I want to be separated from Ash now, left to fend for myself. Besides, we're in this together. I need the council to do whatever it takes to fix me up so we can head home before the Mara make sure there's no one left to welcome us back.

But no one asks what I want.

Ash steers me back to the doors despite my protests and more or less shoves me through. His eyebrows pinch, lips shaping the word "sorry" with a silent lift of the shoulders. Then he slams the door in my face.

10 ABANDONED

'M SURROUNDED BY a crowd of strangers and every single one of them is staring.

I reach up to smooth my mask with trembling fingers. It's not there—I haven't worn one for ages—but right now, I long for the bland anonymity of Refuge's uniforms. Every other face in this crowd is uncovered, but exposing my own bare, grimy skin still feels wrong.

Longing to run back inside and hide behind Ash shudders through me. Instead, I straighten my spine and glare back at the unfamiliar faces. I survived Refuge. I fought the Mara and won. What were mere humans going to do?

"This way." The tall woman with braids—my *grandmother*—touches my shoulder. She must have followed us out. She curls one arm behind me and nudges me down the path, ignoring the crowd. Most of the people obligingly stumble out of the way, still staring, but one boy—slight, perhaps a couple years younger than I am, brown-skinned, with dark hair and features that are almost too pretty—darts closer.

"So you're her, huh?" he says, striking an ostentatiously thoughtful pose, and then pulling a face. "Disappointing, if you ask me."

An older boy with shockingly orange hair jostles him. "Don't be rude, Rei. What if Cady doesn't remember you? What'll you do if she doesn't know you're joking?" He winks. "As you can see, nothing's changed around here. Welcome home anyhow."

The young giant behind him nods and makes a rumbling sound I can't interpret, while a tall girl with long braids standing just to his left gives me a hard look.

"Aleya's teaching right now," a girl with medium-brown hair in a springy cloud around her head says. "And Mogwai got called away, but—"

"Away with you all." The old woman makes a shooing motion. "Give the poor girl some time to get settled before you descend like a cloud of horseflies."

Their names are familiar, and they obviously expect me to know them—friends of Cadence's, maybe?

"Ash's squad," she says helpfully. "Or most of it. Those are their code names they're using, though. Threw me for a minute, or I'd've said hi. Banshee is the one with the braids, in case you were wondering."

Though the large one has to drag the small, comically hyper one—Rei—by the back of his shirt, they all melt into the crowd as ordered and leave us in peace, for which I'm grateful. It's bad enough the way a fog of whispers scratches at me from every side: *can't be—look at her face!— returned—alone?—where are the parents?—the Cole girl— Cadence Cole—Cadence—Cadence!* Having to deal with Cadence's old friends, the ones Ash deserted to come after me, is more than I can face right now.

Our path winds through low hills and vegetation, forcing the crowd to thin. Children chase up and down alongside us for a better look until they are scolded to stay off the roofs— the rolling landscape hides dozens of homes. Windows and doors peek from amidst the greenery, often marked by an extra cluster of colourful flowering plants.

The effect is not unpleasant, visually speaking, but being surrounded by so much nature—*ugh*. The air is full of flying things—some buzzingly alive, others seemingly inanimate floaters. I bat at the stuff that gets too close before I catch myself, conscious of the alarmingly attentive audience.

Though I keep sneaking hopeful glances at the fantastical towers hugging the city walls, our path ends in front of a weathered door with a carved handle below its little round window. The warm, variegated browns of the door set into the side of the hill remind me of Ash's eyes in those quiet moments when he pushes the mist away and lets me see the boy underneath the power.

My breath hitches. I glance back, hoping to see him catching up to us.

No such luck—only strangers return my stare.

"Come inside." The old woman—I can't adjust to calling her grandmother, I just can't—stands in the open doorway. She peers past me. "What are you all looking at? Back to work, the lot of you."

She ducks around me and yanks the door shut as soon as I cross the deep threshold.

The interior is unexpectedly bright. Windows show glimpses of sunshine and purple blossoms. Walls curl into ceiling, painted a soft blue between the raw wood beams radiating from a ringed opening in the middle of the roof. I feel like I've climbed inside the heart of a tree. The counters and shelves lining the walls above wide-planked floors, the doors on the facing wall, the table ringed with upright chairs, and even the two larger chairs in the center of the room are all made of the same warm-toned wood.

Green, purple, and blue fabrics offer a cool splash of contrast in cushions and woven rugs and draped blankets and painted vessels. Baskets hold piles of unidentifiable plant-life; other weedy-looking things are heaped on the counters or hanging from the beams. The smell is . . . is . . .

"Welcome home," she says.

My face flushes and my eyes prickle, welling up and making my nose itch. There's something about the smell of all these plants indoors that's getting to me. It's somehow familiar—and deeply upsetting.

My chest is tight. It's hard to breathe. I pluck the fabric of my shirt away from damp skin and feel behind me for the door. I have to get out—

"What's wrong? Cady?" The woman puts a hand to my forehead. "Are you sick?"

I jolt away, shaking my head.

"Oh, your hair . . ." she flutters one hand at the ragged locks straggling past my ears. Her lips twist unhappily. "Don't worry. It'll grow."

Cadence is silent for once—and just when I could use her help, too.

"I don't—I'm not—" This is ridiculous. I've been in far worse situations before and handled it. Nothing to do but move forward. "Cole. Not Cady. Please."

She blinks rapidly, rocking back on her heels. "Cole—? Cady, you don't—? Sorry, I think I'd better attend after all—"

Mist swells from beneath her skin, silvering her brown wrinkles, dripping down her long braids and clouding over her eyes. She goes very still, so still I'm afraid she's stopped breathing.

I wave a hand in front of her. She doesn't react. I move it toward her mouth to feel for breaths, but encounter resistance a few inches from her skin, as if the mist has gone solid. Like poking a mattress. I can press in a bit, but it pushes back.

I circle, testing the barrier. It's more than whatever Ash had done to keep insects at bay, more like full-body armour—I can't believe Cadence and Ash never mentioned they could do this.

Cadence hums. "If you weren't resisting so hard, you'd remember in the first place. She's off dreamwalking, that's all. You're freaking her out, so she's probably gone to demand answers from Ash."

I could argue, but I have better things to do with this unexpected opportunity to explore. I circle the room, picking up objects from the shelves and counters and trying to guess what they're for.

Some are probably food. These past few days on the road with Ash have introduced a number of new food sources, both plant-based and decidedly not. Quite a number of the unfamiliar foodstuffs have been dried into a form that seems very unpleasant for chewing. I try a bite of a lumpy green thing and spit it out immediately, my tongue working to scrape away the acrid sourness flooding my mouth.

Berries I recognize—and commandeer, cramming handfuls into my mouth as I explore. The first two doors on the far wall lead to smaller, darker rooms, each with a bed, several pegs with colourful woven clothes hanging from them, and a few shelves. Behind the third door I find what I really want but, glancing back to find the old woman still shrouded in silver, I'm not sure I should pass up this opportunity to explore unsupervised.

I make another circuit of the cozy space, this time lingering to handle more of the objects on the shelves and cupboards, though it's still painful to pick things up and that makes me clumsier than usual. I manage to cut myself more than once on the edges of new-to-me tools. I use my forearms for balance on the angled ladder in the middle of the room and work my way carefully up and through the roof to the top of the small hill that shelters the little house.

At first, I'm struck by how beautiful it is—warm and bright, colourful blossoms all mixed in with the wind-swayed grasses. Then I take another step up the ladder and look out over the grass—to a dozen or more curious faces staring back.

I miss a few rungs on my hasty way back down and have to take a moment to let the throbbing pain in my shins and elbows subside.

I wander back to the still figure frozen on one side of the main room. She hasn't moved, the silver mist radiating from her just as thick as ever. Her blank gaze doesn't flicker when I step in front of her. Worried, I move to one side and watch for the rise and fall of her chest.

It's slight, and not nearly as frequent as it should be, but she appears to be breathing. Under the swirling barrier, her colour seems healthy. As healthy as you can be when you've lived as long as she has, at least.

She's a little darker than me, but with the same kind of warm, reddish tone to her skin. Lines crease her forehead and frame her mouth and eyes. Her hair is thick and long, the deep brown strands twined with grey. Fuzzy bits curl out of her braids and spring in an unruly halo around her face. I push my rough-cropped hair back, wondering if it feels the same. If my mother's was like that too—or my father's, for that matter. I search her face as if I'd have any way to recognize either one of them reflected in it. Or even myself.

How many years would it take to look like her? I can't imagine living that long. Although . . . I don't know. I guess I've never really thought about my future that way. Never pictured myself as an adult, growing, changing, getting old.

I peer into the old woman's face and trace lines on my own, making faces and trying to feel where the skin might crease over the years.

Her eyes snap open. The mist sucks back under her skin.

I stumble backward and knock into the shelves, sending things I don't know the name for or use of crashing to the floor. Her gaze never flickers from my face. Her intensity—I kneel and fumble through the broken mess to escape.

She slowly lowers herself beside me.

"You can call me Susan," she says.

My nightmare flashes behind my eyes. *Suzie.*

Something bites my finger, a sharp nip from the shard of a broken dish drawing me back. Susan captures my hands and pulls me free of the fragments.

"Ash just finished giving his report." She tilts my hand to examine the shallow new cut—and the deeper, older damage. So many layers of hurt. "I think I understand now. Is Cadence there, too?"

We both wait for her response, but apparently she's childishly choosing to ignore us.

After a few moments of uncomfortable silence, Susan sighs. "Well, we can come back to that. And to this mess. The council wants to see you again, now that Ash has explained. But first, let's get you cleaned up.

"You were . . . with the council? And Ash?"

Susan closes her eyes for a moment, as if in pain. "You really don't remember, then. Ash said—well, never mind. Hurry and wash up first. I'll get us something to eat, and then it's back to the House of Nine for the both of us."

She bustles about as she speaks, reaching into a bedroom for an armful of clothes, pushing open the door to the bathroom and starting water running.

"These might not fit, but at least they're clean. Gracie won't mind. Soap's on the edge there. You can use it on your hair too." Her hand flutters over the mess on my head, and she sighs again. "Right, lots to do. Better get started. Unless you need help?"

She catches my wrist in a gentler grasp than her brisk tone had led me to expect and examines it again, the wrinkles in her forehead cutting deeper. Her power swells in a halo around her. She holds her free hand out from her body, tapping and twisting the air to no discernable rhythm.

I gasp. My hands come alive with a strange buzzing. It's almost, but not quite, painful. My cuts knit closed and the bruising fades. I make a fist, marveling at the ease. And then I sob, finally realizing what's happening, what her dancing fingers and my vanishing wounds mean.

She's a healer. A dreamweaver, like I . . . was—and yet not alike. She's not slicing into monsters and dragging people around by their deepest desires. She's simply putting broken things to rights.

She's what I could have been. What I was meant to be.

Suddenly I'm horrified. If she's like me—like I was—then she can see *everything*. All that I am. My deepest desires, things I don't even let myself see.

When I fight to escape, she lets me extract myself from her grip without protest. I hesitate, waiting for her to comment on what she's seen. The moment she opens her mouth, I'm gone. I'll be out the door and away before she finishes the first sentence.

But she just steps past me to turn off the running tap. Then she turns and hands me a towel, all in silence. My skin itches and the promise of a clean change of clothes is enough to send me into the bath without another word.

EDUCATION II

IT ALL WENT wrong from start to finish, and in the end, instead of getting my access to the dreamscape returned or healed or whatever it was we had come all this way for, I got sentenced to *school.*

And not even regular school. It's more like preschool. Or remedial classes.

Cadence is not pleased. Ash didn't seem happy about it either, but the council didn't give us any time to talk in private before sending him off, along with his whole squad, so I'm just guessing by the look on his face when they ordered him away on some new mission as punishment for going AWOL after his last one.

Turns out, rescuing me didn't count as permissible grounds to defy orders, and just because he'd snuck off on his own didn't excuse his friends from responsibility. So much for all his big promises.

The Council of Nine Elders seemed to have decided pretty much everything without me. When I showed up, still steaming from the bath and itchy from prying several layers of dirt from my newly scoured hide, they asked a bunch of weird questions I didn't know the answers to. Then they stared at me in silence for a while after that, their eyes glazed with silver and their sour, wrinkled old heads wagging slowly in disappointment or disapproval.

Cadence got pissy and soon refused to respond to anyone's questions.

I got tired of being made to feel like an idiot and told them the only reason I was there was to get my powers back and none of this was even my idea in the first place. If they could just hurry up and fix me or give me a jump-start or something, that'd be great and I'd be right off on my way and out of their hair, thanks.

I was peremptorily informed that I'd flunked my assessment and got myself kicked out of their training program before I'd even started.

Apparently, I don't know anything useful and can't do anything interesting. I'm basically a waste of space, time, and the revered council's energy, or so I gather.

So, now I'll be expected to tag around after Susan every day instead of fighting monsters. If I'm good, I can look forward to joining the littlest kids in training one morning a week. But only if I work hard with Susan and show some promise.

If it seems like I'm taking the news well, that's only because I've been glossing over the part where I tried to claw more than one of the esteemed elders' eyes out—gouged a nice red new tear on the scarred, gate-guarding council member's cheekbone before she planted my face in the floor, too.

They sent me back to Susan's place with an armed escort.

That was last week.

"You're doing it wrong," says Cadence.

"You're doing it wrong," says Susan.

I grit my teeth and pull the twine taut. Another soft green stem crumples against its stake. The long, trailing, leafy end flops to the ground.

"You killed it."

Cadence's voice is amused and reproachful, Susan's dry. She folds beside me in the dirt and demonstrates—again— how to gently catch the string around both plant and stake without snapping or uprooting either.

So far this morning, I've managed to weed the garlic right out of the garden, thin the carrots to nothing but aerated dirt, flatten the neat rows of potato mounds, deadhead every single blossom in sight, and prune the vines to stubs.

I even failed at composting, somehow. I'm still not clear on what the problem was there. Susan keeps trying to explain what I'm doing wrong, and Cadence keeps laughing at me or doing the disembodied spirit version of rolling her eyes (I don't know how it works either, okay?), and I'm just so done with all of it.

All. Of. It.

"Here, just try going a little slower this time," Susan says, pressing a fresh length of twine into my hand.

I let it drop. Her brow furrows. I take in her gentle disappointment, the dirty string, and the row of snapped pea stalks and listing stakes. I jump over them and set off running.

I don't know where I'm headed. Anywhere but here would do, if only I knew how to get someplace *else*.

I hate it here. People keep coming up to me as if I'm *her*. And then like half of them go right ahead and strike up a conversation with Cadence, giving me pitying looks behind silver-dusted eyes the whole time they're chatting because I don't know them and they can't accept that they don't know me. They act like I'm broken. Defective.

Maybe they're right. I don't care.

People call out to her as I storm by. I refuse to stop. Refuse to look into their faces and see the recognition. The pity. The strangers I should know. And the other ones, the ones who had never known Cadence as a child, curious to meet the freak.

I'm learning (relearning?) my way through town. The towers and giant trees make for easy landmarks, though in the areas with long, maze-like aboveground buildings, it can sometimes be hard to see out. Those are mostly places of study or making from what Susan's explained, and I haven't had much reason to go there so far. Instead, I head for the main gate. There are several spots along the enormous wall encircling the city where you can climb nearly to the top and look out over the woods and, more importantly, the road out.

This is not how it was supposed to be. This is not what was supposed to happen. I came here to get my abilities back. To learn how to fight and win. Or relearn, technically. Maybe even to sort things out with Cadence.

I have to get back home. Back to where I'm really from: Refuge, and Freedom, and Under, and all the people I left behind, just months from being devoured by the Mara, or maybe just moments. Every minute I waste here is a possible life I could have saved and the worst of it is, I'm not even making progress toward being able to leave. There was absolutely no point in coming all this way. It hasn't made things better for anyone but Cadence.

Now I'm back to being stuck waiting for someone else to fix things: someone else's power, someone else's plan, someone else's choices and consequences.

It's not okay. But I don't know how to get home on my own, and I don't know how to do what I need to do, be who I need to be, even if I could get back there. And Ash isn't here to talk me down or guide me toward a plan that might actually move me forward, so instead, I stand and stare out over the highway and clench my stomach against the gnawing helplessness that won't go away.

There's movement in the distance. A shout rings out from the walls, causing a mass scramble toward and through the gates. Someone's coming from the outside.

Ash? I lean, narrowing my eyes and raising one hand against the glare.

There are several forms hunched over dark solar bikes, including a few extra wide four-wheeled models towing squat carts heaped high with unidentifiable bundles. But as they near, it becomes obvious Ash isn't with this group. I don't recognize any of them from that first day when his squad tried to talk to me, but they all seem pretty young, and they're dressed in dark, close, tough-looking clothes like Ash's, with cropped or braided hair.

They move like him, too. My cheeks warm, but I scan the long, dusty line of the road anyway, hoping his team is still on their way. Which is stupid, because there's no guarantee he'd be able to help me if he were here.

The distant road remains empty. The returning riders sweep through the gates in such a tide of backslapping, hugs, cheers, and shouted song that I'm glad to be up here and not stuck in the midst of the chaos.

I shudder. All that enthusiasm . . .

" . . . Right." Cadence says, with her equivalent of an eye roll. "Super miserable to be welcomed home. You'd hate it for sure. Oh wait, that already happened."

My shoulders twitch with the urge to swat her. It must catch the attention of someone in the crowd below because the next moment, they're pointing me out on the wall and waving. They shout and beckon me down from my perch, and the only thing for it is to make my escape quick—before they catch me and I'm pulled into the middle of that noisy group.

"Or you could just, you know, make some new friends."

I jump the last few steps to the ground and set off running. Cadence is altogether too comfortable here. We didn't come to make friends or, in her case, reconnect with old ones.

"I know, okay? But what do you want me to do about it? I'm not the one who couldn't make the grade. In kindergarten."

This time, I swat at her, ineffectual as it may be.

Not my fault, not her fault, not anybody's fault, I know—but it's still a crummy situation, and I've had enough, and still I can't fix it, and I can't change it.

Ugh.

I cut a weaving line through town, changing course whenever there are too many people crowding the path ahead. I wind up back at Susan's place, standing on the edge of the poor garden I can't seem to stop killing.

She's not alone.

"Our—Susan—tells me you don't remember us," the strange girl says.

She grins up at me with unexpectedly pale eyes in a more than just sun-darkened face, looking hopeful. Streaks of every shade of brown shimmer through her braids, from a bleached near-blonde to deep earth tones, and her sleeveless tunic is brightly patterned and a little tight too tight.

She clearly spends a lot of time outside, but she's softer looking than the kids I saw at the gates, and younger-looking. Not a fighter, then. And not a hint of the telltale silver dreamwalker's sheen I expect to see.

"Gracie!" Cadence says.

" . . . Sorry," I say. The girl's sunny face falls.

Susan bends to pick up a trowel. "I'll finish up here. Why don't you two head on inside and start without me?"

The girl brushes off her knees and bobs her head. "I'm Grace. We—uh, Cady and I—knew each other. Before. Actually, we're kind of cousins."

I take a step back, shocked beyond words.

Cousins? Despite how hard Ash tried to sell me on the idea of being welcomed back, somehow, I hadn't picked up on the idea that there would still be so much family waiting for me. Or rather, for her.

Susan was one thing, but a kid? What next?

"I can't believe how much you've grown!" Cadence says, ignoring my panic.

Grace cocks her head and furrows her brow but doesn't respond. At least, not to Cadence.

"Sorry for the suddenness, but I, uh. I actually live here? I was staying in Steph's—my sister's—dorm while her squad was away, but now she's back, so, um . . . I guess we'll be roommates?" Her voice tilts up in apologetic question, but she smiles as she brushes past to open the door. "Come on.

We should get started—sounds like you've got a lot to learn!"

"Gracie?" Cadence says. "What—"

Susan shakes her head in my peripheral vision. "Grace can't hear you. She didn't inherit."

Grace pokes her head out the door. "What was that?"

"Your supplies are on the counter, kiddo. I haven't taught her to harvest yet, so just start with the fibres today."

The girl pops back out of sight.

"She can't dreamwalk?" Cadence sounds horrified.

"Don't go making her feel bad about it either, now. She's worked hard to contribute in her own way. Here, take these in while you're at it."

I accept the woven basket, popping an early blackberry into my mouth before taking it inside. The juice is tart, the seeds wedging between my teeth. I'm still not entirely used to actual flavours or food with texture.

"They can't be that bad," Grace raises her eyebrows at my expression, takes the basket from me and rinses the berries in the sink. "So? Are we really going to do this or are you just conning Gran and the council? Promise I won't tell if you are."

I dip my fingers into a bowl on the counter, tangling them in long brown fibres submerged in the water. "What are these?"

She huffs. "Going to be like that, is it?"

"Well, this is fun," Cadence says.

Grace picks up the bowl and carries it to the table. "Come on, get over here. Gran said to start at the beginning."

She untangles a couple strands and holds them dripping over the bowl. Then she drops them again and leans over the table, grabbing my wrist. "Okay, but seriously. You, like, forgot everything? You were top of your class back in the day!"

Cadence snorts. "Don't remind me."

I just stare. It's bad enough dodging the curiosity and pity of strangers on the street who think they know me.

The last thing I need is someone in my very own house making me feel like—

"Like I'm the one who should have survived?" Cadence's voice is flat.

I wince. Then I shake it off. "You're not dead."

"Uh, nope?" Grace says with that strained listening expression again.

"Not talking to you," Cadence and I say at the same time.

Grace's grip tightens. "So it's really true? You're—she's still in there?"

I pull my wrist back and rub it. "We don't want to talk about it. Can we just get on with whatever it is that Susan wants?"

"So weird," she whispers. Then she grins. "Okay, I'll play along. Welcome to weaving for dummies."

SKILLS 12

I HAVE NEVER felt clumsier.

Grace turns out to be five years younger and about five hundred times more graceful as she twists the fibres into long, smooth cords. My attempts—when I don't shred the fibres outright—are scratchy with jagged lumps or so loose they unravel as soon as I let go.

After a couple hours of failed attempts, Susan pokes her nose in, shakes her head, makes us tea, and wanders back out to her garden without comment. My fingers are raw from the damp fibres and my wrists ache from the twisting. My temper's about as frayed as the cords.

"I'm so bored," Cadence announces, echoing Grace's sigh.

I slam my hands on the table, letting my latest attempt unknot itself in a flailing whirl. "I can't do this."

Grace smirks. "Infant."

"I'm here to get my powers back, not help with the chores."

She shrugs. "So you used to have skills. Now you don't. This is where you start."

"Weaving isn't the problem! I just need to be able to see the threads again."

"I wouldn't know anything about that." She laces her hands behind her back and stretches, joints popping, seams straining. "You might not remember, but I'm no good with that stuff. All I know is, the council says you need to relearn the basics and Gran asked me to help. So here we are."

"It's not her fault," Cadence says. "It's yours. Get it together, Cole."

"This is a waste of time," I snap.

"Yeah. It is." Grace rubs both hands across her face, massaging the corners of her eyes. She puffs out a frustrated breath. "Okay. Let's try taking a walk. You can tell me about what you do remember. You know, what's it like where you're from, how the journey back was, that kind of thing. I've never been anywhere."

She pops her head out a window, calls to Susan, and hands me a large basket.

I let it drop. "I don't have time for a walk."

"Fine, stay here and teach yourself." She shrugs and stalks off without me, tidy braids bouncing against her back.

"Cole . . ." Cadence says.

I twist to look at the jumble of crumpled and snapped cords on the table, then down at the blisters on my fingers. I scratch, pressing into the clear fluid until there's a wet burst and the burn of raw skin.

I'm not just being difficult. I'm not.

I didn't choose to leave home and come here. Ash dragged me away from the place I'd only just earned, and now he's not even here to answer for it. Who knows how many have died since I left? How many will die before I fix whatever's blocking my access to magic and get back to them? But instead of healing, or training, or whatever I should be doing, I'm wasting time with an old lady and some kid.

"You don't have a choice," Cadence says. "You're useless without my magic. You'd only get killed if you went back—especially without Ash."

I dig harder into the blistered skin. Red drips from my fingertips.

She's wrong. I have choices, even if I don't have the power I need. Even if the only good choice I have left is to lay low and wait for Ash to come back. With or without my magic, when he returns we're going home. He got me out of the city somehow. I don't see why he can't do the same for my friends.

If I can regain what I have lost, I will. If I can fight, I will. But if all I can do is lay low until Ash returns and lull everyone into a false sense of security until I can force him to help me escape?

Well, then it's time to become a model student.

———— ✳ ————

GRACE DOESN'T SAY anything when I catch up, but her pale eyes arc in what might be a smile. Her pace quickens. With my long legs, I shouldn't have to try too hard to keep up but, true to form, I manage to trip on every exposed root and fallen branch while she strolls along as if the path is as smooth and clear as a concrete corridor.

It feels like the forest starts even before we reach the wall, cultivated patches shading to free-growing ground cover and small brush, then young trees, then not-so-young ones. The buildings step up likewise from the hill- and pit-houses of the rolling center to the taller solid wooden and pressed earth structures as we near the edges, and, finally, the soaring green-and-silver towers and inhabited trees along the inner ring of the wall.

Grace tells me the names of some of the trees and other plants as we pass, repeating them in a few languages. I dutifully mouth the syllables after her, but despair of actually remembering any. All this green looks the same to me.

But I start paying attention when we pass the last tower and stand facing the sharp limit of the wall.

"Don't ever do this alone." Grace grins like she's perfectly well aware there's no way I'll listen.

She leads me to a small gate—more of a door, really—set into the base of the wall. A key hangs from a hook set off to one side. I let out a huff at this evidence of the elders' cluelessness. The city gates are only locked against whatever's on the other side. It's as if, despite my experience, this city was never meant to be a prison.

I take a minute to look around and try to fix the spot in my memory. If I could figure out the way home, this could be a good escape route. Doesn't even seem to be guarded.

Grace ushers me through and locks the gate behind us, dropping the key's cord over her head. I breathe my first breath of free air in a week and sneeze. Nature is denser out here, the air full of pollen and insects and the sharp tang of trees in the sun. I miss the over-processed, dank, and generally toxic air of home.

"This is home," Cadence says.

"Not mine."

Grace squints at me. "Are you talking to her again? How does that even work?"

I shrug. "Ever been haunted? It's like that."

Grace stops walking and flips a braid over her shoulder. "Yeah, I'm gonna need a little more to go on."

"Don't move." I step behind her, grabbing her soft shoulders to hold her in place. She giggles a little, shifting her weight. I lean in real close until my breath makes the tiny strands poking out of her braids quiver and whisper, "You suck at everythiiing."

She jumps and swats me. I laugh.

"I'm not like that," Cadence huffs.

Grace hunches her shoulders and rubs at her ear. "Ugh. Really?"

I nod, lips pressed together.

"Come on, tell her you're joking," Cadence whines.

"Exactly like that," I flap one hand behind my head. "Like there's this irritating fly just behind you nagging, and judging, and pestering you all the time, but you can't ever get rid of it."

"Stop it. She'll really believe you, you know?"

"But she's actually you?" Grace asks. "Like, you're basically talking to yourself, right? Or is it more like your conscience?"

Cadence snickers. "Oh, I like that."

I wrinkle my nose. "No. Definitely not."

"Oh. But . . . I mean, it's Cady, right? Like, she still exists and, um. She remembers me and stuff. Doesn't she?" Grace chews her lip, staring up at me with tragic eyes.

I cave. "Yeah, she remembers you. She remembers all of this. I think."

"Then how come you don't?"

I start walking down the beaten path between the undergrowth, away from the wall. Away from their home, wishing that meant I was headed toward mine, instead of just *away*.

"Stuff happened. It's just how it is."

She rustles along quietly for several minutes, leading me first down clear, well-trampled paths, then along fainter passages through the undergrowth, then, as far as I can tell, into the trackless woods. Every so often she stops to show me things, naming them, explaining how best to harvest them, loading up first the basket she brought for me to carry, then her own. I would have thought we had enough plants growing on our roof, but apparently we're taking *more* back with us.

My feet are getting sore and I'm tempted to abandon the loaded basket when she tugs my sleeve and says, "We're here."

I look around. Trees, bushes, and oh, hey, look at that: more trees, same as before.

I mean, of course there's other stuff. There's dirt and smaller things growing on the ground, and bugs, so many bugs, and rustling that could be birds or small animals or just the wind in the branches. But the point is, there's nothing to see here.

"It's too young to share much yet," she says, reaching out to touch the narrow trunk of one of the smaller trees. "But your mother planted this one when she first learned to gather from the forest. Cadence knows."

I freeze, images of a bleeding, silver-dusted woman slumped across a golden floor flitting behind my eyes. They're not Cadence's memories, the ones that fade from my mind as soon as she shares them. They're Ravel's, painted with the vividness of his childish horror. I reach out shaking, bloodstained fingers—and bark rasps against my fingertips.

"Cadence . . ." I whisper.

"I don't want to talk about it," she says, distant.

Grace touches the bark too, tracing a scar. "Do you miss her?"

I pull back. "No. Like you said, I didn't know her."

She strokes the tree. "I miss her. She was a good teacher. She treated all of us like her own."

Cadence's breath hitches and I feel a pinch deep inside. I don't want to know these things, don't want to picture that dying woman as a planter of trees and a teacher of small children.

"Why did you bring me here?"

"This is what you've forgotten. Weaving doesn't start with dead fibres, it starts with something alive."

She moves to trace a long scar on a much larger tree. The bark has been broken away, exposing a smoother layer beneath. "You came out here as a little girl, like I did, to learn respect. Balance. How to share in life, not just take it for yourself. How to create, and not just destroy."

She moves to a different tree, unscarred, and pauses for a long moment. She just stands there, head down, eyes closed, palm pressed to the trunk. Then she draws a blade from inside her basket.

"We take just a little." She drags the blade near the base of the tree, pressing hard and cutting deep. The bright scent of fresh sap fills the air. "Too much and it will die. You start by learning of limits and boundaries."

Grace pries up the bark and pulls. Cracks splinter further up the trunk She grunts and steps back, leaning with all her weight until the long, narrow strip runs into a branch high on the tree and tears free, showering us with tree-bits on its way down.

"Well, come on." She jerks her chin. "Grab the other end."

I help her gather her harvest, heaping it into a loosely folded pile. "Now what?"

"We use the inner bark of young, straight cedar trees like this one to teach our dreamweavers. And also to make beautiful and useful things—when we're not wasting it on trainees." Her tone is more teasing than mean-spirited, despite the harshness of her words.

I groan, suddenly glad to be hauling big, rough lengths of raw tree instead of fiddling with the small, slippery bits at Susan's table.

"Why bother? There must be easier ways to get what we need."

"Depends what you mean by *easier*. Easier things to grow? To harvest? To work and weave? To wear?"

"All of that. I never used to have to—"

"You did. You just forgot. Don't feel bad. Lots of people forget that what they have doesn't just appear when they need it." She plunks down in the dirt and looks at me expectantly. "How much do you remember learning about the time before?"

I test the ground for dampness with one hand before crouching beside her. I prod the slick, golden inner layer of bark with mingled fascination and disgust.

"So, not a lot then," she says.

Cadence snorts. "Try nothing at all. She never listens."

Grace demonstrates how to break off the rough outer bark from its silky insides. She lowers her voice and slips into an odd singsong: "The people began to look down and in more than they looked up and out and so lost the way of seeing. And in the smallness of their vision, they did not see that they took too much and gave back less. And when their taking outstripped what could be given, the givers began to take back."

She heaps the broken pieces of outer bark at the base of the bleeding tree and watches expectantly until I scrape together a few pieces and scatter them at the foot of the tree as well.

"She means people got greedy and stopped thinking about the consequences of their actions," Cadence says. "The world returns itself to balance, and it's better to be a part of the returning than the chaos destroyed in the process."

I find a small stone on the ground and flick it at Grace. "Whatever. All I want is to get back what I've lost and stop the dying. That sounds like a good balance to me."

Grace balances the stone on her dimpled knuckles and rolls it from index to pinkie and back. "I'm just saying the difference between a hero and a monster is whose dying you're trying to stop."

She flips her hand over, catching the stone. She bounces it for a moment, and then tosses it back to me.

I fumble. The stone falls in the dirt.

13

MONSTERS

THE BARK IS lighter once we've broken off the outer layer and folded it into loose packets, but added to the weight of our already overflowing baskets it means I'm already sweating before we've even lost sight of the harvested trees. The torn blisters on my fingers sting, and the relief I'd felt at leaving behind all the nosy strangers on the other side of the wall is ebbing into frustration. The forest is dirty and busy enough in its own way.

I bump into Grace's back and nearly drop my basket. "Don't tell me you forgot something."

She cocks her head, listening to the wind tossing the branches, or maybe it's small, scurrying animals doing whatever mysterious rustling-type things small animals do, or—

Oh. I can't believe I forgot to worry about the locked-from-the-inside gates.

I square my shoulders and plant myself in front of Grace. I might not have my powers at the moment, but I've certainly been in more fights than her.

Or maybe not. There's a burst of pain and my knees buckle. Did she just kick me?

She hits the dirt beside me, reaching to drag me down again when I try to rise.

"Just stay down and shut up," she hisses.

". . . Cadence?" I try, but she doesn't answer.

I twist my shoulders to free myself from Grace's death grip.

She pinches me hard. "Seriously. Stay. Down."

I glare, but she's too busy staring past me to notice. Her pupils dilate.

It's too late. Whatever was coming for us is already here.

I screw my eyes shut for a moment, wishing. Hoping. Magic, Ash, weapons—oh, if only I had my threads . . . Then I turn to face the nightmare.

Only, it's not.

It's not Mara or any type of water monster I've seen, which makes sense since there's no body of water in sight.

It's hard to focus on it. The sunlight filtering through the trees seems to fall right through it, dancing as the wind tosses branches and shivers leaves.

Its flesh is a rich, ruddy brown and mostly hidden under shifting layers of green. Its head is covered with more of the same—a matting of leaves and twigs and moss softening its form. What face it has is broad, with gnarled, uneven features, and a seamed grain like exposed wood in place of pores.

It blends so well with the forest that it seems to step into and through the trunks of trees and thickets of undergrowth, as if it's a ghost. Or, as if the forest is the ghost and it's the only real thing here.

It looms over us, wafting sap, and pollen, and pitch, and moss, and the dry decay of last season's leaves, and—

I sneeze. Leaves shower over us—a swirling whirlwind that first whispers and then tickles, and any moment now will scratch hard enough to draw blood.

I snatch Grace's basket up and hurl it at the creature. It bounces off and rolls away, scattering its harvest.

"What are you doing?" Grace wraps her arms around my waist and drags me back down.

I struggle, trying to stand, trying to face down the monster. To at least do that much.

But it doesn't seem interested. It leans past to peer at the length of inner bark now splayed over the ground, unraveling from our tumbled baskets. It drifts off to examine the tree we harvested from, running what seems to pass for a hand over the fresh, weeping wound.

Grace's grip loosens. I wriggle out of her grasp and lunge for the blade that must have fallen out of her basket when I threw it. I plant my feet and hold the short, sharp-edged tool out in front of me with both hands, baring my teeth to keep them from chattering.

"You don't understand," she shouts over the whirlwind of leaves.

The green and brown thing looks from the tree to us. I brandish my makeshift weapon.

The leaves swirl faster, blocking my view. I slash, backing toward Grace, uncomfortably aware just how much longer that creature's reach looked than my own.

Then the leaves drop, all at once.

I twist, dancing in a circle to try to get eyes on the monster. I narrowly avoid slicing Grace's cheek.

"Give me that!" Grace wrenches the blade away. "Idiot. What were you going to do with that? Hack it to pieces?"

Her eyes are almost clear with fury—or, no, that's not it at all. She sinks to the ground, still gripping the blade, tears streaking her cheeks.

"Um," I look away, embarrassed for her. "It's okay?"

"No, it isn't," she wails. "You—you thought it was a monster, and you were going to fight it for me even though you can't fight and—and—you could have killed each other!"

I lean over and pat her on the head. It's awkward. I pull my hand back quick.

"Lame," says Cadence. "Your people skills are the worst."

"Shut up."

Grace cries harder, pulling her knees in and making muddy splotches on her increasingly dirty outfit.

"Oh. Not you. Cadence was being a pest."

"Just saying it like it is," Cadence snipes.

"What did I just say?"

"Like that tone's ever worked for you in the past."

"Could you not? It's not a good time, okay?"

"It's never a good time with you. You never listen, even though you know less than nothing, and all you ever do is make it worse, and—"

I ball my hands into fists and focus on the sharp pain of dirt ground into raw flesh.

"Don't you shut me out—" she starts.

"Or what? What'll you do, *Cady*. Oh, right. Nothing. Because you can't. So, just. Shut. Up."

"Are you guys always like that?" Grace is staring open-mouthed, tears forgotten.

I shift my weight. "Um . . ."

"So you don't get along at all? That's gotta suck. But I kind of get it—like me with my sisters."

"You have siblings?"

"Duh," says Cadence. I ignore her.

"Two older sisters," Grace says. "Jess is your age. Banshee, you know? She got sent out with Ash the day you guys got back, which must've made her year. She's had a thing for him for ages. And then Steph's a little younger. She just got back from a training mission today—I was camping out at her place in the dorms while she was gone, remember? They both suck, in case you missed that. Actually, you—uh, well, Cady— hated Jess when she was a kid."

"Yup," says Cadence. "Not too keen on Steph, either. Gracie was a little young to hate, though."

Grace turns her basket right side up and starts repacking its scattered contents.

I follow suit haphazardly. "I can't believe you guys bring kids out here. It's like you're trying to get them eaten."

"Um," Grace delicately tucks a bundle of curly fern heads to one side. "I think you're misunderstanding something."

"I'll say." Cadence sounds amused. "Go ahead. Why don't you explain yourself?"

But Grace just shrugs and finishes filling her basket. She hefts it easily, but I groan when it's my turn. It's a good thing we don't have all that far to go.

Twigs crack, each footstep rustling through drifts of old leaves and new growth overtaking the path. My skin itches with drying sweat and the dirt kicked up by the whirlwind. The basket feels heavier with each step. The adrenaline that propelled me between Grace and that monster is draining fast.

"You know I fought back home, right? In—in the city, I mean." I plod along for a bit before continuing. "Ash explained how there are different monsters, how they emerged as the time before ended. How they were tied to the damage we caused—people, I mean. Back home, we have the Mara—dream-eating monsters—that live in the fog, and other water monsters too, though I don't know as much about those. We saw some more on the journey out, different kinds of water monsters, I mean, but I haven't actually seen—what do you call this kind? A tree monster? A forest monster?—well, I haven't seen that before, but the ones I have seen . . ."

"What?" Grace says after a few moments, a few more steps closer to people and protection.

"I've seen them kill people. Lots of people. Strangers and—and not-strangers. Um. Friends. Or something. And I almost got more killed the last time I tried to fight, which is why I'm here, to get those abilities back. But when that thing came at us, I just—I couldn't watch them take one more. Not in front of me like that."

Cadence snorts. Grace is silent. I can see the wall through the trees now.

"Thank you for telling me." Grace pulls the key over her head, and pauses until she has locked up and replaced it on the hook on the other side. "I feel kinda bad for saying this now, but you should know—that wasn't a monster."

TRAINEE

I STARE AT the gate and wonder if Grace's sanity got locked on the other side. I don't remember her hitting her head.

"Oh, stop being so dramatic," Cadence chides.

Like she has room to talk.

"No, listen." Grace steps closer, bumping me with her basket. "It's an easy mistake to make. Ask almost anyone and they'd probably say the same as you. But think about it. It didn't hurt us."

"It tried."

"That whirlwind? You scared it, that's all. Think of it like a wild animal."

I stare, blankly. That was no squirrel. Cadence laughs.

"Um, or . . . Think about if someone came up to your door and knocked, and then when you opened it they were pointing a knife at you. It looks like they're there to hurt you, but maybe they wanted to borrow a sharpener, or show off their new knife, or sell it to you, or something. Okay, it's not a great analogy, but you get the idea."

"There was a monster. It attacked us. I tried to fight back. You got in the way. Nowhere in that do I remember knocking on a door."

Grace sighs and mutters something about letting Gran sort me out later. I trail along after her, trying to work out what monsters have to do with animals and stupid people who open doors to knife-wielding strangers.

She must be taking a different route back; we're spending longer than we did on the way out in the above-ground-building zone that sits at the base of the towers and giant trees, and along the outer perimeter of the city. Long stretches of wavy, layered earth walls, weathered copper, and age-silvered wood cast shadows on the path. The walls are thick enough to muffle shouts and clacks of impact until we turn a corner.

Grace nods at the sunken courtyard. "Thought you might want to see. Go on, you can get closer, just as long as you don't step into that flat bit."

"What is it?"

"Halfway between the class you should've been in, and the one I'd be in if I weren't me."

It takes little more than a glance to identify the huge courtyard as some kind of training grounds. But these kids aren't learning how to scrub floors or monitor screens like we did in Refuge. This has to be one of Nine Peaks' classes for dreamwalkers. And right now, they're learning to fight.

The inner walls are latticed. Plants grow right up them and along the long beams that span the entire width of the courtyard, casting mottled shadows and shading the trainees as they sweat and struggle below. Earth slopes from ground level down to a rectangle of lighter stuff—maybe sand? Each impact raises a puff of dust.

There are more people moving than I can easily keep track of, but the grounds aren't limitless—no more than a few dozen would fit in here. These kids, like so many in Nine Peaks, all look very different at first glance. But after a few moments, I change my mind.

They all wear their hair cropped or scraped back and tied down tightly. Even the braids are somehow caught close to the head, not loose like Grace and Susan's. The kids all wear close-fitting clothes in dark shades, too. Like Ash, but not identical to his. It's not quite a uniform, then. And they all seem well muscled and confident, even graceful in their movements, though there's a whole range of sizes and shapes tossing each other around in the ring.

I squint, trying not to see Ash in them, setting my teeth against the hollow, left-behind feeling these strangers have unexpectedly triggered. They don't look all that much younger than me, despite Grace's claims. I'm suddenly very conscious of my shapeless, borrowed clothes, my increasingly soft build since leaving home, my ragged shock of hair, well littered with bits of tree and dirt.

But even without all their training, even looking like this, feeling like this, I fought back the Mara. My shoulders straighten. I unknot my fingers from the hem of my shirt.

Cadence snorts. "You think they haven't seen battle? I guarantee you every one of these kids has taken down a monster or two by now. Their trainers will have made sure of it."

Heads tilt across the ring, curious, bored, even irritated gazes swinging our way as she speaks, silver in their eyes. Silver all around them.

My shoulders slump. "Oh."

An adult strides toward me from the other side of the grounds, cutting straight through the crowd. The teens in her path jerk back to their practice with self-consciously upright posture, but the ones on the fringes watch from the corners of their eyes.

Their trainer plants herself in front of me. Hard faced, deeply tanned, deeply scarred, and deeply irritated-looking. I think I remember her from the council meeting when I first arrived. And the un-welcoming committee at the gate.

"Who said you could come here?" she demands.

I start to turn toward Grace and catch myself just in time. It takes an effort to keep my hands loose and relaxed at my sides. "No one."

The trainer's gaze flicks to her anyway. Then back to me. "This isn't your class."

I fold my arms. "So I hear."

Her scars twist in an interesting way when she scowls. I catch myself staring and switch to eyeing the kids training. It's not what I'd pictured. Some stand or sit alone, eyes closed and motionless amidst the whirlwind of activity. Others are paired up, trading blows in acrobatic-looking flurries. Still others seem to practice against an invisible opponent or fend off multiple attackers.

There are weapons and bare hands, dark skin and light, and everywhere I look, shimmering, mist-covered forms. It's chaotic, and bewildering, and some part of me unexpectedly longs to dive in headfirst.

"You like that?" the scarred trainer asks, dragging my attention back to her narrowed eyes. "Good. If you get started now, you might be able to join them in a decade or so."

Cadence bristles. "If it were me, I'd teach her a lesson . . ."

For once, we're on the same page. I cast an ostentatiously dismissive sneer at the training grounds, and something truly ridiculous flies out of my mouth. "Won't need a decade. Won't need a month. Two weeks and I'll beat any student here."

I swallow a gasp and set my teeth against the inevitable slap.

But instead, the trainer smiles instead, slow and twisted. "I look forward to it, *dreamweaver*."

I show my teeth in a vicious grin, fighting to keep my knees locked. What did I just *do*? Those trainee fighters suddenly look a whole lot more intimidating.

I turn on my heel, wobbling just a bit as I march back to Grace. And right past her, and around the corner. Which I promptly collapse against, panting.

Grace races after me, dragging bark in her wake. "That was so cool! You just—and she—and then the look on Steph's face!"

Cadence laughs. I feel ill.

SUSAN LAUGHS TOO, when Grace tells her—possibly because the story comes complete with a re-enactment

95

starring Grace in every role, including an improbable inner monologue by the head trainer, Rocky. Who also happens to be her aunt, as well as one of the Council of Nine, captain of the guard, *and* the one who flunked her out of training in the first place.

I turn my back on the both of them and twist wet strips of tree until my fingers bleed. I can't afford to waste another second.

Step one: master basic skills—like, immediately. Step two: secretly learn everything else there is to know about dreamwalking. Step three: beat whoever I have to into the dust while stupid-face *Rocky* weeps into the dirt.

All in service of regaining my magic and saving my city, of course.

By the time the story ends, Grace catches her breath, and Susan stops chortling, I have a pile of cords as thick as my arm. Too bad the only lengths that aren't untwisting themselves faster than I can replace them are those pinned in place by the weight of the fresh failures on top.

Susan puts one hand on my wrist, stopping me.

I shake her off. "Leave me alone. I'm getting it."

"Yeah, you're definitely not." Grace pinches a ravelling cord between two fingers like a worm, or a twig, or a very skinny snake, or something equally thin and unpleasant.

Her stubby fingers untangle the strands, smooth, and re-twist them into a shining cord. She loops and fastens it around my wrist. "See? Like this."

I yank, but it's too tight to slip off. I need shears . . .

I stop mid-reach, suspicious. "I've almost got it. Stop distracting me."

"So stubborn," Grace says to Susan.

Cadence snorts. "Welcome to my nightmare."

Susan wanders off. The door creaks open behind me, letting in the cool evening air. Goosebumps ripple across my skin.

"I'll leave you to it, then." Grace tugs at the cord around my wrist in passing. "Sweet dreams, grumpy."

I scoff, still twisting, twisting, twisting as blisters burn, and break, and bleed. Ugly, broken cords pile up on the table. Footsteps, the soft thud of a latch as Grace cleans up for bed. Something tugs at the back of my mind but gives up almost immediately.

Alone again.

What was I thinking? I let the knotted strands drop. My hands shake. Grace's wristband gleams, warm brown ripples catching the light.

It looks almost soft. I'm tempted to run my finger along it, but I'd only stain it.

"It's nothing special," Cadence says. "That's literally the most basic thing you can create. It's what they teach toddlers before they have the coordination to weave properly."

I slam my hands down, tipping the bowl. Water splashes across the table.

What does she want from me? I never wanted to come here. I certainly never cared about making perfect beautiful little cords, and farming, and weaving, and fighting my way up the trainee ranks one step at a time, getting treated like I'm some useless wannabe failure instead of—I mean, I already know how to do everything I need to beat the Mara. I've woven the threads of dreams and bound nightmares, without any training at all, and I know how to take back my city.

"Maybe you did, once," Cadence says. "And once upon a time your fingers learned to hold the threads and spin and weave like all the other little kids up here, you just don't remember. So stop pouting and try already."

"I am trying—"

"No, you're whining. You're fighting it every step of the way because you think you're too good for this."

The door slams open, but when Susan enters, it's with a soft step and quiet eyes. I swivel to watch her place a basket by the sink, rinse her hands, dry them, and pull a chair up to the table. She reaches around me, alarmingly close and warm and smelling of growing things, and places her hands over mine.

I yank away, afraid she's going to try to heal me again. I don't want her looking at . . . at *me*. Not now. Not ever. But she gives me an annoyed little jab with her elbow and then takes my hands, covering them.

Her fingers are just as long as my own, if a little thicker at the joints. Her skin is stained in the creases and nail beds, and roughened with callouses and old scars. And if I flinch from her touch and try, repeatedly, to pull away, she doesn't seem to take offence.

Slow, calm, inevitable, she guides my hands to the bowl, gathers fibres, knots and twists, and lays the finished cord to one side. She repeats the process, and again, and the fourth time her hands hover a breath away from my skin as I make the slow, deliberate movements on my own, if only barely.

The result is imperfect—but it holds.

BALANCE

AFTER I PRODUCE ten mostly-even lengths of cord, Susan shows me how to unwork and rework the ruined ones, still without speaking.

I get faster, less clumsy. The old pile shrinks, a new one forming on the other side of me, until there are none left to fix.

"Congratulations," Cadence says. "You can now keep up with the toddlers."

"I seem to remember it taking you more than a day to master these . . ." Susan raises her eyebrows.

"I was *two*, gran."

I shove my chair back and head for the door. I don't have time for this.

"It's dark out," says Susan. "And you missed dinner."

"Not hungry."

I slam the door, though it's not Susan I'm angry with and she doesn't deserve me mistreating her home.

The night is still, but for a late-evening breeze stirring the garden. Good. I don't want an audience.

"But they'd be so amused," Cadence says.

I slide my feet apart and bring up my arms, hitting out at the air with closed fists as if I'm facing an invisible opponent.

I need to teach myself to fight at least as well as those kids I saw today. By myself. Within the next fourteen days.

While also mastering everything else they know, because I'm not sure I even have fourteen days to spare away from Ange and the rest of the poor souls stuck within the barrier. Two weeks seems like an impossible amount of time to build my skills, and also far, far too long to wait. But this is the only path forward I can see right now, so I'd better get started.

I don't have any time to eat, or sleep, or fail—or feel like an idiot. I jab at the air a few more times, aware of just how lame I must look, but a little less chilly with each attempt. When I try a sidekick, I stagger off the path. A dusty, herbal smell springs from the crushed leaves.

"I wish you wouldn't."

I scramble out of the garden. Susan stands in the doorway, wrapped in a bold-patterned blanket. Warm light streams out around her.

"Sorry," I mutter, turning my back on her and planting my feet. "I'll be careful."

"Just come inside. Flailing around in the dark won't get you any closer to passing an assessment or showing up your juniors."

But the door thumps closed when I make no move to obey. The night seems darker and colder. I check behind me to make sure she's gone, and try another kick. The garden leaps up and smacks me in the face. I sneeze and roll off a fragrant patch of fresh-crushed herbs.

"The bane of gardens everywhere," Cadence says. "At least your clumsiness is legendary."

I drive a fist into the ground and discover it's not just made of dirt.

"That'll leave a bruise."

I chuck the sharp stone in her general direction. Which is nowhere.

"Next time, just toss it at your own head. Maybe it'll knock something useful loose."

I brush myself off and limp back to the path. "If I go inside, will you shut up?"

I hope she says yes. I'm sore and shivering and grimy and almost ready to quit— except I can't.

"You don't always have to do things the hardest way," she says, sounding more serious. "You think I don't want you to get my power back and take down Refuge, too?"

"You've done nothing but get in my way since before we got here."

"They killed my parents. They took my memories, my body. They put you in charge. How could I not want revenge?"

"I was raised by monsters that taught me I was broken. My friends have been killed in front of me—more are probably dying right now. Just when I'd finally found a place and a purpose and the power to stop the dying, I lost it all. And now the one person who was supposed to be on my side won't stop dragging me down. So, please, tell me again how much better you are at everything,."

"All right, over there?" A stranger looms in the shadows a few feet away.

I jump at the sound and backpedal for the door before he can get any closer.

The stranger grumbles but doesn't chase me in. Susan leans out and waves reassuringly over my shoulder. It's probably just a neighbour out for an evening stroll.

Sudden warmth burns my chilled skin, and the smell of cooking makes my stomach grumble. I slump inside without a word, feeling like the world's biggest loser.

Susan waits for me to wash and eat before saying anything. She clears away the dishes and hands me one of my twisted cords, not as perfect as Grace's but still holding its shape, more or less.

"You couldn't do it this morning. Now you can. What changed?"

I blink, heavy and slow with sudden exhaustion. "I don't know. "I got better?"

She hums. "Oh? How? When?"

I long to pillow my head on my arms and close my eyes. Instead, I turn the cord over, looking at the fine strands as they melt into one another. "Don't remember. It just clicked."

"No." She taps the back of my hand. "You learned by touch, not thought. Thinking about it didn't help. Learning where it came from, digging into your motivation to learn, none of that made a difference in your ability."

I roll the cord between blistered fingers and wince.

"What did you see in the woods?"

I rub my eyes, not sure what brought on this sudden change of topic. "Trees?"

She gives me a look.

"Uh, Grace showed me how to harvest bark so it doesn't kill the tree, and then we carried it back."

"Good, what else?"

"We were attacked by a strange monster. Not a water monster, some other kind. Forest-monster, I guess. But then it just kind of went away again. Grace didn't tell you about it?"

"She did. She said you tried to fight it for her."

I blush, look down at my hands, scratch at a blister. "I knew she didn't have magic, so—"

"Neither do you."

I bite back a retort. She's right. It had been like that last day in Freedom, standing against the attack, reaching for something to hit back with and finding nothing at the ends of my fingers but air. "I had to do something."

"Why?" But she doesn't wait for me to respond. "You wanted to help a friend. Protect her. That's good but dangerous. You're a child right now. You don't have the tools to understand, or to take action."

I wave the cord at her. "And this is supposed to help?"

"Balance," she says, taking it from me. "Pull too hard and it breaks. Twist too tightly and it warps; not tightly enough and it unravels. But when you started respecting the material, really feeling it, you stopped hurting it and yourself. That was not a monster today."

The light rippling over the cord has me so hypnotized I nearly miss her last comment.

"What?"

"The creature you and Grace encountered in the forest. It wasn't a monster."

"Sure looked like one." I shudder: its inhuman form, that whirlwind of cutting leaves it sent at us . . .

"You want to learn to fight."

It's not a question. I nod anyway. Obviously.

"Why?"

"To save my home. My friends."

"Then tomorrow you will learn what makes a monster."

"I don't have time to waste." But the words slur and drag. I'm heavy with tiredness and confusion, and if my frustration can't even push back the need for sleep, it certainly can't shake Susan off as she shoos me off to bed.

I stumble against the new bed wedged into my room. Grace curls a little tighter under the covers in the other and groans. I blink, slowly coming to the conclusion that yes, she should be there—and then I yawn, and tumble into darkness.

GRACE CHIRPS ME awake too early and keeps up a steady stream of chatter as we eat, garden, tour a new-to-me section of the city that holds workshops, repair shops, plant nurseries and an odd mix of garden-and-laboratory buildings where people wander around scribbling things while prodding at plants or playing with dirt. Then we harvest, cook (or, in my case, burn food and learn some more about composting), eat again, pointlessly twist more slippery strands of tree, progress to simple woven patterns, discuss but don't actually start working with beads and thread, cook and eat yet again, and practice simple stances and blocks in the garden as night falls.

Turns out most people learn the basics of fighting around here, dreamwalker or no. Grace is happy enough to pass along what she knows, though she says it's more about understanding your body and maintaining basic fitness than fighting anything, or anyone. Still, what little she's able to show me is more than I knew this morning.

She changes the subject when I ask about Susan's cryptic late-night lecture, and Susan refuses to bite when I bring up monsters in passing.

And then I've lost another day. I've barely learned anything. I have less than two weeks to catch up to and pass the younger students, and I just want to sleep but I can't afford to, and—

Susan hands me some tea and settles back into her chair. "What did you learn?"

"Nothing useful. I'm running out of time and you made me do chores all day!" If I sound like I'm sulking, it's only because I am.

"Did I? What a shame." She sips her tea. "And what did you learn about monsters?"

"They love torturing me?" I cut my eyes at her meaningfully.

Susan smiles. "Good."

I wonder if I can put in for a transfer. Isn't there anywhere else I could stay? Another teacher I could be assigned?

"Where do monsters come from?" she continues.

The answer catches in my throat. From the fog. But also from the water, and apparently, from the trees, and—

"Borders," I say, a little proud of myself for the insight. "They come from the edges of things."

Susan leans in. "Good. That's perceptive, and true. But incomplete—you had it right the first time. Monsters come from us. Which is why the creature you saw in the woods yesterday wasn't one."

"Sure looked like it."

"No doubt." She's laughing at me.

I stand, eyeing the door.

"Sit down. We're not done here, not until you know what you can and cannot get into a fight with."

I keep walking.

"They're our fault."

I stop.

"The monsters. The others have always existed—the unseen, or rarely seen, creatures born of wave and wood. But we who could see them knew them as . . . perhaps not friends, but not enemies, either. We left each other alone. Until we didn't."

"They look like monsters."

"They look like themselves. We're the ones who made monsters of them. They're of the earth and the waters. When we hurt it, we hurt them. When the damage became too great, they rose against us. It was self-defence."

I turn on her, getting in her face like she's the enemy, like she's the one I have to defeat.

She catches my wrists, the beginnings of a silver mist trickling along her skin. "You're angry. You've seen what they can do. I understand. But it's our fault as much as theirs."

"They struck first."

"No. We did. They responded, tried to stop us. All creatures react to their environments. Theirs was killing them, so they fought back."

"You don't know anything."

"I know what you and Grace saw in the forest did not want to hurt you. I know what you fought in that poor shattered city of yours desperately wanted to hurt you, and you it."

"It held us captive! For generations! It killed, over and over again, and wanted more!" My face is hot, fists clenched. I tear away from her and slam the door to my room.

She's insane. No wonder she hasn't been teaching me properly—she's trying to protect the monsters.

FURY

I T GETS EASIER after I stop listening to Susan. Grace seems worried but willing enough to help, even when I insist on ignoring our chores and training far away from Susan's house every day. It's bad enough living with the enemy—I don't have to let her ruin my chances entirely.

Away from Susan's corrupting influence, Grace is more willing to show me what I need to know. Drills to improve dexterity, free from the limitations of slippery strands and tangling threads. Stances for defensive and offensive attacks. Strike patterns—even I can tell she's not great at them, but the clumsy moves she shows me are bound to be more useful than learning how to thin carrots and train vines.

After two days, I'm no longer tripping over my feet every time I move. Maybe I can pull this off.

But by a week in, and with only a week to go until the challenge, I'm stuck. Grace doesn't have anything new for me to learn. I've even snuck over to watch some training sessions, memorizing and trying to copy the way the students move on my own later, striking against the side of a building or pulling the blows with Grace as a moving target.

The process frustrates both of us, creating little more than bruises. Cadence occasionally comes up with something helpful. More often, she sulks and interjects snarky commentary on my inadequacies.

And then Grace does something truly terrible.

"This is Steph. Say hi to Cady and Cole, Steph."

Grace's sister is a little taller than her, with the same round face, but darker of skin, eye, and expression. She's stocky, but her sleeveless tunic and scraped-back hair show none of Grace's softness.

"Freak," says Steph. It's not clear which of us she's addressing until my feet leave the ground.

By the time I coax air back into my lungs and blink most of the stars away, she's looming over me with a curious expression. I'm completely unable to work out how that a solid-looking girl went from standing a few feet away, to having her foot planted in my midsection, to me going airborne in a single whirling second.

She rolls back onto her heels.

"Huh. You really are broken."

I swat her outstretched hand and scuttle backwards on my hands and heels. "Go away."

The girl laughs. "Cool. Monster-bait talks."

"Steph!" Grace cries.

"Chill. I'll stay. Seems fun." She bares her teeth at me. It's not a friendly expression. "Heard what you said, 'bout beating the best of us by the end of next week. That'll be me. You're welcome to try today if you'd like a head start."

I curl tighter. Then uncurl into one of Grace's defensive postures, feet braced, elbows out. Steph whistles.

"Wow, you're all mouth, arent'cha. That's the worst stance I've ever seen, and that's saying something with Gracie here."

She jerks a thumb at her red-faced little sister. I take advantage of the momentary distraction to try a surprise attack. Only, I'm the one who goes sailing through the air. Again.

"Nice try. Crappy form. Go again."

I could roll in the dirt in a ball of pain. Instead, I dive at Grace's stupid sister again, and again, until she works up a sweat and my head's spinning too hard for me to stay on my feet.

"Not too bad," my new tormenter says. "If you were, like, six. Maybe. No talent, of course, but you're persistent. You might make it into the babies' class now. Same time tomorrow?"

I spit in the dirt at her feet. She laughs. I glare.

Then I nod. "Tomorrow."

Steph swaggers off.

I flop back down, sweat plastering my hair and clothes to my skin. "Seriously?"

"I didn't have anything more to teach you," Grace says. "It was either get beat down by Steph on your own time and maybe learn something, or in front of the whole class, with Auntie Rocky gloating from the sidelines."

"I don't like your family."

Grace nods understandingly and helps me up. "Follow me."

She trots off, braids bouncing. I limp after her, too sore to protest.

She leads me to the wall and unlocks the small side gate we used last time.

I make a point of looking back over my shoulder. I'd been thinking more along the lines of a bath and something to eat, maybe even going over some of those moves Steph showed off and trying to figure out how they'd worked if I had the energy after dinner . . . But Grace steps over the threshold, tosses the key at my feet, and sets off into the forest.

I could lock the door behind her and head home. Except there are monsters out there, and even my rudimentary fighting skills have to be better than hers. Or, about the same, apparently. But still, two incompetents wandering in the forest are better than one, right?

Cursing with a selection of the interesting new words I've picked up watching the trainees, I stagger through the gate, lock it behind me, and jog after Grace. I snag one of her braids and give it a tug.

"Ouch?" She cuts her eyes at me but keeps up her pace. "Don't be mad. I want to show you something."

"I want to sleep."

"No, you don't."

Since she's right, I keep my mouth shut and focus on cataloguing bruises as we make our way through the woods.

It's not the least pleasant thing I've done all day. If I didn't have to be on alert for monsters, or creatures, or whatever, it might even be kind of nice. There are bright wildflowers scattered around, and a whole lot of shades of green that I'm starting to be able to tell apart, and if there's quite a lot of suspicious rustling, I can chalk that up to wind in the trees and harmless little forest creatures.

The rustling gets louder. I snatch at Grace's sleeve, but she just tugs it out of my grip and keeps going. And then we break through the trees.

It's a stream, complete with a small cascade rippling down from higher ground. It's strangely peaceful—and apparently, free of monsters.

Grace gives me this crazy huge grin and walks backward until her heels are teetering over the bank. Then she drops, folding into a serene puddle at the very edge of the stream. Her pale eyes, the exact soft green and brown hues of the burbling water reflected between dark lashes, flutter closed. She seems to breathe in the breeze, and the rushing water, and the fresh, clean scent of this place, and grow larger with it. Brighter.

Mist creeps across her skin, paling its surface with a faint silver cast.

"Hi Cady." It's barely a whisper, too quiet to hear over the small waterfall if I hadn't seen her lips move.

"Hi Gracie," Cadence says.

Grace just tapped into the dreamscape.

I have the sudden urge to shove her into the stream.

"Cole's annoyed," Cadence says.

If Grace answers, I don't hear it. Her face is still, under its faint silver covering.

"Yeah, she'll wait . . . I know, right?" Cadence laughs. "Okay, but if you'd seen . . . hmm. Uh huh. Seriously? Wish I'd been . . . Okay, yeah. Yeah, I hear everything she does, so . . . Cool, go for it. I'll be here."

Grace's eyes open. The mist fades back under her skin. She grins. "She's really there!"

I dive back into the forest.

"Wait," she crashes after me. "Don't be like that. I can be friends with both of you like this."

I turn on her, and she almost falls over trying to reverse direction. "You said you couldn't do that stuff. I thought you were locked out, like—"

Like me.

"I can't. Usually. Except for in that one spot. Even there, the connection's weak. I couldn't do what you did, Cole. I can't fight. I can barely communicate. If Cady weren't so strong to begin with, she probably couldn't even hear me. But if even I can cross over to the dreamscape like this, maybe there's something, or somewhere, that'd boost your connection too."

"A magical forest stream is hardly going to help me fight the Mara."

"But something else might," Grace says. "Like a certain type of wood, or a rock, or—"

"So, what? I should wander the forest touching everything to see if it can unlock my powers?"

I slap the nearest tree in frustration. And, if I'm honest, hope.

I'd be happy to tuck a few twigs in my pocket if that's all it takes to get back everything I've lost.

17

TALISMAN

I STOMP THROUGH the woods, hefting stones, thwacking branches, and splashing through puddles while Grace watches for traces of mist.

It's infuriating to be wasting time looking for a magical solution instead of getting back to my real training. Except—Wasn't magic what I'd been missing all along? If I could get my ability to tap the dreamscape back, I wouldn't need to bother with boring training and stupid challenges and impressing those idiots in Nine Peaks anyway.

"Not that." Grace unexpectedly smacks my reaching hand. "Those burn."

The leafy green thing in question doesn't look any different than a dozen other bushes between the trees, but I plant my palm on the rough, thick trunk behind it instead. "This isn't working."

She shrugs. "It could take a while. Or it could all be a wasted effort. It's not like I'm an expert."

A stone. A twig. A mushroom. I paw through the forest floor, discarding one bit of junk after another. We've already tried hanging out by a couple different ponds and streams, and wasted too much time sitting at the side of Grace's little cascade waiting for something to happen. Trying to make something happen.

But between Grace's vestigial talents and my own brief and untutored experience tapping into the dreamscape, I'm not sure we even know what we're looking for.

Cadence, on the other hand . . .

She sighs. "Don't you think I'd have helped by now if I could? The only path I know besides being a natural like me"—I swear she pauses to bat non-existent eyelashes before continuing—"is to get into dreamwalker training, and you didn't even qualify for that."

"Maybe we've just been trying the wrong things," I say, without much hope. "Or looking at it the wrong way? Obviously, this is a weird case. How does it work for normal people?"

"It doesn't." Grace has been following my half of the conversation, and chimes in. "Normal people can't dreamwalk. Most can't even see creatures, never mind fight monsters."

"So what's different about the ones who can?"

"It's partly hereditary," Cadence says. "The ability is passed down over generations. It's a whole thing. People get weird about it."

"What is the dreamscape?" Grace asks overtop of her. "Where do you go when you dreamwalk?"

"Cadence says access to the magic is hereditary," I tell Grace.

She holds a finger up. "I'm not adopted, so there's more to it than that. Hang on—. We'll come back to that. First, answer my question."

"It's . . ." It felt like travelling, like that time when Ash had been in the infirmary, and then suddenly in Freedom when I'd needed him. But, thinking back, there had been people around at least some of the times I'd tapped in, people who would have said something if I'd suddenly vanished and reappeared, so my body had to have stayed in one place.

Whenever I'd seen Ash, or Susan, or even Grace, briefly, draw on the magic, they went all silver, but they mostly hadn't actually moved, so—"We don't go anywhere, not really."

"Wrong," says Cadence.

"Actually, we do and we can," says Grace. "Just because your body stays in one place doesn't mean the rest of you isn't travelling. And just because dreamwalkers don't often fully move through the dreamscape to another location doesn't mean they can't. So, if the dreamscape is a place both the inner self and the whole self can travel through, what is it?"

"You know this," Cadence says unhelpfully.

I think about accessing the dreamscape—back when I could. "I was on the rooftop of Refuge, mostly. At night. There were stars out. But, also other places. Sometimes right nearby, other times on different floors, or outside the tower entirely."

Grace's eyes gleam. "Refuge? Is that a place in your city?" But she shakes off her curiosity with a visible reluctance. "You're being too specific. The dreamscape might appear as familiar places, or take you to different locations, but that's not what it *is*."

"She's not gonna get it," Cadence says, forgetting Grace can't hear her.

But Grace seems to have arrived at the same conclusion. "It's okay. The answer isn't that simple anyway. Gran explained about monsters, right? How they happen at the edges of us and *other*, when we warp what was already there? It's kind of like that. If the regular world can be defined as what exists outside of us, the dreamscape is what's inside. But not just inside you, or me, or Cadence, or whatever. It's like insideness itself. All the insides of everything at once."

Which makes about as much sense as wandering through the forest tapping trees to see if they grant me magic. So I huff at her and dart away down a faint track in the woods, slapping my hands against everything I come across while Cadence snickers and Grace puffs along in my wake.

And then, unexpectedly, the trees become familiar. My fingers hover above the newly scarred trunk where we harvested the bark only a week ago. Nearby is the smaller tree my forgotten mother planted. This is where that monster—creature—appeared.

If anything out here is magic or can give me back what I've lost, it's this. My hands tremble, first brushing the rough, fragrant bark and, when nothing happens, tapping, pressing, digging in as if I can rip what I need from its heartwood.

My nails sting with splinters. Sap gums my fingers.

I work myself in closer—feet braced between roots, bushes scratching my knees, both hands pressing into the trunk. I lean my forehead against the long scar, inhale the clean scent of sap and silently beg, *Here, please, let it be here. Give me back what I need, so I can escape this place so full of everyone's memories but my own. Give me back myself so I can go home and do what I was meant for. Please, please, please.*

Begging gives way to raging. I claw at the living wood— pounding, tearing, kicking—until I'm left clinging to the trunk, sobbing like a child, afraid to let go, whispering: *sorry, sorry.*

And it reaches back. Not to draw me in, but to push me away.

Grace gasps. A branch-like hand pries me from the tree, thrusting from the trunk like the ghost of the tree is bursting out.

I land in the dirt, hard. The creature looms over me, the one we met in this wood a week ago or one very like it. It has the same gnarled features set in an alien expression that defies interpretation. Its makeshift covering flutters as it moves, shedding bits of moss and leaves that drop soft and green and land brown and crisp. The smell of growing things in the sun sharpens and deepens around us, spicy and honeyed at once. It makes no sound, but for creaking and the susurrus of murmuring leaves.

It doesn't move to attack—so I do. I jump to my feet and draw on everything I've learned from Steph, from watching the trainees at their drills, and from practicing alone in the dark for hours on end. I scream silently with each blow: *give it back*.

And, immovable as the tree before me, the creature takes my blows and my words and grants nothing in return but a steady rain of dead leaves and withered moss, though it grows no less for it.

When I am exhausted and my attacks limited to hanging from its limbs and trying to drag it down with dead weight, it gently shakes me to the ground. And then the monster of the forest holds something out: a knotted lump of silky-grained, red-brown wood twice the size of my closed fist.

By the time it lands, heavy and unexpectedly warm in my cupped palms, the creature has dissolved to nothing and Grace and I are alone in the woods once more.

BELONGING

WE TAKE THE knot of wood back to Grace's cascade. Side by side, eyes closed, we listen to the rushing water. And we reach for magic.

But when I open my eyes, only Grace is silvered in a thin sheen of mist.

I hurl the useless bit of wood into the stream and watch it bob away on the water.

Then I wade in after the stupid thing, grumbling with every slippery step at myself, at tree-monsters and their wordless cursed gifts, at gross, messy, impossibly inconvenient nature in general. I'm drenched to the hips by the time I catch it again.

Grace is still where I left her at the side of the stream, though not, as far as I can tell, chatting with Cadence this time. I stretch out on the bank to dry in the sun, one hand on the damp bit of wood that fits itself so perfectly to the shape of my hand, and breathe through the panic.

What if I never get my magic back? What if it's just not possible?

I'll have my revenge against Refuge no matter what happens. The Mara's hunger is unstoppable; eventually, it will devour even its servants. Maryam's corrupt reign will fail. But Ange and her family, and all the others besides, will die too.

I'm supposed to save them. I'm the only one who can. It's what I'm meant for. And yet, every time I try to fight for them, return to them, get the power to save them, I only seem to get further from my goal.

Ash is gone. Sent someplace I've never heard of and could never find, I'm sure, even if someone had bothered to tell me where he's gone. Without him, I don't know how to get back home, how to cross the barrier and return to my city, how to fight back against the Mara without being able to see and manipulate the threads, or against Refuge without the ability to stop the monsters.

I shiver, despite the sun overhead. But even in the midst of horror, I know there's a warm bath and a soft bed waiting for me, and that's perhaps what I'm most afraid of.

I didn't return to the welcome Ash had promised—that homecoming was always meant for Cadence. But that doesn't mean there's nothing here for me. Nothing to tempt me into comfortable complacency.

I palm the knot of wood and fit my fingers into its satin-grained twists and grooves. I could belong here, with Grace, and Susan—even Steph seems to be warming up to me. Well, perhaps not. But I could learn to grow things. Get better at weaving. Maybe even earn my way into training. Not in a week, but eventually.

I'd work my way up to going on missions, eventually. Probably. There'd be other cities to save. Ash would return, and I might eventually forgive him for leaving, for abandoning his promise, if it meant I could go with him. Even if I can't get back to what I've been, to the kind of power that stops monsters in their tracks, I'm sure I could learn enough to help.

I could make a place for myself here.

I roll over and gag, hanging my head over the bank and spitting bile. The vision, all soft and content and comfortable, turns my stomach and sends me trembling with revulsion. I wipe my mouth, shove to my feet, and hurl the knotted bit of wood deep into the forest where I'll never have to look at it again.

It bounces and crashes louder and longer than I expected.

Then it flies back out of the trees and bumps to a stop at my feet.

"Really, flame?" says the forest. "I thought you'd be happy to see me."

I kick the possessed thing back the way it came and yank Grace to her feet, dragging her stumbling behind me before she's had a chance to shake off her trance.

"Cole, no!" the forest calls behind me, and then curses.

"Who was that?" Grace pants, struggling to keep up. "What happened? What's wrong?"

I tighten my grip. "The woods are haunted."

We're both wheezing by the time Nine Peaks' wall comes into sight, but I don't slow until we reach the gate. I snatch the key over my head and fumble it three times before it clicks into the lock.

Once inside, door safely slammed to and locked behind us, we both collapse.

Grace hangs her head between her knees, heaving. "What did you see out there?"

"I didn't see anything. I heard a ghost. Not that tree-looking creature or monster or whatever. Someone I knew."

"You're sure?"

"I mean, he wasn't actually dead the last time I saw him, but it couldn't have been anyone else."

She runs the back of her arm across her face, scrubbing away sweat. She's flushed, bright eyes narrowed. "But you didn't see anything. And you definitely weren't dreamwalking?"

I shrug. "If I had been, would I have been able to yank you back like that?"

She thinks about it, sighs, and hauls herself up the wall to stand. "I need to report this. If you want to get another training session in with Steph, you'd better hurry and meet her. She's about to get busy."

I groan. "I thought that wasn't until later?"

"It is later. You remember how to get there?"

I roll my eyes and stump away on leaden legs.

"Cole?" she calls after me. "You're sure you didn't see anything?"

I flap a hand at her and keep scuffing toward the unofficial sparring ring we've established in a quiet corner between long, windowless structures.

I've spent most of my life obsessing about death and believing I was haunted. You'd think I'd cope better with a real ghost, but . . . Ravel *died*? Dead—and haunting me. How did he—his ghost—even find me? How many more are on their way . . . ?

When I've reached our sparring ring, I take a running leap at Steph, hoping to gain the edge with a surprise attack and outrun my dread at the same time. She knocks me into the dirt.

"Nice try. You and Gracie spend all day coming up with that?" She stomps, kicking up dust where I'd been sprawled on my back only a moment before.

I skitter back, trying to put distance between us and find a less vulnerable position at the same time. "Spur of the moment inspiration."

I snatch a long, flexible branch from the side of our sparring circle and fold my hand around it lightly, fingers outstretched and thumb curled in. It's meant to mimic threads since my talents are—were—better oriented to manipulating them directly than using blades like Ash, or the hand-to-hand Steph excels at. We've already established I'm more likely to damage to myself than her when handling practice blades, and as I just demonstrated, my direct combat skills usually end with me eating dirt.

I snap the skinny branch in the younger girl's direction. She twists aside. If I can keep it touching her for more than a five-count, I win. So far my record is half a second.

I flick my arm. The branch whips away and back so fast its end blurs.

She leans; watches it swish harmlessly through the air. "Keep those fingers spread. Rotate, not pinch."

I snap the branch against the ground. It shudders out of my grip.

Cadence and Steph snicker, trading friendly insults. Steph circles, poking me with her own stick every so often to remind me to keep moving while I flail my branch and pretend it's a handful of magical string.

If anything, I seem to be getting worse.

"You know this is all pointless if you can't tap in." She jabs me in the ribs.

I swat her away. My branch folds against hers and springs back, thwapping me in the face.

"Combat skills aren't what get you into the program; they're what keep us in," she says. "You'll have to show at least a little talent."

"So why're you teaching me?" I flick the branch back and forth with a humming swish to keep her at bay. "Why waste your time if I don't have a chance."

"Maybe I just like seeing you wallow in the dirt." She pivots, drops, and lunges faster than I can redirect my branch's force, sweeping my feet out from under me.

I land hard, gagging until I can coax air back into my lungs. Steph grins but she gives me a hand up all the same.

I attack. She rebuffs; I hit the dirt. She attacks; I try to block . . . and end up in the same place.

"You'd think she'd at least have learned to fall properly by now," Cadence says.

"Hopeless," agrees Steph.

But she waits for me to brush myself off. She's practically bouncing in place, but she doesn't move to attack until I've planted my feet and raised the increasingly limp branch.

Then we hear the crunch of footsteps approaching. She snatches my branch and throws it aside with her stick moments before the boy rounds the corner.

"There you are." He drops out of a run without a sign of sweat. "Meet at the training grounds."

He's dressed like Steph, well muscled but baby-faced to the extent that I wonder if he's closer to Grace's age. He glances at the discarded bits of tree on the ground, apparently identifying them as practice weapons, and eyes me with interest. "She gonna be ready?"

"Don't you have somewhere to be?" Steph snaps.

The boy's smirk doesn't quite mask the flush that reddens his ears. He saunters off, but as soon as he rounds the corner, the footsteps kick back into a run.

I swipe sweat from my face and ask, with admirable nonchalance, "What's going on?"

Steph shrugs. "We're wanted. Could be a new mission, or an attack, or some other kind of emergency. Or auntie got bored and dreamed up a new training routine she can't wait to inflict on us. Either way, looks like you're off the hook for today."

Grace must have raised the alarm. The trainees are getting called out to, what? Comb the woods for ghosts? Do their weapons even work on ghosts?

"Obviously," Cadence says. "How else could you have fought off the Mara?"

GHOSTS

I DROP MY stick. "The Mara are ghosts?"

"Not exactly," Cadence sounds bored. "But neither is Ravel if you ask me. Which you should have."

"You heard him too? Back by the stream?"

"I heard the same thing you did. You just never asked. Which, again, could have made things a whole lot simpler. But now you need to get back to Gran."

Then, apparently in revenge, she refuses to answer any more of my questions. So I take the long way back, watching people dash around in controlled alarm. Little kids dart in circles waving toy weapons like miniatures of the sticks and branches Steph's been using to train me, which is depressing. Eager-looking teens in dark combat gear and securely holstered weaponry quick-march in packs, and more than a few of their elders seem to be marshalling, too. The rumours spread: under attack, enemy lurking in the woods, protect the borders, send out scouts, a squad, no, a whole division.

The whispers dry up when they catch sight of me. Tight smiles, wary eyes, or worried, or pitying. One lady even tells me to go on home like I'm one of the little kids getting shooed inside away from the threat.

Soon enough, the streets clear and the clusters of movement wheel away, and there's nothing much to do besides lurk by the main gates and watch for signs of a ghostly attack, or head back to Susan's place and wait for news.

So, of course, I head to the gates.

Which turns out to be a boring move. A solid row of dreamwalkers bars my way. They won't let me up on the wall, where I could get a better view. They won't tell me anything. They won't even talk to Cadence when she tries to get answers.

I circle around and try one of the side gates, but guards are everywhere now. They keep warning me off. Every door is buried behind bristling strangers.

I keep thinking I'll run into Steph and the other trainees that I challenged last week, but after covering maybe a third of the wall from the inside, I still haven't seen them. They're either stationed at a different gate, or they've been sent out to deal with the threat.

Curiosity gives way to thirst and a growing desire to get off my feet, so I drag myself home. Back to Susan's, I mean—twisting around to check behind me every few steps and make sure I'm not missing anything important.

When I get there, the house is empty. I slam through the motions of getting a drink, shedding dirt in my wake, too afraid to miss any new developments by wasting time with anything so mundane as washing up.

But somewhere between downing that cup of water and craning my neck to watch the door and the window in turn, I must have put my head down. The next thing I know, I'm picking it up off the table.

Susan stands in the doorway. She looks from the dirty floor to me. "Really?"

I ignore the fact that we haven't been on speaking terms for days now, and also the related fact that I don't trust her, in favour of getting some answers. "What happened? Did they find the ghost?"

"Bath. Now."

"I know, sorry, it's just—is it over? What happened?"

She sidesteps the mess, opens the bathroom door and points.

"I'll clean up after. What did they find? Was there a fight? Did we win?"

Her mouth tightens. I'm starting to think it's not the dirty floor that has her upset. But when she speaks, her tone is surprisingly gentle. "You don't need to worry. I'll explain after."

"Oh, just go wash already," Cadence grumbles.

It's the fastest I've ever scrubbed down in my life. Susan refuses to answer any questions until after I've swept and wiped up the dirt I tracked in the door, too, which at the very least must mean that whatever happened can't have been too dramatic. Though, what do I know? Maybe she just wants to have clean floors when the invading ghostly hordes descend.

Susan cooks in silence, and then we both have to eat even though it's the middle of the night—still without answers—and then, settling in her chair with mugs of tea for the both of us, she tips her head. "Now, what was it you wanted to know?"

I could scream.

Deep breath. Unclench fists. Okay. "Oh, nothing much. Just wondered if that ghost Grace and I met in the woods came back, maybe with a ghost army? Seeing as how we scrambled our entire fighting force this afternoon? Which, by the way, I wasn't aware included you—"

"She's retired," Cadence says helpfully.

"Semi-retired." Susan sips her tea, watching me over the rim of the cup. "Was that all?"

This time I nearly do scream, emitting a high-pitched shriek like a boiling kettle before clamping my lips.

Susan grins. "Good news: there was no attack, ghostly or otherwise. You're lucky you didn't get called out; you had a nice peaceful day at home while the rest of us charged about defending against an imaginary enemy."

"I didn't make it up. Cadence heard too—"

"Sit down." She flaps her hand at me. "I wasn't accusing you of lying."

I perch on the edge of my seat stubbornly, tea growing cold beside me. "We heard him."

"Okay. Tell me all about your ghost." She settles back in her chair like she's getting ready for some kind of bedtime story.

"I'm not making this up." I pause, but she doesn't argue. Just sips her tea expectantly, if a little louder than strictly necessary. "It was Ravel. I know it was."

"Oh? How?"

"His voice. What he said. No one talks like him. No one calls me . . . that." Goosebumps ripple over my skin. Why isn't Ash here? Why is Ravel haunting me? I thought I'd come to terms with him, with the way he'd been.

"Calls you what?" she asks.

I glare.

She blinks innocently. "So you just knew it was this Ravel from his voice. But you didn't see anything?"

"Can you see ghosts?" I mean to sound sarcastic, but a note of curiosity creeps in.

Her eyes crinkle, but all she says is, "So, basically, you saw a bunch of trees and heard the voice of an old friend?"

"He wasn't a friend."

"That's one way of putting it," Cadence says.

Susan's eyes widen. She sits up a little straighter. "Noted. So this not-friend, you knew him back in—"

"He was the son of the leader of Refuge." Cadence takes over. "And a wannabe rebel. A creepy, controlling jerk, but he had his uses."

Susan looks like she's waiting for me to argue.

I shrug. "What she said."

"Did he hurt you? Is he dangerous?"

"Not anymore," says Cadence.

Dangerous? He'd caused harm. Cost lives. Almost cost me mine.

He'd also tried to sacrifice his own to save it. I'm certainly no longer dazzled by him, no longer overwhelmed beyond reason, but neither will I make the mistake of thinking him harmless, nor powerless, nor even, simply, an enemy.

"Always. Especially when he was trying to help." My tone is mocking, but the words fall like stones on the rug, with a nearly audible thud.

It was true of more than just Ravel. I'm not sure if that makes me feel more forgiving of him, or more wary of everyone else. Especially myself.

"How much did he know about us?" Susan seems alert, but not alarmed.

"Nothing," Cadence says. Susan still looks to me for confirmation.

I feel just a tad smug about that. "He saw me dreamwalk. Saw me fight. He has memories of when we first arrived and Cadence's parents dying,"—Susan blinks fast, a sudden sheen to her eyes—"and he seemed to have some idea of what we could do. But I don't think he could actually see much more than the silvering. He didn't seem to notice the threads or even the Mara—"

"That's what they called their monsters," Cadence interrupts. "Anyway, we never told him anything so if he found out something out, it wasn't our fault."

"But you do think he knew you were from outside the city?"

"I guess," I say. "But nothing more."

"So he couldn't possibly have found you all this way away?"

"I don't think ghosts care about distance—"

But Cadence speaks over me again. "He was good at finding out secrets. If anyone could have figured it out, he would have. But not from us."

"Did anyone else know where you were from? Where you were going? Did you ever say anything to him, or even near him, or around those under his influence, about Nine Peaks?"

"No," I say.

"Yes," says Cadence. "Maybe. Ash might've mentioned it to, um, some people."

Susan's fingers tighten around her teacup. "He knows better. What people?"

Cadence doesn't answer, so our grandmother frowns at me instead.

I fidget, knowing it makes me look guilty but helpless not to. "Don't look at me. I didn't even know we were leaving until it was too late."

"Cadence?" asks Susan.

"It was nothing. Just some kid," she finally says.

"What kid?"

"There was this little girl. Her family helped him when he first arrived. She'd been separated from her dad and wanted help getting him back. It was hard for Ash to leave her behind. He talked too much, maybe, but she was just a kid . . ."

Lily. Ash had told Lily? Then, somehow, Ravel had gotten a hold of her? Would he have hurt her?

To get to me? Maybe. Probably.

Ugh. I'd liked it better when I'd thought he was a ghost. "Okay, so maybe he could have found out where we were headed. There's still the barrier—"

"Um," Cadence interrupts. "Ash might have mentioned something about that too . . ."

"Time for bed." Susan jolts to her feet.

"I still have questions."

"Bed." She follows up the order by marching into her room and closing the door.

"Somebody's in trouble," Cadence singsongs.

20

SPARKS

SUSAN IS GONE before I get up the next morning. Grace refuses to answer questions in her place. I should be panicking about losing my challenge—six days away, now—but I'm distracted by the tingle of unseen eyes on the back of my neck.

If Ravel could haunt—or hunt—me from the forest, I don't see any reason he couldn't haunt me from inside these walls. Or worse.

It's one thing to *think* about Ravel. I can bring reason to bear on his actions, his motivations, considering each piece of evidence and laying them down in tidy rows where they can't hurt me. But the way I feel—I keep pushing it off at arms' length to keep from going under, the memories of being lost in what he wanted and who he would have made of me sparking a swelling surge of panic that threatens to paralyze me.

So, instead, I practice the forms Steph has been teaching me, building up muscle and balance if nothing else. But I keep flinching, imaginary knots of wood flying at me out of my blind spot. Grace gets fed up and makes me sit on the ground with my eyes closed and my hands clasped. I keep peeking until she adds a blindfold. It only makes me jumpier.

"Focus." She raps the top of my head, which doesn't help.

"I can't. This is a waste of time."

"You're a waste of time." She pats my shoulder to soften the retort. I only flinch on the first pat. "Meditation is the first step to unlocking your abilities."

"I thought playing with string was the first step? Or forest gathering? Or basic stances . . ."

"Different paths. That was for weavers. Like handing a stick to a dreamwalker. And meditating for dreamspeakers."

"But I am a dreamwalker. And weaver. And—"

"You *were* a dreamweaver. And we're all—well, not me so much, but the rest of you—dreamwalkers. Weapon-based and hand-to-hand fighting are just for the lowest rung of travellers. Um, maybe don't mention that around Steph, 'kay? The point is, weaving's rare and kind of a big deal, but you said you'd done it before, and your family was known for unusual talent in working the threads, so we started you there."

"Then why am I sitting in the dirt?"

"'Cause you suck at everything else," Cadence says.

"It's even less common than weaving," Grace says. "And not nearly so powerful, but there are also dreamspeakers, and the first step in their training is—"

"Sitting in the dirt?"

"—Meditating. Which looks a lot like sitting in the dirt, yes. You must've noticed a few speakers at the training hall. Basically, they've moved on from the need to fight on the physical plane. Instead, they just tap the dreamscape and work from there. Which is what you need to do, either way."

"Wait, so then why have I been letting Steph beat me up every day?"

"Entertainment value?" Cadence suggests.

"Trainees usually learn a little bit of everything, to explore and test their talents," Grace says. "And you haven't been showing much of an aptitude for weaving. We figured, with your challenge coming up, even if you couldn't dreamwalk, you might as well learn how to defend yourself."

I'm going to fail, aren't I?

"Definitely," says Cadence.

"Anyway, now we're giving this a shot," says Grace, glossing over my woeful lack of combat aptitude. "Sit still and try to feel what's around you. Reach for those threads."

I roll my eyes behind closed lids and flutter my fingers sarcastically.

"Not with your hands."

I fold them neatly in my lap and imagine throwing pebbles at Grace's head.

"Wrong image," says Cadence.

I growl and shift, already getting numb. The ground is cold. A dusty, earthy smell clogs my nose and scratches the back of my throat. It looked flat here when I sat down, but I can feel clumps of earth or stones or something poking up.

"Are you even going to try or can we go inside now?" says Cadence.

I roll my shoulders and make an effort to settle. Abstract patterns of ruddy light and shadow twist behind my closed eyelids. The breeze ruffles my hair, cool on my skin, wafting in the musty, nose-tickling scents of herbs and distant flowers.

There's a scuffing sound from Grace. Voices in the distance. Buzzing—some kind of insect.

My skin crawls, waiting for the brush of wings and the creep of tiny legs.

"Wrong life-form," says Cadence. "Try for something bigger."

Oh, so she's helping now?

"Nah, just bored. But please, do keep wasting our time. Not like we're on a deadline or anything."

I pound my fist against the dirt in lieu of her face and something sparks behind my eyes. Clawing both hands into the earth on either side of me brings it jittering in and out of focus: a tangled web of shadows and bright lines as if I'm facing the sun with my eyes closed.

Except I can feel its heat on the back of my neck. And those aren't veins wavering at the edges of my awareness.

"Don't get excited," Grace says, her voice too even. "Just stay with it."

My lids flutter with the effort not to scrunch in concentration. Phantom threads pulse in and out of focus in time with my heart, my breath slowing to match.

"That's it," Grace says. "Find the balance."

I dig deeper into the cool earth, knuckles aching. Grit stabs deep under one nail. I snatch the hand to my chest, losing the tenuous connection.

"Well?" I wave the bloody digit in Grace's direction.

She looks down. "I don't know how to tell you this . . ."

"But it's hopeless," Cadence finishes. "You're better off giving up now."

"But it worked!" Grace squeals, jumping up and dragging me with her as she bounces in a tight circle.

I go stiff, elbows out in self-defence. But I'm practically fizzing inside. It's the first time I've so much as caught a glimpse of the dreamscape since fighting off the Mara. Maybe I have a chance after all?

"Yes, fine, you might've poppsed a few sparklies," Cadence says. "Don't get too excited. You're hardly ready to dive back into battle."

The fizzing stops, replaced by a stone in my gut.

Grace stops bouncing. "What's wrong? You finally made progress!"

I mumble something about it hardly being anything and try to pull away. But she leans in, so close I can feel the heat of her breath.

"Stop squirming. I just want to see." She smooshes my face to keep me trapped.

I blink fast and stare into the middle distance as if that'll make it less awkward.

"So jealous," she says. "It's cool how it mirrors your mask. Even the fade-out is pretty."

I stop trying to push her away. "Fade out?"

Her fingers trace across my cheeks. "The way the silver pulls back under your skin. Not much surfaced, but it's slowest to fade in your eyes and over these marks above and below."

She backs off—finally—and I suck in air fast before she can crowd my space again.

"Good work. Now try to do it again." She plops down and pats the ground.

I ease down, my finger throbbing where grit lodged under the nail—

"Poor baby," Cadence says with all the sympathy of someone who's forgotten human sensation. "Have not! You're just a whiner."

I knuckle both fists into the ground in response, going up on my knees to put more force into it. But this time, nothing flickers behind my eyes.

I uncurl and press fingertips to the earth, biting back a yelp. Nothing but pain sparks to life.

"Be patient," Grace says, sounding anything but. "Give it a minute. Feel for the connection, don't force it. Reach out, don't grab."

My fingers flex, stubbornly digging deeper, but I focus on relaxing just a little with each breath, listening and feeling for the life around me buzzing and rustling and . . . crunching?

"You're needed," says Susan.

I jump up, hiding my hands in my shirt as if I've been up to something I shouldn't be.

It's more than the interruption that puts me on edge. Her voice was abrupt, distant—or maybe that's just weariness dulling her tone. Her face might be tense, but her shoulders sag with exhaustion.

"Cole just had a breakthrough." Grace bounces up to Susan as if she hasn't noticed anything's wrong.

"I need you to come with me," Susan's glance takes in the dirt clinging to my clothes, my grubby hands, even the drop of blood seeping from the pricked nail. "Now."

I tilt a reassuring smile in Grace's direction. "Finish later?"

She nods, brows furrowing. She doesn't know what's wrong, then.

Susan's already walking away.

"Is it the ghost from the woods? Is Ash back? Am I in trouble?" I hurry to catch up, voice pitched low, ducking my head as strangers pass.

"The Council of Nine wishes to speak with you. You haven't done anything wrong. Just answer their questions. Truthfully, girls."

"Both of us?" Cadence asks.

"They can hardly question you separately."

When she puts it that way, this sounds more like an interrogation. I hunch my shoulders and wish I could go back to sit in the dirt with Grace.

What have I done now?

REUNION

I 'VE BEEN HERE before. That might be why I notice more details the second time around.

Or it might be the way I'm doing anything I can to avoid looking to the front of the room.

Heavy timber holds up the roof and lines the walls. Much of it is carved and painted in stylized patterns that shift from angular and sparse to whorled and intricate to smooth and heavy and back again as they wrap around the room. Woven and stitched hangings show still more varied designs.

I squint to compare the lean figures of a woven hanging with the blocky carvings behind it. Why do they work so well together when they should clash horribly? And why am I acting like a crazy person, staring into the shadows?

"You're not listening. I don't care what he said," Cadence insists, annoyed. "Ravel is not a friend. I did not guide him here. Cole did not bring him or help him in any way. Neither did Ash. Anything he's done, that's on him, not us."

"She's right. I found my own way here. Vi—Cole—she saved my life. Saved a number of my people's lives, too. But they're still dying. We need more help. Hers, or someone like her, if you can't spare her . . ." Ravel might be here asking for help, but he lolls back in his chair, nonchalant. Everything under control. No threat here.

I'm not convinced. Even bound and bedraggled, he's dangerous. He never should have been able to find his way out of the city, never mind track me all the way up here. I avoid looking at him, desperate to avoid feeling anything at all, especially here, under the council's scrutiny.

The elders of the Council of Nine watch, sharp-eyed and silent, as their apparent spokeswoman—my nemesis, Grace's Aunt Rocky—turns to me. "You deny all involvement with this man?"

"I have nothing to do with him. I want nothing to do with him," Cadence says.

They can hear her just fine—a faint silver glow lights their eyes and a dusting of mist hovers over their skin, proof of their connection to the dreamscape—but still they stare at me.

"Answer the question, child." Susan's voice is remote, her silver gaze just as inhuman as the other council members' when she turns it on me.

I tighten interlaced fingers to keep them still. "I did not invite, guide, nor otherwise aid or encourage this person to follow us here."

"That was not the question. What is your relationship?"

"He means nothing to us." Cadence has escalated from mildly irritated to full on outraged.

Ravel raises an eloquent dark eyebrow over those startling gold eyes of his. "Flame?"

What do I tell them?

We obviously know each other, but how can I sum up our twisted history in a way they'll comprehend? That small boy, watching—obsessing—over a stranger from afar, present at the worst moment of my—Cadence's—life, when our parents were killed. And years later, his unexpected offer of protection when I needed it most. An ally I was so desperate to claim that I was willing to ignore his controlling, manipulative, even abusive nature.

But in the end, he'd willingly put himself in danger for me . . . been willing to die, even, to save me . . .

What was Ravel to me, really? More than a stranger, less than a friend, possibly an enemy, certainly devious, dangerous, willing to sacrifice anything and anyone he deemed fit—

"That's enough," the scarred woman says, lifting a hand.

An unseen hook digs into my gut and yanks. Silver glows at the edge of my vision. I hold my hands out, each finger limned in the same mist that shimmers over the councilmembers. "How . . . ?"

"You are one of ours," she says, waving a hand in dismissal. "Just because you can't access your abilities at will doesn't mean we can't. We needed your honesty. Now we have it."

Wait, what?

Susan won't meet my eyes.

I plant myself in front of her chair, rigid with the betrayal. "All this time?"

She shakes her head mutely. The elder beside her, Ash's grandfather, reaches for me, scarves rustling. She raises one hand, just a twitch of her worn fingers, and he stops.

"All this training and struggling to access the dreamscape on my own, and you could have turned it on like flicking a switch?" I don't yell, though the harsh whisper claws at my throat like a scream.

"You don't understand," says Cadence. "It's not the same."

Susan nods.

"Flame—" Ravel starts.

"You," I whirl on him, and for once, I have no problem owning that stupid nickname. Fury burns through every inch of me. "You don't get to speak. You don't get to be here after you—you—"

"Flame, they're dying." His voice is ragged; his cocky attitude discarded like a crumpled mask. "We need you back."

No. How dare he even ask? As if he's the one who cares? As if I'd do it for him? As if it wasn't my plan all along, wasn't what I'd been working so hard for all this time, wasn't—

"She can't," Cadence says.

The scarred elder echoes her nastily for Ravel's benefit, or maybe for mine. "Remove him," she orders.

The nearest elder reaches a mist-silvered finger into the air as if plucking an invisible string. Ravel's searching gaze shutters. He slumps, bindings keeping him from toppling from his chair.

Part of me is relieved. The rest is furious. "What did you do? He wasn't hurting anyone."

Susan still won't look at me. The others watch with austere disapprobation as if I'm a small child—someone else's—throwing a tantrum.

"Does she need to be here?" one asks.

"They're debating," Cadence says when no answer is forthcoming.

I pace. Silver-glazed eyes swivel to follow in otherwise stone faces.

I'm tempted to turn on my heel and stalk out without another word. Ravel can fend for himself, or not. There's no reason to make his fate my problem.

But what he said just before they knocked him out—I have to know more.

How many have died? And who? Faces flicker before my eyes: Ange, Lily, hapless Amy . . . Sam, who I barely managed to bring back to them. They have no way to defend themselves from attack, not without me.

Or someone like me.

I plant my feet against the darkness that rages at the edges of my vision. "Send a team."

There's no response. But this is what needs to happen. I've been trying as hard as I can, but even with today's breakthrough, I'm way too far from the kind of power needed to save anyone, much less a whole city's worth of people. I take the part of me that insists this is my job, my calling, my purpose, and shove it as deep and as far away as I can.

It doesn't need to be me. It doesn't even have to be Ash.

"Send help," I repeat, louder. "He might not be a good person, but Ravel's telling the truth. There are still people in that city that need saving. Send a squad to help them."

The stone faces crack, one by one, though the silver doesn't bleed fully from their eyes. "No."

"You don't understand. There's no one there who can fight back. Why do you train your people to fight if not for this? Send them out before it's too late!"

"Cole." Cadence's voice is tight, near breaking.

"The lost cannot be saved." The response is inflectionless, coming from many throats at once, eerily like the layered, echoing tones of the Mara. "No more lives will be spent on that city."

But one face reflects the horror I feel at their response. Susan's forehead is knotted over eyes silvered with more than just magic.

"You can't abandon them!" I plead with her alone.

But she's not the one who answers. Her fellows speak as if with one voice: "The decision is made. As for the boy, he will be permitted to serve. Be thankful. In following you here, his life has been spared."

I look at Ravel, limp and ragged and helpless in his chair and wonder if he wouldn't rather have stayed to be eaten by monsters. Of all the people to be saved, why him?

No. I can't accept it. I won't.

"You have no choice," Rocky says as the silver fades back under the elders' skins—along with their spying ways, if I have any luck left. "You are powerless, and we have spent enough lives on that deathtrap of a city."

I hunt for a sympathetic face, a way out of this nightmare, something, anything. There has to be some argument, something I can say or do to persuade them . . .

"You're dismissed." A flat, merciless order.

"I won't just leave like—"

"As you wish."

The floor rushes up to meet me.

COMPANY

I WAKE UP to the sight of a familiar wood-and-plaster ceiling, and spend the next few moments pushing away the sick weight of a bad dream.

Voices in the next room drag the nightmare into reality.

"She did what?" Susan laughs over the clatter-slosh-clink of dishes.

"You should have seen it!" Ravel's voice is smooth, confident. The master manipulator at the height of his powers.

I stumble through the doorway, scrubbing sleep from my eyes and trailing knotted bedding.

"You're up." She raises a soapy hand in greeting, smiling, though she won't quite meet my eyes.

"Sleepyhead," Ravel calls, flicking a dishtowel in my direction.

Ravel. Casually doing chores in Susan's kitchen.

He looks strange without his usual ostentatious paint and ornamentation, his dark tangle of tattoos mostly hidden under a bright oversized tunic and baggy trousers—obviously borrowed.

My head spins. Do I chase him out the door or confront Susan first? Could I manage both at the same time?

"Or you could play it cool," Cadence says. "Pretend you've accepted the council's orders and then do your own thing when they're not looking. Always worked out pretty well for me and Ash."

Susan pours a glass of water and places it on the table. "Sit. Breathe. I'm sure you have questions."

Ravel hangs his towel neatly on the drying rack and slides into a seat across from me. "Been a while, huh, flame?"

His tone is friendly, bland even, but when Susan turns to grab plates, he holds a single finger in front of his mouth, widening his eyes meaningfully. "Maybe I can help bring you up to speed while we eat?"

Susan sets the table and turns back to the counter.

"As you may remember, the esteemed elders denied my petition." He picks up a plate and angles it, inspecting both sides with exaggerated curiosity. "And since I wasn't supposed to know about this delightful place in the first place, I'm now under house arrest with my favourite person."

He grins over the plate. Cadence gags.

"I'm helping you get settled and become a productive member of our community," Susan corrects, plopping a loaf of bread in the middle of the table. "You've been invited to join us, since your home is . . ."

She darts a glance at me, then bustles away without finishing.

"So, basically, I'm your new roomie—again." Ravel reaches for the loaf.

"We only have two rooms." I hitch a thumb at the doors. "And they're both fully occupied. Guess you'll have to find some other place to crash."

"We'll make space," Susan calls, busy at the counter.

Ravel shrugs. "Housemate, then, if you're going to be pedantic. Oh, here—I brought something for you."

I freeze, flipping through the possibilities. Glitter? Mask? Drugged drinks? Severed head?

He unveils a chunk of wood with a flourish. It's alarmingly familiar.

"What have you got there?" Susan peers over his shoulder.

Ravel shrugs. "Flame chucked it at my head out in the woods, so I figured it must be important to her."

"If only he'd actually been a ghost," Cadence says, mirroring my thoughts.

I snatch the knot of wood from him. "It's nothing."

He plucks it back. "Really? I'll hold onto it then. I like it. Shiny."

He runs his fingers over its twists and hollows. Traces of black polish and paint still stain his hands.

Susan holds out her upturned palm.

He shrugs and passes it over. "Or I could make a gift of it?"

Susan brings the cursed thing to her face, seeming to breathe it in. Mist swirls from her skin to the wood, making it look like a knobbled extension of her hand.

Creepy.

The silver ebbs from her eyes as she finally meets mine. "Where did you get this?"

"Uh, the woods?"

"Let me rephrase: who gave this to you?"

Now she wants to talk to me? Not interested.

"Some tree-creature gave it to her," Cadence says.

Traitor.

Susan's lips twitch—almost, but not quite a smile, which doesn't make a lot of sense, but then, what does anymore?

"You need to keep this close," she says. "It's a gift. Don't take it lightly."

"What did I miss?" Ravel asks, tracking the bit of wood as if he regrets handing it over so easily.

"Monsters are giving me presents now," I say, baring my teeth. "Things have changed, in case you hadn't heard."

He returns the kind of wolfish grin I wish I could pull off. "Oh, I'm counting on it, flame."

"That's unkind." Susan holds the forest's "gift" out. When I don't move to take it, she plants it on the table in front of me. "That wasn't a monster and you know it."

Enough of this. I head for the door.

"Aren't you going to eat?"

I swing back, intercept Ravel mid-reach, and snatch the bit of wood away, if only because he wants it and I'm not above punishing him. "Not hungry."

"Where are you going?"

"Out."

"I really think we need to——"

The door slams shut on her last word—and bounces open again. Ravel bounds after me, calling his thanks over Susan's protest.

I pick up my pace.

"Good, now we can talk," he says, loping along without breaking a sweat.

Or that's what I expect. But when I glance out of the corner of my eye, his teeth are set and the skin around his eyes tight. His steps, though fast, fall in a lopsided rhythm. He's limping.

The thought of what must have been a brutal journey cheers me up.

"I have nothing to say to you."

"No worries, flame, I've plenty of news." He grabs my shoulder.

I spin, smacking him away with one of the practiced moves Steph has taught me. I don't pull it off as well as she does, but it's more than enough to send Ravel staggering.

"Don't want to hear it," I snap, to cover my surprise—and the unexpected wave of panic his fleeting touch had sparked.

But after a few steps, I hesitate. "Ange is . . . ?"

"They haven't reached Under. Yet. But, Cole . . . it's going to be soon. It's bad. We need you back. I—I wouldn't have come if there were any other way."

I hate it when he sounds like this. Honest and real and vulnerable. The scared little boy peeking out from his hiding place, not the dazzling and treacherous young master of Freedom. I raise a foot to take another step away from his manipulation and find myself pivoting to face him despite myself. I set my shoulders and widen my stance to keep from curling into a protective ball.

He looks around. "Is this a good place to talk? We don't want anyone listening in . . ."

The path's empty, and the windows on the nearest buildings are closed. No one to overhear—or to come to my rescue. I want to run away, but sick curiosity pins me in place. "It's fine. But I really can't help you. You saw what happened, the last time I—"

"Trust me, the last thing I wanted to do was drag you back into danger. But there's no one else—"

Grace rounds the corner with a huge grin. "Hi! You must be Cole's ghost. I'm—"

"Waiting for me, I know." I cut between them, steering her away. "Sorry, I know I'm late. We should get going. No time to waste."

"Ravel. Lovely to meet you." He swoops to plant a kiss on Grace's hand with an absurd flourish. She blushes. He smolders.

"Get a room," Cadence says.

"Any friend of flame's is a friend of mine." Ravel tucks Grace's arm in his. "I'd love to hear how you two met."

"Nope." I grab her other arm and pull. "Gotta go. Busy day. Important things. No time to waste."

"About that," Grace says. "Turns out your friend will be joining us. The elders decided you two need special treatment. *Gran* and I have just been appointed as instructors of the new remedial class."

"Remedial?" Ravel says with distaste.

"No way," I interrupt. "It's not like he can learn anyway. He's not one of us."

"He actually beat your assessment score. Apparently he 'has potential.' So it's back to basics for both of you. Um, Steph said she'd come around later, though, so there's that."

I don't even know where to start.

"What's a 'Gran'?" Ravel asks.

"Hmm? Oh, Susan's my grandmother."

Ravel leans in under the pretense of getting a better look.

Grace bats her eyes. "See the resemblance?" She preens and giggles at the stream of compliments coming her way.

"This is a waste of time," Cadence says. "Ditch him."

I couldn't agree more.

REMEDIAL

I WALK FAST to escape their banter.

It's not just how irritating they're being, or even Ravel's history of manipulative and cold-blooded behaviour that's the problem. Time is running out for Ange and everyone else back home, and I'm so far from being back in fighting form it's as if I haven't started.

Which is why I can't afford to waste any more time persuading Grace to ditch Ravel.

I veer off toward a quiet patch where a thin strip of orchard borders a cultivated area of mixed crops and press both hands to the soft earth. I close my eyes and reach—

But irritation is the only thing that fills my senses. That, and the chirping and cooing of a couple of idiots.

"What's she doing?" Ravel stage whispers.

"Meditating." Grace practically stands on top of me.

I take a deep breath and try to block them out.

"It's the only thing that seems to help," she continues. "She' terrible at weaving, and my sister has been trying to teach her to fight, but she hasn't been making much progress on that front, either."

I dig my fingers deeper into the soil. Focus. Breathe. Block them out.

A thump shakes the ground. Sudden warmth heats my back.

"Am I doing it right?" Ravel's voice, too close.

Something brushes my hands, and I swat, connecting with a satisfying smack.

"Ouch," he says. "I feel something. I think it's working."

Grace laughs. "Connection is the first step. I'm not sure meditation is your path, though. Come on, I'll teach you to weave."

"No, I'm getting something here." He hums. "Yes, yes, I feel it, a whole world opening up before my eyes—"

I hiss with irritation and scoot a few inches away. Focus. Focus . . .

It's no good. I whirl on Ravel. His eyes are closed, lips upturned in a smirk.

I kick him. Not as hard as I could, but it's enough to send him sprawling. Anger flashes across his face. But he blanks it out in an instant and raises his hands in mock surrender.

"This isn't a game," I snarl. "Go play somewhere else. I have real work to do."

"He was just—" Grace starts.

"You don't get it. People are dying out there. Who's going to stop it? Not you. Not him. Not your precious council."

She backpedals. But I'm in no mood to let this go.

"Did you forget? Think I was like you? Playing at power to fit in or sooth my pride or whatever? I can't afford to fail. People are counting on me. My friends are counting on me."

"We're your friends," Ravel says, coming up to put an arm around Grace.

She's slack jawed and pale, not because a beast who sacrifices human beings to feed his own desperate lust for power has her in his grasp, but because I've hurt her. Obviously the only thing left to do is turn on him instead. He's had it coming for a long time. "Friends don't try to feed each other to monsters."

His mouth flattens. "That wasn't—"

I bristle, bracing for his defence, preparing for him to turn it around on me, to make his crimes somehow my failure, or maybe to turn to Grace for sympathy. His deviousness is beyond my capacity for understanding,

I know that much. I'll just have to be ready for his lies this time, poised to hit back harder than whatever he can throw at me.

But instead of fighting back, he just sighs, visibly deflating. "You know what? Never mind. You're right. I was an ass. I used you and I'd do it again. I'm doing it right now, chasing you down to drag back into my mess because I can't handle it alone."

He pats Grace reassuringly, pulls away, and drops to his knees in the dirt, turning dangerous eyes up at me. "I need you, flame. I've betrayed everyone who ever looked to me for help, and I can't make that right without you. So, here I am making trouble for you yet again."

He raises his hands in an attitude of supplication, though his mouth quirks at the edges even in this show of humility.

And a show it is, for manipulation is in his nature, just as being pushy is in Cadence's.

"Hey! Don't you ever lump me in with him," she complains. "You know he's no good. We don't need him."

I close my eyes. Take a deep breath. Reach for the expressionless, emotionless calm I learned under Refuge's harsh tutelage. If he won't fight fair, there's only one thing left to do.

When I face them again, I am ice all the way through. "I'm walking away now."

This time only silence follows me.

IT'S THE LAST day before my big showdown, and I'm no closer to winning that idiotic challenge than when I first made it.

I haven't even been able to find my way back to that almost-vision of threads, though I've broken every nail and scratched my fingers to bloody shreds trying to claw that connection back from the earth. I've huddled in what feels like every clearing, garden, and quiet stretch of pathway in town, and even snuck out of Nine Peaks to try various groves and out by the stream, but no luck.

Susan made a bed up for Ravel in her main room that first night, and he's been staying with her ever since. He still insists on calling us roommates at every opportunity. Grace spends all her time hanging on him, begging for glamorous stories of Freedom as she and Susan teach him to master everything I've failed at. Even Steph has been falling all over herself to teach him to spar.

As far as I know, despite his newfound skills in gardening, weaving, housework and fighting, he can't actually dreamwalk, but I'm not about to enquire. Whenever I enter the room, their happy chattering stops and they all stare. Their questions are tentative, neutral, their attempts at humour forced. I refuse to respond, refuse to so much as look in their direction. No matter what I do or say, I can't seem to counteract Ravel's charm offensive. But that doesn't mean I have to be party to it.

The night before my challenge, Grace finds me pounding my hands into the packed dirt in front of the side gate we use most often.

She sits down without comment. Her quiet, even breaths are calming.

I relax ever so slightly, fists uncurling, senses expanding. There's a brush of—something. A sense of light—but my eyes are closed. A fluttering at the edges of my awareness, a pulse, a tangle of threads—

"You really don't notice stuff, do you?" she says.

I let out a soft hiss of frustration. Almost. I was almost there.

"You've never asked me where my parents are."

I frown, squeezing my eyes tighter shut, drilling fingers deeper into the cool soil where I've scraped and scratched it to some measure of softness.

"They died when I was four. Left us with my dad's family, went off on some mission and never returned. For the longest time, no one even told us they'd died. We just kept waiting." The breeze rustles around us, carrying a scent of night-blooming blossoms. "You're not ready. You won't win tomorrow. You can barely tap in, never mind cross over."

I let my head fall back. The rest of me follows, stretching out on the ground in utter exhaustion. "I have to try."

But the image of myself, bleeding into the sand of the training ring while the entire city points and laughs, won't let me go. My pulse picks up, cold sweat beading on my skin, because as bad as public humiliation is going to be, there are worse things than failing in front of my enemies—and, if these people would abandon my entire city to the monsters, then they are my enemies.

My embarrassment would be nothing compared to the true cost of tomorrow's failure.

"Ravel told me," Grace interrupts my horror. She scoops up a handful of dirt and lets it patter back down like gritty tears scattered across the earth. "You were right. I don't know what its like to see people killed right in front of me. I don't know what it's like to fight for the lives of my friends. But there are things you don't understand, either.

"There is not one single person here who hasn't lost someone they loved. No one wants you to fail. They just don't want to see more of your life wasted. You only just came back to us."

"But they're willing to abandon a city full of people?"

Her shoulders slump. "It's not that simple. The council has to weigh the costs, choose the battles we have a chance of winning. They have other priorities to consider. Our missions are about more than just fighting monsters."

"It's a whole city!" I take a breath, lower my voice. "They're my friends, Grace. And even if they weren't, they don't deserve to die."

"The council's made its decision. They're not going send anyone out." The words are harsh, but she leans against me in silent apology.

I close my eyes. "It doesn't matter what happens tomorrow, does it? They never had any intention of helping me, of sending me back, even if I could fight properly. Did Ash know? When he brought me here?"

"Ash can be . . . determined, when it comes to his goals. He would have put your safety first, I know that much. I don't think it occurred to him he'd be sent away after bringing you back."

I wrap my arms around my knees and rock, grieving all my plans, all my hopes. My friends, and all the others who will fall to the nightmares.

Lily, her family who'd only just reunited. Ange, still fighting for a better future for all of us, even after Cass's death. The hunger of the Mara rampaging unchecked until there's no one left.

My ability to combat the Mara isn't coming back. The council won't send anyone in my place, and Ash won't be able to fix anything, even if he returns tonight.

I hadn't realized just how much I was relying on his return to set things right until this moment.

I keep making the same mistakes. I'd pinned my hopes on him saving the day in Refuge, too. And before that, tried to rely on Refuge's rules for protection, and then on Ravel and his ridiculous little kingdom. But in the end, there'd been no one but me to stand against the Mara and—

Hang on. Ravel. Escaped.

"And good riddance," Cadence says.

No, that's—I'd known Ash could move through the barrier around the city and take me across it. But Ravel . . . He got out *on his own.*

I jump to my feet, buzzing with the implications. Grace stumbles to her feet, knocked off balance by my sudden move. I turn and seize her hand.

"Where's Ravel?"

She studies me. "I'll show you, if you tell me why you want to know."

"I'll explain on the way."

24
SHOWDOWN

I KNOW WHAT I have to do. But when I lead Ravel back to the unguarded side gate, Steph is waiting for us.

She doesn't say anything, not at first. She just plants herself, solid and unmoving, in front of the key. The look on her face makes me cringe. But I won't be turned aside.

I motion Ravel to wait, and settle into a guard position, the one she's drilled me on relentlessly. Not that it does me much good. She waits for me to get nervous enough to attack, and puts a quick, painful end to my first attempt—and the dozen or so increasingly desperate ones that follow.

Ravel stands back and watches me eat dirt over and over again, wincing and calling encouragement, but not interfering. Not that he could beat Steph in a fair fight either.

When I can no longer summon the energy to pick myself up off the ground, Steph stands over me and scowls. Then she puts out her hand and pulls me to a sitting position.

"That was the real fight," she says. "I won. Tomorrow, you will."

I can't do anything but stare—and wobble, almost too worn out to hold myself upright. If her goal was to keep us from running away tonight, she's accomplished it admirably.

"Would it kill you to explain?" Grace must have joined us at some point during the fight. "Sorry, Cole. She was just supposed to stall until I could finish talking to the others. We're coming with you." She beams, practically bouncing in place.

I scrunch my eyes and shake my head. I must've hit it harder than I'd thought on one of those falls . . .

"Not you, Gracie," Steph growls. "Nightwitch squad only."

"If you don't want me telling Auntie Rocky on you, you'll let me do whatever and go wherever I want," Grace says smugly, sounding more like Cadence than I've ever heard from her.

I draw my knees up and ask, carefully, "Who's doing what now?"

The answer, as far as I can make it out between sisterly squabbling, and assorted references to people and things I've never heard of, seems to be that my city's plight has stirred the hearts of the younger residents of Nine Peaks, despite their elders' apathy.

Steph will throw tomorrow's fight in my favour—thus explaining her grumpy trouncing of my unsuspecting self this evening—to create chaos and give the other trainees time to steal bikes and supplies.

"That's the worst plan I've ever heard." I groan my way to a more-or-less upright position and make a half-hearted effort to dust myself off. "Remind me how witches fit into it again?"

"Steph's squad is Nightwitch," Ravel says helpfully. "Or they will be, once they graduate. Assuming they graduate—apparently wandering off on unsanctioned missions is a no-no. She'd like you to refer to her as 'Yaga, now, by the way."

Steph—who I am absolutely never going to call, uh, whatever that was he just said—shows her teeth. Grace rolls her eyes.

"How do you even know that?" I ask, because, of the dozens of questions buzzing around inside my head, that might be the only one I actually have the capacity to process right now.

Ravel shrugs modestly. "I listen."

I WAKE UP flailing, blind to everything except a semi-conscious but urgent demand for *air*. My mouth and nose are covered, shoulders pinned.

"Shh," Cadence hisses. "You'll wake Grace."

Which isn't the most helpful comment under the circumstances, but it does make me look for her. I can't find her—because Ravel is in the way. When he catches my gaze, he lets up, just a little.

"I'm going to let go. Don't scream, okay?"

I nod frantically and gasp as soon as he removes his hands.

"Shh!" he and Cadence whisper at the same time.

"Don't wake Grace," Cadence says. "And get up already. We don't have much time."

I'm stiff, and clumsy, and every bruise from Steph's trouncing throbs—but I manage to wallow my way off the bed with only a moderate amount of groaning. I shake off Ravel's touch when he tries to help, but follow him to the main room all the same, and through it to the front garden. He eases the door shut behind us without a sound.

Now what?

"It's time to go," Cadence says.

"We need to leave, right now." Ravel picks up a pack from the side of the path and hands it to me.

My brain must still be oxygen deprived, because I shrug it on and follow him obediently for a few steps before it clicks that something's not right. "Why didn't we wake Grace up? I thought she and Steph were coming with us? And we're not leaving until tomorrow, or later today, whatever."

Ravel raises his eyebrows. "Weren't you just playing along? You really want to be responsible for the deaths of a bunch of kids? I thought you had a whole thing about that."

I stare, openmouthed. That's not—well, sure, Grace can't defend herself and we'll have to find a way to keep her out of danger, but Steph, she's strong. Her squad mates are all dreamwalkers, maybe not fully trained ones yet, but—*Oh.*

Oh no.

I've been too caught up in my own powerlessness, at least relative to nearly everyone else here. I've forgotten what it's like. What the Mara are like. Even Ash couldn't stop them on his own, not completely and not for long, not after I lost my ability to fight them.

I groan, letting my head slump back. The cold, distant stars laugh humourlessly at my foolishness. Though Steph and her friends can run circles around me, they're, what, only fourteen, fifteen? At least a couple years away from Ash's level of competency, and the elders had refused to send even a fully trained squad . . .

And that's what it comes down to. Am I willing to risk the lives of children to save my people? Am I going to lead back a bunch of half-trained teens younger than I am to sacrifice themselves to do what I can't?

I can't stop the dying by bringing more to be slaughtered.

I slump to my knees, dumping Ravel's pack in the dirt.

He scoops it up and dusts it off. "I worked hard to get that, you know. And the bike."

"There's no point. We can't—"

"Oh, stop feeling sorry for yourself," Cadence snaps. "Just because you didn't think ahead doesn't mean no one else did. Obviously we can't just abandon everyone."

I shake my head. "I won't let Grace and Steph and their friends die for us. Even to save Ange, and Lily, and—"

"Uh, flame?" Ravel puts out a hand, which I ignore. "I think you're misunderstanding something. Just because the kiddies' plan is no good doesn't mean we're out of options."

And something he said earlier finally clicks. ". . . You said something about a bike?"

He grins. "You and me are about to enjoy some quality time together. Roadtrip!"

He singsongs the last word, and then looks around guiltily, as if afraid someone will overhear.

"So he's a moron," Cadence sniffs, unfairly, considering her own penchant for silliness. "But we need to get back to the city, and I happen to know he stole a map along with the bike."

I take a deep breath and hold it. Back to plan A: cut and run all the way back home, Ravel in tow. We still have no way to fight the Mara. But if it's just the two of us, maybe we can get in—and out—without needing to.

Ravel crossed the barrier once. If he can do it again—and, more importantly, take people across with him, like Ash did—even if we can only rescue one person, it'll be worth it.

ROADTRIP

W E REACH THE side gate a few hours before dawn. If things back home are progressing as fast as Ravel said, there's no time to waste.

Plus, I just so happen to have one other excellent reason to get out of town early today. Fake-winning a fixed challenge would hardly have been much better than for-real-losing it. Now that I'm running away from it, I can admit that even if, by some miracle, I managed to win that challenge on my own, it was never going to help me get back what I've lost. Issuing it was one of the dumbest things I've done, and that's saying a lot

I'd have liked to steal one of the more stable and cargo-friendly four-wheelers, but it would never have fit through the side gate. Instead, we wheel a solar bike out the narrow door in the wall and take turns trying to toss the key back over after locking it. The bike is unwieldy and heavier than I expected. Forcing it down the straggling forest paths in the general direction of the main road is hard enough without the added (and futile) effort to be as quiet as possible.

Grace had said the elders would send a squad after us as soon as they figured out we'd gone—thus the point of creating as much chaos as possible at the challenge and, ideally, making sure they didn't want to see our faces for a good long while. Looking back, I'm not sure that would have worked. Now we'll never have to find out.

Hopefully Grace and Steph will just assume I'm off doing some last-minute panic training until it's too late. But even if we're careful, and lucky, we're not likely to even manage as much as half a day's head start. Not much margin for two city kids with a stolen map and only the barest idea of how to navigate. Just keeping the bike upright and pointed in the right direction is hard enough, even once we reach the relative smoothness of the main road.

At which point I insist on driving. Or piloting. Or whatever you call it.

It doesn't go well at first, but neither we nor the bike break, and I figure it's important to start as I mean to finish. Plus, even if there's no way around spending the next few days being jolted and jittered to pieces on the back of this awful two-wheeled torture device, I don't intend to be the one stuck wearing the backpack this time.

Ravel's uncharacteristically compliant. I figure he's happy to have gotten his way and be heading back to the city. Cadence sulks, unhappy we had to take her least favourite person in the world along for the ride, despite the fact that she's the one who pointed out we needed him. If I can live with being stuck on a bike with him for the sake of our friends' lives, she can suck it up. Apparently, she's at least on board enough with the plan that she points out when our map's upside down.

The bike's lights don't illuminate far enough ahead for me to feel comfortable rolling along much faster than walking pace in the dark, but we've cleared the trees by the time the sky starts to brighten. It's actually a little easier to steer once we get going faster, though the poor condition of the road slows us back down in the worst stretches. I'm worried about monsters approaching without me noticing— I can't exactly afford to take in the scenery while driving— but it's not like there's much I can do even if we do get attacked, so I refuse to surrender the front seat.

We're weaving through crumbling switchbacks up a mountainside when the bike finally gives up.

"Why'd you stop?" Ravel rocks forward as if to nudge the bike back into motion.

"It needs to recharge." I hop off and wait for him to realize I'm serious, then flip the charging panels out of the sides once he's clear. "Shouldn't take too long."

He shrugs the pack off and starts rummaging. I yank it away, do some rummaging of my own, and hand him a single apple.

"That's it?"

I grab one for myself and close up the pack. I'm amazed at how far we've managed to come already, but even so, if he hasn't figured out how woefully undersupplied for a rescue mission we are, I'm not about to break it down for him.

Instead, I wander along the roadside, stretching my legs and examining the terrain: raw-edged rock, scrubby yellow-and-green bushes, wisps of long grass and dust, lots and lots of dust. A narrow thread of water weaves along the bottom of the canyon, too distant and shallow to be much of a threat.

It reminds me a little of where Ash fought the great battle of the turtle "monster" on the way up. It's a lot funnier in hindsight.

I still keep to the middle of the road, wary of the rattlers Ash warned of. If only he were here, instead of—

"So," Ravel strolls up, munching his apple. "Excited to get home?"

I take a big bite of mine and turn away.

"Yeah, me too. Not that all this nature isn't nice." He circles, trying to get in front of me. I pivot again. "Scenic. Not my style, but some might find it appealing. Romantic, even."

Cadence snorts. I chomp my apple, the grit we kicked up on the bike squeaking between my teeth. Front seat comes with extra bug splatting and dirt eating. But when Ravel goes quiet, I peek over my shoulder. He's just standing there, staring. Not at me, either. I squint along his line of sight, checking for signs of pursuit, but there's nothing there. Just dusty plants, and rock, and sky.

"What are we doing out here?" His voice is a rough whisper. His eyes seem faded, nearly colourless in the brilliant sunlight; a lamp that shines brightest in the dark. Then he shakes off the moment and pulls on his usual mask of arrogance. "I don't think nature agrees with you, flame. You look a wreck."

I grunt, pivoting toward the bike to check its progress and hide the flush racing up my neck. We're both dusty from the road—but that's not what he means.

I'd refused to discuss it with Susan, but Cadence was all too happy to hash it out with her within earshot. They figured the stuff I'd been fed in Refuge had messed with my body, and now I'd been off it for a while, I was catching up with all the normal changes but at ten times the speed.

It almost makes me miss Noosh. It might've been bland, and frankly, disgusting, but it was better than greasy hair and angry-looking, painful skin and—and . . . other stuff.

"You're a normal size for your age," Cadence says primly. "And even that sad excuse for training you were doing was bound to put some muscle on."

"I don't care about that."

"Uh huh."

"What was that?" Ravel pops up on the other side of the bike.

I glare. "You don't look so hot either, you know."

He gasps and clutches his oversized, loaned shirt in mock horror. "Now, I know that can't be true. No need to get defensive."

I snap the charging panels back into the frame. "Pick up the pack. Time to go."

THE CHARGE LASTS well into the night, but the fourth time I jolt off the road and have to wrestle the bike back, Ravel puts his foot down.

I'm too tired to argue. Too tired to peel myself off the bike, too. He more or less has to haul me down, at which point we realize we didn't actually pack blankets or mats or anything useful for sleeping.

I lose track of time—slumping against the bike that, in turn, is propped against a tree while Ravel rifles through woefully inadequate supplies and curses—and find it again when the sun is suddenly overhead.

I'm sore, and stiff, and starving. Ravel's curled around my feet with one arm slung across my calves and the other pillowed under his cheek.

He looks younger, vulnerable, without the armour of his layered ornamentation. The dark curves and angles of his tattoos look faded in the sunlight where they disappear under his shirt. His hair flops low on his forehead, his lashes deepening the bruised hollows under his eyes. He doesn't look strong enough, big enough, *mean* enough to have done as much damage as I know him to have.

I scrunch my face and shake the sleep off, jerking my legs free. I stumble to my feet, dancing and stamping against the pins-and-needles. He moans and curls his arms over his face, snuggling into a ball.

Whatever. Let him sleep. I could use a minute to myself, anyway. That way, I'll be fresh, and fed, and ready to scornfully prod him onto his feet and then the back of the bike before he's awake enough to be annoying.

Unfortunately, I hadn't remembered to flip out the bike's charging units to catch that early morning sun before passing out, so we coast to a stop again late in the morning.

This time, we're on the downslope, almost to a bridge when we run out of power. And I'm pretty sure that river isn't empty.

FISHING

RAVEL SAUNTERS OVER to the edge of the bank, yelps, and backpedals. Cadence laughs.

I drop into a defensive crouch, not that it will do much good if the monsters come after us, but the rearing necks and flicking tails subside when we show no further movement.

Ravel scuttles back several steps, breathing fast. Then he dusts himself off. "So, about lunch."

"You could try fishing," Cadence cackles. I snort.

His affected nonchalance fades into a cautious grin. "I take it I wasn't in any danger?"

We laugh harder.

He rolls his eyes and scuffs off to dig up something to eat from the pack. I let him forage for himself this time.

He tosses me an apple. It bounces across the road and over the bank. The splashing that follows is louder and goes on longer than a single piece of fruit warrants.

We hustle several feet back up the mountain, abandoning the bike to its fate. When nothing chases, I perch on a convenient rock to consider our next move. We'll have to cross that river somehow.

Ravel sidles over and squats on his heels. He offers me half his apple.

"Gross." I wave it off, but my stomach growls.

He cocks an eyebrow and waves the apple under my nose. I give him a shove. He catches his balance and proceeds to munch away without comment while we both pointedly ignore the gurgling noises coming from my midsection.

"I knew about Ange," Ravel says, finally, chucking the core behind him.

"Hmm?"

"Her little underground empire. How she and Cass were spying and running rescue missions. I always knew. We were friends when we were younger, you know."

"Uh huh."

"No, really. It's not like they were all that stealthy. You think I wouldn't notice my own staff sneaking around behind my back?"

I stretch my arms behind my back and listen to the joints pop. "You know I didn't believe you the first time you brought it up. What's with the repeat performance?"

He shrugs.

We sit and listen to the river and pretend it's just the water roaring.

"You think I'm the bad guy," he says, finally. "Okay, yeah, I've done a lot of bad things, but—"

I look at him sideways.

His shoulders droop. "I know. I sucked. But you have to understand, it's complicated. I did what I had to. I tried to make it better. I—"

I walk back to the bike.

"Flame?" He trails after. "I'm messing this up, aren't I? I just wanted to . . ."

It's working. Without my attention, his protests weaken. He doesn't have any power I don't give him. At least, that's what I've been hoping, but—

"No." His wheedling tone transforms, taking on sharp-edges. "You know what? I'm not doing it. I won't apologize for all of it. I did what I had to. I swear some of it even made things better. For some people. Sometimes. I got you out, didn't I?"

I let my head fall back. Breathe through the rage his words stir. The insincere apologies are one thing. This show of honesty, manufactured in yet another attempt to trick me into believing in him.

Once enough tension's drained that I can trust my voice, I turn. I measure each word out, low and steady. "You almost got me killed. More than once. If anything good came out of it, you certainly don't get the credit."

He opens his mouth, but I bring up a hand to stop him. "Oh, and let's be clear. If anyone saved me, it was me. Not you. Not even Ash."

Ravel scowls.

"Don't start."

"Just wondering where your knight in shining armour is at. Seems to me he hasn't been around much." He gestures expansively, as if inviting me to look for myself.

Cadence chokes on a retort he won't be able to hear anyway.

I concentrate on the bike, checking the power levels and wiping dust from the charging panels to speed their efficiency. I could speed off without him. Let him try to find his own way back—on foot.

But it's a silly fantasy, and one I don't let myself indulge in it for more than a moment. If I didn't need to use him more than I feared him using me again, we wouldn't be having this argument.

Still . . . I give the bike one last wistful pat before returning to reality. "We should get going."

"Flame—"

Nope. Enough of that. "My name is Cole."

"That's just the ID given to you by your oppressors," he sneers.

I twist to glare at him, biting off each word. "My name is Cole."

His lips thin. "He gets to call you Cady."

"My name is Cole. Not 'flame.' Not 'Victoire' or 'Cady' or 'Cadence.' Cole. Now, get the pack and get back on the bike."

He sulks his way over to the pack but stops with one hand on the straps. "You haven't eaten yet."

"On the bike. Now."

As a strategy, "take charge and shut down the whining" may or may not be the most effective way to deal with his manipulation, but it definitely makes me feel better. I shove the charging panels into place, stowing them in the hollows on either side of the frame, and mount up. What remains of the old bridge lists, piles missing, sections cracking or half-submerged. Without a dreamwalker to fend off the river monsters, our best hope of getting across in one piece is to hit it at top speed. But from a standing start, that speed won't be nearly as fast as I'd like.

I mentally plot the most promising course through potholes, slick river water, and debris, grit my teeth, and urge the bike forward. Seconds before we hit the bridge it kicks up another notch faster, as if it's as afraid of what lies beneath as I am.

I'm halfway up the incline on the other side when I work out why my back feels unusually well ventilated.

"Don't worry about it," Cadence says. "Might as well finish the climb first."

I push the bike harder in agreement, just for a heartbeat. Two. Three.

Then I let gravity pull us to a halt.

"Don't want to burn out the engine." I say it out loud for Cadence, the mountain, and anyone else listening who might mistake my intentions.

Ravel has no power here. Neither do I. He knew our only chance was to outrun the monsters.

So there are only two reasons he could have for getting off when he did. And whether the river monsters got him or he chose to bail, I can't help him.

Like an idiot, I can't help looking back all the same.

"No, really, you go on ahead. I'll catch up." Ravel waves from the middle of the bridge and dances back as a huge splash sends water surging toward him.

Moron.

Cadence hums agreement.

I stalk down the side of the mountain, catching up a jagged, loose bit of it to hurl when I reach the bottom. It scrapes past Ravel's head—just—and smacks into the reaching tentacle. The monster roars in pain, or maybe just irritation, others joining in with screeches that send both Ravel and I to our knees, hands clapped over our ears.

"Not. Helping." Ravel's lips shape the words, but I can't actually hear past the splashing and howling as river monsters surge into the air and scrabble for purchase on the bridge.

I stumble back, reaching for more chunks of rock to throw for lack of a better plan. But when I bring my hand back to hurl another stone, there's a pause in the attack.

"Are they . . . watching you?" Cadence whispers.

I hold my breath and wave the stone in a slow arc. What seem to pass for faces tilt to follow. That the monsters have some form of intelligence doesn't surprise me. That they can show restraint, or fear, does. It makes them seem like . . . something else.

Not monsters. Creatures. Like the one Grace and I met in the forest.

What had Susan said about it—that it would only fight back in self-defence? Something about us hurting it first?

Sweat traces a cold line down my back. My arm trembles, the stone heavy in my hand. I don't lower it. But I do risk a glance away, scanning the riverbanks in both directions for signs of human habitation. A town. Even a single house. Some indication that we'd started this fight. Some hint that, like Susan believed, we'd made these monsters.

But, aside from the bridge itself, I can't find any noticeably human mark left on this landscape.

"That doesn't mean anything," Cadence says. "There could be a whole city just around the bend. Or a flood wiped out the houses. Or—"

I lower the stone. The river monsters—the *creatures*—had made their presence known when we approached. But they hadn't actually attacked until I hit first. Had they merely been warning us of their presence? Or had they been lying in wait?

"Flame?" Ravel follows the stone's path with as much interest as the creatures, though his attention is understandably split.

Even when he slides a cautious foot forward, they don't take their focus off me. I place my makeshift weapon on the ground and ease back, nodding to him.

"We won't hurt you," I say over Cadence's protests.

Ravel's eyes widen, but he creeps another few steps toward me before the creatures seem to notice. They hiss, shifting toward him. I raise both hands to show they're empty and nod for him to follow suit.

"Just let him through, and we'll go away and leave you in peace." I stand as still as possible and do my best to make my voice slow and soothing.

It doesn't come easily; Ravel is the persuasive one. Staying out of it and pretending nothing's wrong is more my speed. But if I'm going to try to save a whole city, I should probably start practicing heroism sans magic now anyway.

"Yeah, that and he has our only map," Cadence says.

Ravel flinches away from my sudden and, from his point of view, unexpected glare. The creatures turn on him.

He yells. They screech. I lunge. He puts on a burst of speed, ducking and swerving around snapping jaws and flailing tentacles.

There's a tearing crunch, one shark-toothed maw closing from behind, and he goes down with a yell. I jump forward without thinking, hurtling for the bridge to, I can only assume, get eaten alongside this absolute idiot of a not-quite-enemy.

The monster drags Ravel into the air and shakes him like it's trying to snap his neck. From this angle—*why am I on the bridge what was I thinking I'm gonna die*—I can see the monster's mouthful is mostly backpack.

There's a shredding sound and the contents of the pack drop, along with Ravel. The monsters dive in every direction, distracted by the sudden bouncing scatter of colourful hail.

One piece rolls toward me. But instead of something useful like our map, or even a stray apple, it's only that stupid knot of wood again. I pick it up anyway in the sudden, eerie silence that falls between bending and rising again.

They're all looking at me. Ravel, sopping with monster-drool and half the river. The inhabitants of said river seem suddenly less interested in our scattered provisions than in the one object that happened to make its way to me.

I extend it hesitantly. Their oil-slick eyes follow, teeth dripping, tentacles curling and uncurling hypnotically. I take one step, two, mincing until my toe nudges Ravel's knee. I prod, hardly daring to breathe, much less speak, but he seems to get the message. I back away, careful to keep the knot in plain sight as Ravel creeps along beside me.

And then, impossibly, we're on solid ground and, a heartbeat later, racing up the side of the mountain to get away from the splashing, roaring danger at its base.

We don't stop until we reach the bike. Ravel collapses at its base, panting. His pant leg is ragged, blood seeping through, and his cheek is raw from that stone that almost-but-not-quite missed him. His back under his tattered shirt looks better than expected, though—the monster really did get mostly the pack. He's lucky it went for him with its teeth instead of the tentacles. He's even luckier I stopped and went back for him in the first place.

I drape myself over the bike and let my heartbeat settle from a full-out gallop to a thudding trot before kicking him in the ribs.

"Next time you decide to give in to that death wish of yours, give me the map first."

27

PURSUIT

B ETWEEN CHARGING INEFFICIENCIES, river monster showdowns, and getting lost a half-dozen times already (we tend to realize only when the road dead-ends), I'm pretty sure whatever extra margin we had from pursuit has shrunk to nothing.

But we have to be close now. How many more mountains could there really be before we hit the coast?

Still, I can't stop checking behind us. We've stopped waiting for the bike to charge, taking turns pushing it when it runs down, even in the rain. And its not just pursuit from Nine Peaks I have to worry about. My nightmares are catching up.

The dead of Refuge haunt my sleep and half of my waking hours, too. Cadence and Ravel take turns talking to keep me focused—which would work better if they could actually hear one another. Whatever dreamwalker potential Ravel has, apparently it doesn't extend to hearing Cadence, and every time he speaks over her just makes her more pissed off.

"Have you noticed how the trees on the ridge look like people from the corners of your eyes?" Ravel says. "I keep thinking there's someone watching us."

I grunt. My foot sloshes in the mud filling my shoe, while the shoe slips in the mud outside, only in a slightly different direction. There's mud everywhere, including the insides of everything we're wearing. It's been raining for two days, and we won't be able to recharge the bike until it stops.

"Still think nature is romantic?" Cadence says, but the snide remark is lost on Ravel, as usual, and I don't bother repeating it for him.

I slide and stagger with each step, blisters growing and bursting and growing again. It's my turn to push, but Ravel leans into the bike from the other side, stabilizing and providing more than his fair share of forward momentum.

I should be appreciative of his efforts, but the extra effort it takes to keep both the bike and myself upright is something I desperately need to stay focused on the here and now, the only way I can even begin to push back against what gnaws at the edges of my mind.

"Hey, so listen. We need to talk about how we're going to—" His voice fades out as the dead rise.

The day is already dark with rain, but its edges grow even darker, hollowing out until the only things that seem real are the bodies hovering before me.

Some, I know well. The long dead. The familiar ones I failed to save, glaring and gesticulating and howling in raw, deafening whispers that slip in and out of static.

This isn't the dreamscape—I'm almost certain it's not. It's not my magic returning, nor the Mara, but the ghosts of my city calling me back. Warning—and urging. And there are more of them every day.

I'm running out of time. I try not to look when they descend, afraid to see the faces of friends among their numbers, but I know it's only a matter of time until I will.

The living world returns gradually, the whispers of the ghostly horde ebbing amidst the rush of icy raindrops, the only warmth in the world the twin points where Ravel grips my shoulders and shakes.

We've been through this enough times by now that I shouldn't see worry in his eyes, pale yellow like a guttering candle, wavering behind a sheet of rain and the inky fringe plastered against his scalp.

The mud slurps underfoot as I struggle to find my balance, reluctant to release its hold. I reach down to haul the dropped bike from its grip and Ravel shoulders between us, getting both the bike and me upright and moving forward, if barely.

"We need to find shelter," he says, leaning close. Only, I'm the one leaning.

I shake my head. Somehow, my cheek ends up against his shoulder. I can't summon the energy to move away. "Nowhere to stop. No time."

"Pull it together," Cadence grumbles, but she's not the one slogging through the mountains in the rain, and I'm too worn out to argue.

"Tell me." My teeth chatter. "You wanted to talk. About something. Before . . ."

His grip tightens. "It can wait."

"Talk."

He reaches over to adjust something on the bike. I sway, shivering all the harder in his absence. I hate feeling this pathetic.

I stumble to the other side of the bike. It holds me up, more than the other way around, but this way is better. Distance is better.

Ravel's shoulders stiffen, sending me back to that day not so long ago in a warm, clean-ish room when he raged and raved and took out his fear of rejection on me. He's been more enemy than ally to me, and yet here we are. Somewhere along the way, I lost all the fear of him I had left, and most of the anger.

"You know better than to trust him," Cadence says.

I agree. But I'm alone in the mountains. And he's the one here with me. He's sacrificed and suffered just for a chance to go back and fight.

Power-hungry he may be, but the truth is he's nearly as powerless and desperate as I am to save our people right now. And they are our people, if for no other reason than that no one else seems to care to save them.

But that doesn't make him trustworthy.

"Cole," he says. Not "flame" or "Victoire" or any of the other pet names meant to shove me into the shape of who he wants me to be. "I need to tell you something."

"So talk." It's less a rush of adrenaline than a trickle. But it pushes back the cold, if only for a few more steps. I shake off exhaustion and focus. "Tell me."

"There are things you don't know," he says. I growl in frustration, but he hurries on before I can get a more articulate complaint out. "There's no way you could. I shouldn't know most of them either. I'm not even sure where to start. But maybe it can help us come up with a better plan, so . . ."

A plan. What a wonderful, impossible, idea. All our plans keep blowing up in our faces. But, sure, why not come up with a new one?

"How do you think I found you?" The corner of his mouth lifts in a wry smile. "I didn't have a decent map. I certainly didn't trail you and then hide out in the woods for weeks."

I don't bother pointing out there are so many impossibilities to his presence I'd long since given up trying to get answers. None of it makes sense. How did he get out of the city in this first place? Past the Mara, and the water monsters, and the barrier? How did he even know I'd left, never mind where I'd gone?

The only thing I could guess was he'd somehow heard I'd taken off without realizing how useless I'd become, and stormed down to Under to demand answers, but . . .

Oh no.

"Is she okay?"

He stops pushing for a moment. I stagger as the bike slides out from under me.

"Who?" he asks, leaning back in to stabilize us.

"Ange. What did you do to her? If you hurt her—"

"Why would I—look, like I said, Ange and I have been friends since before you even got to Refuge. She owes me her life a hundred times over. Trust me, she's fine."

"Then how—"

"I can feel you," he says. Then he swallows. "That sounded weird. I mean . . . I can, uh, feel . . . Where you are? When I want to? Ever since you arrived in the city?"

He keeps glancing at me, then away, like a guilty child. But it's far from the weirdest thing I've encountered over the last few months.

"Do you have any other abilities? Useful ones?"

Cadence snorts. "He wishes."

"Um. It's not an ability, exactly. Not magic, or even something I've trained myself to master. It's more like . . . technology?"

I've had more than enough of that question in his voice. "I'm not mad at you." At least, not about this.

He closes his eyes. "You don't understand."

"I don't care what you call it. Magical powers. Technology. Purple brain sparks. Just tell me what you can do. Or,"—when he still hesitates—"just start with what you have done."

He pushes the bike with renewed energy—hard enough I have to scramble to keep up.

"You know about the Influence. I can talk to the Mara, sure, but I don't know if that's part of it or if . . . Anyway, there's the way people listen to me, do what I say. And I can find you and, uh, if there were others like you, I'd probably be able to find them, too. It has something to do with the tattoos—they're not just for show, you know. But it's more than that, I think. Monsters like the Mara don't like me, exactly, but they don't seem to think I'm all that tasty, either. Substances don't have the same effect on me. And I can pass through barriers."

"Barriers like—"

"Yeah, apparently I can leave the city whenever I want."

I'd figured that much out already, given that he had just up and appeared outside Nine Peaks. But the real question, the one that matters so much I'm almost afraid to ask, is: "Can you take others with you?"

"Dunno. Never tried. Can you?"

I shrug, but our bare shadow of a plan is starting to coalesce. Ash obviously got me out of the city somehow, but he's no longer around to help. And if he, or someone like him, could have brought everyone out of the reach of the Mara, I have to assume we wouldn't be in this mess to begin with. Which means it's not just a matter of being able to remove people from the city, but convincing them to actually leave.

"Totally. No big deal," Cadence mocks. "You're great at convincing people."

"Maybe not, but he is."

"I'm what?" Ravel asks, hearing only my half of the conversation, as usual.

"Persuasive. And able to cross barriers. If you can take people with you, that's all we need."

Between his ability to cross the barrier and his Influence, whether that really was some kind of talent, or technology—whatever he meant by *that*—or just the inherent power of being the son of the mayor and deliverer of the Mara's favourite treats, it means we might have a real chance.

I wonder if it occurs to him that he never needed me to begin with. I hold my breath, but his grin shows no sign of cutting me out of the plan, and I'm not about to give up now.

I set out to save my city. If Ravel is the tool I need to do it, good enough.

"Sure. Just keep telling yourself that," Cadence says.

DESOLATION

TURNS OUT THE journey through the mountains was the easy part. Apparently they had been mostly uninhabited in the time before, which means no one had bothered bombing them to bits. The monster threat there wasn't as big to begin with. But the wide valley between the mountains and the sea had evidently once been packed with people.

Some of this story I picked up from Grace and Susan. Ravel knows even more, or at least is willing to share more than they were. He tells me bits and pieces as we pick our way across twisted bridges and shattered roads.

There was once a whole chain of cities between the mountains and the water, not just ours. Our city held on the longest as the waters rose, ignoring the signs until it was too late, or maybe just too stupid and greedy to abandon their holdings. The sea covered the land and made islands of the towers, and still the people did not leave, even as monsters rose from the waves and the Mara stalked their halls in the sky.

This is where their stories diverge because Susan said the monsters hemmed our city in and trapped us there to contain our ability to cause further damage, and Ravel says it was our people who made the barrier in the first place. He says it was meant to protect us—and it did when the bombs started going off. Apparently, someone had decided that the best way to take back the land would be levelling it, without regard for either the people living there or the monsters hunting them.

Clearly, that didn't work. The only traces of human life in this broken wasteland are ancient and decaying, but monsters still snarl in the depths of night and surge under every bridge we cross.

Between the end of the mountains and the uneven blotch of the city rising from the waters at the edge of the coast, we find rivers where there should be roads, lakes where there should be fields, and all too often, decaying skeletons of mammoth constructions barring our way. I thought I'd at least be able to find my way back to the first camp we made on our way out, the one near the haunted village, but even that turns out to be beyond me.

In the end, it's Cadence who saves us from getting eaten in the wilderness.

Have I mentioned we're exhausted? Because, between the ghosts-behind-my-eyes nightmares and the monstrous-actually-screaming-in-the-dark nightmares, both Ravel and I have bags under our eyes big enough to haul a second bike in.

Which makes it all the more irritating when Cadence chirps that she totally knows the way, and why are we wasting all this time going in circles?

"Not in the mood." I snap.

She's been uncharacteristically quiet lately, other than that persistent and monotonous humming, but I still don't have the energy for her games right now.

"For what?" Ravel asks.

"Hmm? Oh, Cadence's messing around again."

He doesn't even raise his eyebrows at that anymore. "Shut up, Cadence. The grown-ups are tired today."

"But I really do know the way!" she whines.

"Shut up, Cadence." I second, enjoying the way Ravel said "grown-ups."

We may be screwing this up, but it's kind of nice not being the only screw-up for a change. It'd be even nicer if the stakes weren't so high. At this rate, I can't believe pursuit hasn't caught up to us already, and I can't let myself think too hard about the other thing. The thing where the Mara have had weeks now to do as they will . . .

"What if I can find us a good camping spot for tonight?" Cadence interrupts, dogged. "If I'm right, will you believe that I know the way?"

I shrug, stumble over a weed, and thwack my elbow on the side of the bike trying not to face-plant.

Ravel looks over in concern, but I do this often enough he doesn't bother dashing over to check on me anymore. That or the fit I threw the last time he tried has finally taught him better. I kick my way free of entangling vegetation and rub my elbow.

"Cadence says she knows a good spot to stop for the night," I say by way of explanation.

"Does she have a lead on dinner, too?"

"Oh, right," Cadence says. "You guys eat. Sorry, not too many options out here—unless you want to fish?"

"That's a nope on dinner." I lean into the bike, pushing until I can't feel the hollowness of my stomach. "But I'm thinking we give her a shot on finding a place to sleep. She couldn't be any worse than you at it."

Ravel gives me a look that says I have no room to talk, which is fair.

There's still blood on his sleeve from a surprise attack two nights ago. My suggestion to camp at the foot of a rare intact wall hadn't factored in the things apparently living just on the other side of it. Those monsters were small, but they could climb. And bite.

"Your call," is all he says.

I expected gloating from Cadence, but she guides us to a mostly-standing building with a minimum of fuss. It's small enough we can scout its single-story of remaining rooms and be reasonably confident it's unoccupied before the light fades. There's even one room with all four walls and a door intact. The only window is high and narrow. It's dark but as secure as anything we can hope to find out here.

"Not bad," I admit. We wheel the bike in and lean it against the door as extra insurance.

"She have any other surprises in store for us?" Ravel asks, reaching up thoughtlessly to unsling the pack—the one that lies in tatters on a mountain bridge a few days' travel back.

Cadence giggles.

The hair on the back of my neck prickles. She never acts this playful around him.

Ravel looks up sharply, sensing more than seeing the change. "What?"

"Oh, nothing much," she teases. "Just saved you, is all. The squad from Nine Peaks would've run right into us if I hadn't helped."

"How do you know? Where are they? Are they here?" My pulse kicks into high gear, blood rushing in my ears, which is entirely unproductive, since all I want to do is press up against the wall and listen for approaching footsteps.

"What's going on?" Ravel puts himself between me and the door, preparing for an attack.

"Shh," she says. "They'll hear you if you're not quiet."

I reach for Ravel's shoulder. He pivots away from the door and sinks to the floor without a word, following the pressure of my hand. Even on full alert, part of me marvels at the grace of his movements, which just goes to show how exhausted I've become.

I shake away the distraction. "Explain."

Cadence hums. "Should I? You never believe me."

I growl. Ravel edges closer. "What—"

"Oh, fine," she sighs. "Will you stop freaking out if I tell you I can feel them? Listen in on their plans?"

That's . . . possible, I guess. "Who?"

"Not Ash," she says, puncturing the bubble of hope I hadn't realized was inflating. "Not anyone you know. The elders made sure of that."

Ravel taps my knee in silent question. I brush him off.

"You're not going to tell him? He's feeling left out."

I ignore her taunting. "What do they want?"

"Us. They were sent to bring us back."

I close my eyes. Too late. We wasted our head start and now they've caught up.

"It's okay," Cadence says, in a disquieting, hollow tone. "I can keep them from finding us, just like earlier. They'll pass us and make for the city. I'll listen in on their plans. We'll be able to stay just out of reach until it's too late for them to stop us."

I strain my ears. All I hear, beyond the rasp of my breaths, and Ravel's, is the creaking and popping of the decaying structure around us. But now I wonder: that rustling outside the window, is it the wind in the weeds, or the stealthy footsteps of trackers surrounding us?

"We're safe here. I promise," she says. "Now, you'd better explain to that idiot or he'll go and blow it all."

Ravel is up on one knee, ready to launch himself at whatever threat is coming.

I sigh and tug his sleeve until he drops down again. I whisper the news against his ear. He smells of sweat and dust and, still, after all we've been through, just the faintest hint of the oversweet, spiced air of Freedom.

When I finish, he turns to look at me. There's so little light left that our heads bump.

I jerk back, sprawling off balance and almost hit the floor with a thud. His arm around me muffles the impact, spilling us both in the dust, tense and panting.

"Wow, so stealthy," says Cadence.

SEAWEED

E XHAUSTED OR NOT, there's no way I can sleep after Cadence's announcement. I prop myself against one spongy wall and stare at the door, twitching with every muffled noise from outside.

But the next thing I know, the angle of the room has changed, and the light. Ravel rolls over and blinks sleepily at me from across the room. My far-too-empty stomach gurgles. I clap my hands over it and wince.

Cadence laughs. "It's fine. They're long gone—no need to keep quiet now. We should get going, though. They'll be harder to follow if they're too far ahead."

We leave the bike behind after Cadence promises she can help us find it again if needed. We can't risk the noise of it giving our position away.

Without its grumbling company, I'm able to make out a strangely familiar sound: a low, drawn-out noise that calls to something in me. I've taken a half-dozen steps before Ravel snags my arm. I shake him off and continue a few more before the fence comes into view.

I hadn't realized Cadence had brought us so close to the place Ash had first stopped on our way out of the city after all. We've just spent the night in the remains of a building down the hill from it. And I hadn't expected the haunted village to still call to me so strongly.

"Flame?" Ravel keeps pace beside me, tugging at my sleeve. "I think that's the wrong way."

I ignore him, pushing through high grass and low bushes to reach past the rotten boards. I hook my fingers into chain link and shiver at the familiarity.

Ash had said this was a broken, abandoned place—a fake village overrun by monsters. Cadence had said it wasn't safe—

"It isn't," she insists. "You need to come away. We're losing time, remember?"

—But it still doesn't *feel* dangerous. Just alien. And when twigs brush my fingers from the other side of the links and a clump of leaves and bushes nod at me, I get the sense it's more than just the breeze driving them.

I close my hand around the twigs, still listening to that low, distant murmuring—and in the place of the dry sticks are the familiar knots and whorls of a satin-grained bit of wood.

I can't remember having seen it since we fled the river monsters in the mountains . . .

The whispering of the wind in the leaves and that low sound overlap, forming an oddly melodious pattern and I can almost hear, almost make it out—

"There's no time for this," Cadence says, urgently, her pitch rising. "We have our own monsters back home to worry about. Cole! Hey!"

I shake my head, suddenly dizzy. I'd forgotten how this place affected me. How these monsters were able to get inside my head. And yet, even knowing their threat, there was something about this place, the way if felt, the sounds that almost made sense, would make sense if I could just listen for another moment—

"What's wrong?" Flame?" Ravel nudges me. "Didn't you want to get going?"

I blink. Then I backpedal, so fast we almost both go down trying to get out of each other's ways. I slip and fumble my way down the low hill to where we'd started, trembling. Whatever lives on the other side of that fence can make me see things, hear things, feel things that aren't there. If I hadn't had both him and Cadence pestering me, pulling me back, I'm not sure I'd have been able to stop myself from crossing over to the monsters. I need to get out of this place before they can cast their spell on me again.

Ravel prods for answers that I have no intention of giving him—even if I could. Instead, I ignore him and focus on getting us back on track. The bike is where we left it. We have no supplies to gather anyway. It's time to go—well past time.

The group pursuing us from Nine Peaks must be a good size—a full squad, even. The trail they left in the weeds and dirt might have been enough to follow even without Cadence's help. With it, we make good time toward the coast, dropping back from the direct route only when she warns we're getting too close to remain undetected.

By nightfall, the yellow stain of our city is visible on the horizon. The barrier gives it a weird, dome-like appearance, toxic fog blurring our view of the towers within.

"Tomorrow?" I whisper, despite Cadence's assurances we're more than shouting distance away from our pursuers.

Ravel shakes his head. "Probably not. It takes more time than you'd think to cross all that. And I'd rather not do it in the dark if we can help it."

He's right—no sense risking a night crossing now we're so near.

But then the nightmares close in. The dead are multiplying, their voices calling out to me; ghosts now mixed with what I desperately hope are just memories. Suzannah, ancient and young, dead and alive and dead again. Lifor, rebellious and hurting and trapped. Lily, clinging to Ash and begging us to save her father, Ange's face blanching behind her. In the relentless storm of it all, I even catch sight of Maryam, withering and renewed and broken down once more, her face impassive and her eyes glittering with malevolence.

Victims and friends, enemies and strangers, all crying out to be saved. Or avenged.

And, just at the end as Ravel pulls me out of the nightmare, a new face. A memory of the child Cadence and I had been stares out at me, dark eyes brightening with a silver sheen—and draining to liquid black.

I wake with a gasp, shivering in Ravel's arms. I scramble to my feet in the grey light of a hazy, drizzling dawn, pushing him away. "Today. We go in today."

He hesitates, looking up with all the fear and vulnerability of the lost ones haunting my dreams. And then he stands, shoulders pulling straight, jaw hardening. "It's a good day for an invasion."

BETWEEN CADENCE'S GUIDANCE and Ravel's memories of the map and his journey out, we manage to forge our own path back to the city without running into the squad from Nine Peaks. We even make it before dark, if only just, though we're weaving on our feet and faint with hunger and exhaustion by the time we stand at the edge of the water and look out—and up—at the barrier before us.

The ocean laps at the gritty shore, deceptively calm. The dome over the city looks like a dingy sheet of glass slicing the water in two. It juts high above our heads, just the faintest suggestion of an arc catching the setting sun and scattering its bloody hues across that vast surface, obscuring what lays within.

"You're sure you can cross?" I ask.

Ravel shrugs. "I did it once before, didn't I? The real question is, can I get you across with me."

He tries for a grin, but it falls flat as we consider the image of me slipping down the wrong side of that glassine surface and into the waves below—yet another type of barrier to worry about—while he steps through alone.

I crouch down and reach out to the icy water, wetting the tip of my finger before Ravel yanks me back.

"Not a good idea." He doesn't let go until we're several feet from the edge. "No sense giving them a taste for you."

"How do we get there"—I wave an arm at the malignant churn of fog on the other side of the barrier—"if we can't go into the water?"

Kind of the wrong question to be asking since I don't remember learning to swim.

"I do," Cadence says unhelpfully. "It's not that hard."

Ravel shoves hair back from his forehead and grimaces. "I was planning to wait until the tide went out and—"

"Nope. Next."

"Lure in a bunch of sea monsters and hop across on their backs?" Cadence suggests.

"Uh, find something that floats?" he offers.

"Make some wings and a tower and glide at it from above?"

"Build a really tall ladder and tip it against the side?"

"Dig a tunnel under the water?"

"Catch a sea monster and ride it across?"

"She already said that." I roll my eyes. Amusing as all their absurdly creative solutions are, none of them get us into the city tonight. "How did you get out in the first place?"

He points at the barrier in front of us. "The tide was out. I walked."

"When does it go out again?"

He shrugs. Cadence does her version of a shrug, which is pointed silence. I scrub my hands over my face. "Okay. No sea monsters. No bridges. No waiting and absolutely nothing that requires constructing anything. What are we left with?"

"We could look for a boat," Ravel says. "Or boat-like floating objects."

"Do you see a boat?" Cadence says.

Even in the dying light, it's obvious none of the debris within view is going to do the job, even if we knew how to propel it in the right direction once we got it on the water. But that reminds me of something.

"How did Ash get in, again—and get me out?"

"Old train tunnels, remember?" Cadence says. "They're mostly flooded, but Ash waited until the tide was at its lowest, swam as far as the barrier, and dreamwalked to the other side. Trust me. You're better off swimming from right here if you want to go that route."

"Are there more sea monsters in the tunnels?"

"Nah. More bodies. The trains were still running when it flooded."

I shudder. As it happens, I do remember Ash mentioning something about that. Great. Like I needed more ghosts to worry about.

Ravel steps closer, looking concerned. Instead of bringing him up to speed, I head for the water. "How fast can you swim?"

"Not fast enough."

I make it two steps into the water before he tackles me. I land on my shoulder. Wet sand and slimy water plants spray up into my face. I roll to my knees and scrub a sodden and gritty sleeve across my face. He doesn't back off, wrestling in the sand to drag me further from the water's edge.

When my vision clears, I see why.

There's only one at first, its head a sudden stillness in the relentless motion of the waves that separate us from our goal. And then it surges, up out of the water and toward the shore. There's a flash of too-many-too-sharp-too-white—

I shoulder Ravel aside to scramble up the shore faster.

It keeps on coming—*so fast, too fast, what were we thinking*—and stops. The waves surge toward us, and subside.

Ravel and I clutch at each other and stare as the sea monster submerges, all those teeth and tentacles vanishing under the waves until there's just the glittering eyes and slick dome cresting.

It's watching us.

"It has been watching for a while," Cadence says. "You just weren't paying attention."

Easy for her to sound calm. She's not the one at risk of getting her arm chomped off by a vicious sea monster. Or twisted off. Or chomped-and-twisted at the same time. My imagination is capable of coming up with several possibilities at once, each worse than the last.

"Can it come on land?" I back away slowly, without taking my eyes off of that eerie stillness amidst the waves.

"Probably?" Ravel has a death grip on the back of my shirt as if he thinks I'll make a break for the water at any moment.

Yeah, not likely.

But then I have the most horrible idea.

"Go find something to float on." I point inland.

"Lame," Cadence complains. "My ideas were better. Those things can definitely knock you off a boat if they want to."

I wait as Ravel stalks off. Every few steps, he cranes his neck to make sure I'm not making another suicidal run for the ocean behind his back. I shoo him along and turn to scrape together armfuls of seaweed from the stinking piles heaped along the shoreline.

"Um, if you're planning to distract them, I'm pretty sure they'd rather chew on you than rotting plants," Cadence says.

I keep right on heaping up the weeds, grimacing at the way they squish between my fingers. Small creatures skitter from their hiding places in the rubbery fronds. I grind my teeth to keep from shrieking when some sharp-legged thing scrabbles across my hand.

But, by the time Ravel returns dragging a large chunk of debris, I've amassed a pile of the stuff large enough to hide behind—if we hunker down and get cozy.

I wave for him to drop his makeshift raft and join me behind the newly assembled seaweed bunker.

"I'm afraid to ask." He wrinkles his nose against the fetid reek.

I tug him closer, whisper: "Camouflage. We'll wait until it's too dark to see, pile it on the raft, and float across."

He's shaking his head before I can finish. "Never going to work. They might not be able to smell us or see us, but they've been watching the whole time. I'm pretty sure even a monster can see through this plan. Besides, the water level's different on the other side. If I walked across at low tide, that means we'd have to dive to cross now. Why don't we just wait—"

"No. We do this tonight."

I know he thinks I'm being unreasonable, but something is telling me we can't afford to wait much longer. The nightmares are calling me back for a reason—to regain my lost powers, to save the lives of my friends before it's too late, to return to who and where I'm meant to be . . .

Or that's what I want to believe—and Cadence's silence in the face of my delusions gives me hope that we really are still special, still necessary, still destined to be heroes.

Because the alternative is that I'm truly haunted, or going crazy. The harsh reality is Ange, and Lily and her dad, and all the others on the other side of that barrier might be able to survive another night without rescue, but I'm not sure I can.

CROSSING

R AVEL ISN'T HAPPY about it, but when I threaten to get on the crude raft by myself if I have to, he gives in and helps me shift the heap of decaying weeds onto it and drag the whole mess to the water's edge.

We can't help the scraping, much as I wish we could. When Cadence calls out a warning, it's alarming, but not surprising. Our pathetic attempts at stealth have still tipped off our pursuers, but maybe we can turn that to our benefit.

Shouts ring out in the distance, clouds cover the moon, and we slip into the water. Our first attempts at paddling succeed in little more than knocking seaweed over the edge, but with a little whispered negotiation—and a lot of yelling on Cadence's part—we work out a system.

Belly down in seaweed, icy waves lapping over the edge, I clutch a smaller bit of debris in my left hand and draw it carefully through the water, counting slowly in my head before lifting and starting the next stroke. On the other side of the raft, Ravel does the same. We're not moving fast, but that's kind of the point. We want to fly under the radar until our diversion arrives.

The shouts get closer. I catch my name, and Ravel's, over the pounding in my ears and the creak of our raft. There's splashing as the voices near, and then crashing and a kind of hollow roar as the monsters go hurtling past, disrupting the wave pattern we're only just getting the hang of. We paddle faster in their wake.

A sudden jolt sends me rolling off the side of the raft. I lose my makeshift paddle trying to scramble back up. Something grabs my leg and yanks.

I shout. Water closes over my head, filling my mouth with brine. I flail, hitting out in every direction.

One of my blows must have connected with something important. My hand breaks the surface, and then my head. I suck in a lungful of air before something new gets ahold of me.

"Quiet." Ravel hauls me against the raft.

It takes several breathless seconds of scrabbling, splinters digging under my nails and into the soft undersides of my arms, but I manage to get a reasonably firm hold on the waterlogged surface.

The raft bumps against the barrier with the motion of the waves. I curl my legs to my chest, and float, unable to climb back into our seaweed nest but wary of teeth in the depths beneath us.

Now we're here, this seems like a stupid plan.

Ravel uses the raft to pull himself toward the barrier. He flattens one hand against it, and the dingy tint ripples as if he's dipped a finger in still water. He presses harder, his hand sinking into the surface, sending yellowish waves pulsing along the glassine surface.

I inch closer. Ravel notices me coming and pulls back to help me balance while I press my own hand against it. The barrier offers a spongy, dense resistance. When I push harder, it oozes up around my fingers with a strangely vibrating pressure.

He drifts back, letting go of my arm, and the sensation changes, the surface hardening instantly around my hand with a buzzing sensation that rapidly escalates from mild to excruciating. I'd scream, except the buzzing has taken over, knotting every muscle in agony and freezing my breath.

Cadence shrieks for me, though the sound of her voice is distant, dimming—

Ravel's touch snaps the barrier's hold.

I jolt back, sinking below the waves before I remember to reach for the raft's buoyancy. I manage to gain some purchase with my good hand on a rough patch, but my burned hand slips off an oddly familiar knobbled shape.

We must have shoveled that stupid knot of wood onto the raft along with the seaweed. The cold water, or maybe shock, seems to have numbed the pain of my burn, but at least on my second try I remember to heave with my elbows instead of my hands.

"What happened?" Ravel trails his fingers against the barrier.

I shudder. "Don't touch it."

He taps the surface. It ripples. "Did it do something to you?"

"It tried to kill me!"

He raises an eyebrow. "Are you sure? You seem fine." The eyebrow goes down when I shove my injured hand in his face. "Huh. That's kind of cool."

In the sickly illumination of the barrier, it doesn't look so much burned as scarred, or maybe tattooed, undulating patterns etched from my fingertips to my wrist. I make a fist, the heat fading, the pain cooled to mere stiffness.

So I'm floating in sea monster-infested waters beside a mysterious, faintly luminescent dome that seemingly wants to kill me, and I don't know how to swim. But we still haven't reached the best part, which is when Cadence reminds us: "You know there's nothing on the other side, right? Except rocks? Because you have to dive down to the tunnel Ravel used?"

WE DON'T DIVE so much as sink in tandem, Ravel pulling us down the side of the barrier until Cadence tells me to stop. I squeeze his hand twice in the agreed-upon signal.

My lungs feel like they're going to burst, which helps distract from the certainty that a sea monster is about to take a bite out of us every time something brushes past.

It doesn't stop me from dreading the barrier and wondering if I'll burn up or drown first. Which is silly. Obviously, I'll burn while drowning.

I tense so hard against the impending anguish that I miss the moment we cross over. Ravel has to prod me into opening my eyes and breathing again.

The air is stale, with a noxious tang that tastes like coming home. I run my fingers along the rough floor and try not to sob with relief. I try to stand and get no further than a crouch before I knock into something with a dull clang. My head rings.

"Sorry," Ravel's voice is muffled by the scrape of his movements. "It's a little tight in here. Just a sec."

There's rustling, a click, and then a bluish glow outlines Ravel's silhouette. More rustling, as he digs through a well-stuffed pack. Apparently, he planned ahead for our return. I'm impressed despite myself.

The glow of a small lamp lights up the side of his face as he reaches back to me. "Eat this. It'll help with the shivering."

I'm shaking so hard my teeth chatter. My stomach cramps at the idea of food after far too long. The packet jumps from my hand when he passes it to me and lands on the floor with a small but pronounced crunch.

"Probably poisoned anyway," Cadence says.

Not comforting. Or helpful.

Ravel fishes it out of the dust, unwraps, and holds the oblong thing until I can get a grip on it. It's painfully sweet. I don't recognize it from my time in Freedom, where food tended toward the sparse and decorative, nor does it resemble the pale but plentiful stuff grown by Under. All the shaking makes it hard to chew, but if it is poison, it must be slow acting.

Ravel produces a blanket for each of us and munches his way through a few bites of the sweet, dry food before turning away. "It gets bigger up ahead. We can change there."

The walls curve around us, explaining why I'd bumped my head when we first came through. It's not so much a small tunnel as a very large pipe, but it opens out into another that's big enough to walk side by side without brushing the walls.

Ravel drapes his blanket over the light to dim it and we peel off waterlogged travel clothes. We leave them in a heap, little more than rags, and fumble into blessedly dry fabric. When he uncovers the light once more, I realize the dark, loose garments must've come from Ange. Huh.

"S—so, uh, when did you actually start working together?" I garble the words, but all the shivering does seem to be dying down. Marginally.

"Together?"

"You and Ange."

He quirks the kind of grin that brings back memories of black paint and gold ornaments and dancing the night away in the fever-dreamtime between one of my worlds shattering and the next. "When have we not been working together?"

"You're not part of Under."

"No?" He turns and leads the way down this new, wider tunnel. "I'm the one who brought it to life, flame. How did you think Ange and her band of runaways survived down here?"

I still don't believe his story—he was nobody's friend or ally last time I was in this city—but it's a good question. I've seen the boundary close up and have the—scars? The marks on my hand certainly don't look like burns anymore, or not fresh ones at least—anyway, the evidence to prove it. Nothing and nobody from this city gets in or out.

Except for Ravel, apparently.

Between the flooding and the monsters, it's not easy to survive here, especially without access to the rigorously maintained life-support infrastructure of Refuge. Ange's people have built some ingenious solutions from scavenged materials, but there were enough of them—and enough survivors clinging to life on the surface—that they couldn't be getting by solely on foraged scraps from the bones of the old city.

Could they? Or had Ravel really been slipping them resources behind Refuge's back all this time?

He can say what he likes for now, but I'll have other means of getting the truth soon. "So that's where we're headed now, right? To Ange?"

Ravel leads the way through the maze of tunnels without answering. I remember too late that this is my mission. I hadn't planned to tag along behind him—or Ash, or Ange, or even Cadence—like usual. But I'm lost in these tunnels, and he's the one with the ability to cross the barrier, and I don't know how to take back control, or if I even should anymore.

"Is that what you want," he says, finally. "To see Ange first?"

My steps stutter to a halt, and he looks back over his shoulder, one eyebrow raised as if he's actually interested in what I want. As if it really is up to me to decide what we should do next. As if he's waiting on me, instead of pushing for his own way.

It's what I need from him—but it's not how Ravel operates, which means this is a new trick of his, pretending to let me choose while actually being the one in the lead the whole time. It almost gets me.

But two can play at this game. "Where do you think we should go?"

". . . Ange is fine."

"This is painful. What are you even doing?" Cadence grumbles, missing the point of the game.

"Changed my mind," I say, testing my theory and him at the same time. "I think we should swing by Freedom first, check on the situation."

He perks up. "Yeah? I think that's the right call, too."

Score one for me?

TUNNELS

W E DON'T EVEN make it near the edges of Freedom before the ghosts descend.

I'd hoped the attacks, or nightmares, or visions, or whatever would stop when I returned to the city. Wasn't that what they wanted?

So much for that. One moment I'm stumbling along behind Ravel, and the next I'm caught in the void, the faces of the familiar dead and strangers alike making their deafening pleas and accusations before the darkness swallows them one after the next.

But this time, I don't wait in agony to see who's joined their ranks.

I made it within the boundary. If it's a warning they want to issue, it's misplaced; I'm here now. I'll do what I can to stop the dying and save the living.

My resolve doesn't silence the ghosts, though. It takes Victoire to do that.

I pull on the icy mask of her self-assured poise and dismiss them. They go, fading into the shadows of my mind. Their message remains, a hollow echo bouncing through the empty spaces: *We're coming—for you.*

That's new.

Victoire smiles a slow, hungry smile that says, *not if I get you first.*

I wake gasping, one hand to my face to hold the memory of a mask I no longer wear from slipping and exposing my vulnerability.

I haven't been Victoire since before I fought the Mara in Freedom—and won. I haven't spared her so much as a thought since I woke in Under after that battle, even when Ravel showed up, called me by her name. Because that's all she was: a borrowed identity, a convenient shell to hide the parts of myself I couldn't accept or acknowledge.

Wasn't she?

The timing is too suspicious. Is Victoire connected to the loss of my ability to tap the dreamspace, somehow?

I reach a shaking hand out in breathless hope. For a moment, I see them: countless threads drifting and twining through the air. But these phantoms too fade before my eyes. I drive my fist into the ground in disappointment, and hiss at the pain. Ravel turns to look.

"You finished?" he says, tense. He shifts his gaze back toward the dim tunnel ahead. "We should hurry."

I scramble to my feet. "How much further?"

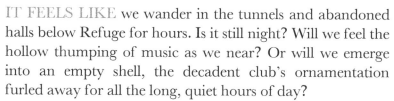

IT FEELS LIKE we wander in the tunnels and abandoned halls below Refuge for hours. Is it still night? Will we feel the hollow thumping of music as we near? Or will we emerge into an empty shell, the decadent club's ornamentation furled away for all the long, quiet hours of day?

But when the sweet-sharp scent of Freedom floats through the air, neither music nor cavernous stillness greets us. The thick wall hangings of the club are still on display, though ragged and stained, the swirling lights picking out heavy damage to both floor and ceiling. There are no screams, no voices of any kind to mark the Mara's attacks, though their work is evident.

Freedom is open—and empty.

Ravel looks stricken, eyes wide and jaw slack as he takes it in. I touch his arm, but he makes no attempt to hide his horror from me.

"There are no bodies." I have to repeat myself twice, pointing toward the broken but abandoned floor. "If the Mara got them all, there'd be . . . evidence."

He winces. Nods, eyes closed as if he's absorbing my words, weighing them. I don't think it's an act. He really is falling apart at the idea of death overtaking these halls— again. It's a new and better look for him, and it weighs me down with an unexpected burden of hope.

I squeeze his hand. "We need to check for survivors. You try down there."

We're in the middle of the chain of halls that make up Freedom. I point him toward the early rooms, the safest ones, even though they are the closest to the Refuge access point I'm most familiar with.

In the other direction, the halls get darker. I'm afraid of what might be lurking in the black hall—the room of sacrifice. I'll check it myself, though I'm aware of the absurdity of shielding this man from death when he's knowingly sacrificed lives to the Mara to get what he wanted.

But, twisted as his actions were, he seems to think of the dancers as his people in some way. Not friends, or equals, but perhaps subjects. Or pets. Creatures under his domain. I'm not sure if he's more in shock at their supposed deaths, or the lack of anyone to rule over.

I'm probably being stupid, pitying him. I'm surprised Cadence isn't telling me so right this minute. Why should I protect him?

I try, all the same. But he trails along behind me, stubbornly refusing to go where I would send him, and so we discover each new broken and desolate hall together.

The damage worsens as we round each new corner. Our shoes scuff through grit and debris and dark stains that I refuse to stop to examine. But we find no one, dead or alive.

Retracing our steps, we search in the other direction, and then in the side chambers concealed behind the hangings, checking staging and supply rooms with no success.

I keep expecting the Mara to descend.

Is it possible they've devoured all the living, not just in Freedom, but in Refuge and the city outside as well? Have their hunger and their power grown to the point that they can devour our forms entire, and not just the life that lies within?

Finally, we're forced to admit Freedom has been abandoned. The Mara don't make an appearance, though the hairs prickling at the back of my neck suggest something must be watching. I guide a staggering, shell-shocked Ravel out of the halls of the club and into a dusty service corridor before speaking.

"We'll find them. They can't all be gone."

His gaze sharpens. "Liar."

"Fine. The Mara chomped them all up, right down to the bones, and we've come too late. Better?"

He chokes, eyes blazing.

But I'm not afraid of him anymore. I find that I haven't been for a long time. I turn on my heel. "I'm going to check on Ange. Come if you want."

It's a bluff, of course. It's possible there are still some living tucked away into some corner of the city. Perhaps the dust-dimmed dancers of Freedom and the Noosh-dulled workers of Refuge finally woke up and decided to remove themselves from the scene of carnage. If they already admit they are in danger that will make what I have to do next that much easier.

I choose to hold out hope there's someone left here to save—which means I'll need Ravel's help sooner than later.

It has been a while since I navigated these corridors and tunnels. Luckily, Ravel catches up quickly. Finding my way back to Ange isn't easy, especially when she is not where I left her.

The rooms are all empty in Under, too. At first, I think we're in the wrong place, but when Ravel leads me to the makeshift recovery room I stayed in, its cots overturned and trailing bedding, I have to accept Ange and her people are gone, too.

The damage isn't as bad down here, though cracks spider web across the floor and the ceiling has crumbled in places. Did the Mara come for them, too? The monsters had never ventured this far below the surface before, not on dry ground.

I kick my old cot hard enough to send it screeching across the floor. Dust sifts from the ceiling, powdering the shiny surface of a dark object half-buried in trailing sheets.

It's a mask. A deep purple mask that once belonged to a man I got killed.

Ange is alive.

32

CLUES

RAVEL STARES AT the mask without a flicker of recognition, but I'd know it anywhere. It once belonged to Cass.

The last time I saw it, Ange was wearing it in mourning as we rushed to save Ash from torture at the hands of the twisted, Mara-ridden enforcer, Serovate.

It's a message.

I race out of the room, ignoring Ravel's shout. I round a corner and trip over rubble from a caved-in ceiling.

"Where are you going?" he pants. I backtrack, peering around each corner in search of familiar landmarks. "What is it?"

"She left it for me." I take a few steps down an unfamiliar hallway and retrace them. "She knew I'd come back. She wanted me to find it."

"Okay. Sure. And now you're lost?"

I refuse to dignify that with an answer.

He sighs. "Just tell me where you're trying to go, flame."

"There was a room. Where that possessed enforcer held Ash, tortured him, when you . . ."

"Had you kidnapped? Drugged? Forced to participate in human sacrifice?" Exhaustion is etched on his face. "Sure, why not? Let's go visit a torture chamber."

He navigates without hesitation, jaw set, though we both can't help watching out of the corners of our eyes for movement, signs of life, even signs of death that could answer the question of what happened to strip this place of all life.

The door is closed when we reach it, hiding a room I never expected to return to.

Ravel gestures, inviting me to enter first. I hesitate, flashing back to images of Ash's torn and broken body tacked to the wall; sobbing children cowering behind the monstrously mundane form of Serovate; sharp-edged implements strewn across a blood-spattered tray.

I haul open the door, stale air rolling toward us. Ravel holds out the light. I step into the dark room. And trip, the lamp arcing away as I scramble to catch myself. It flickers wildly when it lands, but doesn't go out.

I don't know what I expected, but it wasn't this. There are piles and piles of stuff heaped all over: not debris, or bodies, not Ange and her people waiting to welcome us home—a distant hope, but one I'd harboured until this moment. There's hardly room to move, the floor is so piled with bundles and boxes and mismatched heaps of random objects. And, right in my path, that stupid "gift" from the forest that I swear keeps following me around. I'm not sure why Ravel thinks it's funny—or how he has the energy to play games right now—but I'm not amused.

I give the thing a hard kick, sending it crashing into the depths of the room where I'm sure he won't find it easy to retrieve.

Why would Ange send me here? Did I misunderstand her message? Or was the mask a meaningless accident, dropped during some fight and left behind? Still, I don't remember her ever wearing or even storing her club costumes anywhere but in Freedom.

Ravel recovers our light and finds it a safe perch on one of the nearer piles. He picks up one object, then the next, sifting through the seemingly random collection. His face lights up. "It's all here. Food. Clothing. Weapons. Trade goods. Everything we prepared for an escape. They saved it."

I study the piles instead of meeting his gaze. The supplies might have survived, but where were the people?

Was this Ange's last message? Take what you will and go?

I can't accept that. I blink away the sting of tears and turn back to the closed door. "Let's get out of here."

Again, Ravel follows without comment or question. Marvelling at his uncharacteristic obedience distracts from the tightness in my chest, even if it is part of some larger ploy in his eternal quest for power.

This time, I find my way without his help. But when I reach for the door leading into that long, dreaded stairwell back to the first home I remember, he catches my hand.

"Are you sure?"

My fingers tighten on the handle, knuckles paling. Of course I am.

Of course I'm not.

But what else is there? "I have to know."

He hands me a square of dark fabric and shakes out a second into a black cloak. "After you, flame."

ALL THAT TRAINING with Steph is paying off. Even exhausted by the journey, I match Ravel's pace up the stairs. Our breaths echo in the silence of the first couple floors, though by the time we reach the third landing, I realize we'll actually need to check every level to be sure. But if there is any life left in the Towers of Refuge, it's most likely to be on the highest floors, where it's safer.

We don't get that far. There's light under the door at the sixth floor's landing and a rustling sound. Something is still alive on the other side. I want to believe it's something human. Maybe even someone we know. If we're lucky.

But this is the sixth floor, where they send those in need of correction—all too often a euphemism for elimination. There is less shielding down here, less protection against the Mara. I'd hoped Refuge would have abandoned the floor when they realized the danger.

I should have known better.

Ravel tugs my sleeve, motioning to descend a few steps before whispering in my ear, "I'll go in first. Follow right behind and be ready to fight."

I shrug him aside. "I'm better trained." He lifts a sardonic eyebrow at that. "Whatever. I'm going first. Follow if you want."

Then, before he can argue or I can start to worry about our distinct lack of weapons, I hurtle up the last few steps and shoulder the door open.

Something soft and very solid gets in my way. The stranger and I clutch each other in an ungainly dance before I catch my balance and wits enough to sweep his feet out from under him.

Once I pin him, noting a poorly maintained white enforcer's uniform as I wrestle his hands behind his back, I look up to see a second enforcer staring slack-jawed. Ravel grins over the man's shoulder. I cut my eyes at him meaningfully and he winks. Then he disarms the enforcer, stifling his shouts with a mouthful of torn cloak.

We take turns shredding our cloaks for makeshift bindings, moving as quietly as we can. It's not normal for enforcers to guard the stairways like this, especially not at this time of night. Not when Refuge has so many better ways to make sure its people don't stray. But if these two are here, there could be more around. If anything, it is strange no one has come to check on the shouting.

When we split up to tiptoe down the halls and peek around the corner, the reason for the silence becomes horrifyingly obvious. Long cracks splinter through the drywall. Portions of the ceiling have crumbled, exposing dangling wires and dripping pipes. The floors are cratered, thin carpet shredded and mixed with concrete and dark stains. Worse are the gaping dark holes of empty doorways.

I'm afraid to get closer; I don't want to see what lies beyond.

It shouldn't feel like a shock. The Mara have always haunted this floor, though nowhere near to this extent. But the last time I saw one of their victims here, it was an empty-eyed but otherwise pristine corpse. Some part of me had been holding out hope what I had accomplished during the battle in Freedom had, if not broken them, at least weakened them. Slowed them down.

Ravel storms back to the nearest guard and kicks him, repeatedly, before turning on the next. Both are moaning behind their gags by the time I drag him off.

His punch would have had me rolling beside them if I didn't have the benefits of Steph's training to draw on. Instead of backing off, I press in, shoving him against the wall.

"They—they had no chance." He chokes on the words, grimacing as if to hold back the welling in his eyes. "I didn't think—I could have got them out, flame. I should have, before—"

Before he came after me. So he did realize he could have saved them on his own.

I glance back the way he came, gaze skipping past rubble and snagging on an empty doorframe. Is it wrong that the very last thing I want to do right now is to go look? Is it cowardly to want to ignore the cost of his actions, his selfishness—and mine?

But it's not my fault my magic vanished overnight. I never chose to leave. That's all on Ash, who isn't even here to face the consequences.

It's not my fault Ravel chose to come after me, either. If he'd just tried to save them on his own, instead of fixating on me in the first place . . .

There's something there, something about him and me that I hadn't faced until just this moment. But there's no time to tease it out because there's one door in sight that remains intact. It's the one that leads to the main dormitory.

And someone's knocking on the other side.

LIVESTOCK

I REACH THE door first.

The knocking stops when I turn the handle. It doesn't open. The banging starts up harder than ever, desperate but muffled cries rising behind it.

Ravel elbows me aside to wrench at the door, hurling himself shoulder-first at it when the handle refuses to turn. I dart to the bound enforcers and rifle through their pockets, ignoring their moaning. If I focus, I can almost quell the churning disgust at the way these idiots not only locked up survivors in this death trap but also stayed to guard the only escape route.

At least their presence means a key is within easy reach. The banging stops the moment it scrapes into the lock.

I yank the door open. Ravel shoves past. He wheels back with a shout as it flings wide. There's a rush of one-two-four-*many* people stampeding into the hallway.

I flatten myself against the nearest wall, losing sight of Ravel. Strangers in a mix of Refuge uniforms, Under's more sedate dress, and Freedom's extravagant costumes pounce on the bound and clearly terrified enforcers.

A tug on my sleeve distracts from the impending carnage. I look down into the face of a ghost—no, a living child, one with familiar hazel eyes and tight curls.

Lily scowls up at me. "Took you long enough."

The impulse to offer reassurance takes me off guard. My hand hovers over her head, wavers across to her shoulder, and retreats limply to my side. "Is—are you alone?"

"Uh, no?" She sweeps a pointed glance at the crowd around us. "Are you? Where's my Ash?"

I search with her, though not for Ash. It shouldn't annoy me that she insists on the possessive, especially right now. She's just a child, and I have more important things to worry about.

It still bothers me. To tamp the frustration down, I focus all the harder on the tide of strangers. I pick out familiar faces here and there, but not the one I want to see. The child's mother pokes her head out the door, sparking a moment's worth of excitement that dampens at her timid wave. Amy isn't the one I'm looking, though she sidles out to stand beside us, crowded by Sam at her elbow.

I watch the opening expectantly as the stream of people trickles to a stop. Ravel is the last one out, looking uncharacteristically ragged and disoriented.

"So? Where is she?" He cranes his neck.

The crowd quiets around us, heads turning to watch, voices murmuring. They are looking to us for instruction. Us—not their leader.

"Where is Ange?" My voice comes out steady, carrying none of the shrill panic swelling in my chest.

Feet shuffle, gazes drop, and Lily's small, warm hand slips into mine. "They took her."

I look at Ravel. He stares back, wide-eyed and pale.

"He can't help you," Cadence says.

I startle. It's been a while since she last spoke. Foolish instinct has me scrambling for arguments, but the pressure of a small hand yanks me back into the moment.

Instead of pulling back, running away, waiting for Ravel to come up with something—anything—I drop to my knees, bringing myself down to the level of a pair of serious hazel eyes. "Tell me everything."

I DON'T ACTUALLY remember being Lily's age, but I'm sure I lacked her composure.

Cadence's roaring silence confirms the suspicion. The child recounts the days between my departure and return spent helping her aunt rally stragglers and stockpile goods in a remarkably even tone. It barely wavers when she gets to the part when enforcers descended and ripped Ange away from the rest of the group, dragging her off and locking them all into unprotected dorms without light or food.

Lily doesn't ask me to rescue her. She just watches, silent trust in her unwavering gaze.

It makes what I have to do next so much worse.

"It's the only choice," Cadence says, sympathetic for once. "You can't sacrifice the mission for one woman."

I catch Ravel's eye and he nods, slow and solemn. Though I'm very well aware he is not one to shrink from necessary sacrifice—particularly someone else's sacrifice—if he told me the truth then he has known Ange longer than anyone.

Maybe Ravel even cares for her somewhere in his malformed little stone of a heart.

I shut out the sight of too many people looking to me for answers, for direction, for hope. Just for a moment, I stop and let myself feel what it was like to have power. To risk the safe plan for the one my heart sings. To have options.

But this time, I have nothing that hasn't been given to me by foolishly trusting strangers. No magic to change our intolerable reality. This time, I can't fight the monsters.

But I can save the child in front of me. At least I can do that.

I smile at Lily, though my skin is tight with anguish. Amy's arms go around her daughter and the child relaxes, relieved someone has come along to make it all better.

If only.

I lead the way, and the crowd follows, unquestioning. Ravel walks at my shoulder, silently supporting this show of leadership. But it doesn't take much—these people are afraid and, in the absence of the leader they know, desperate for someone to take on the burden and show them the way.

And if some small part of me thrills that the someone they need happens to be me, well, there are worse things. Things like hoping for the impossible. Like dreaming of running off and rescuing my friend instead.

"The mission is what matters," Cadence says. "Get them across, and then you can worry about the ones left behind."

So I lead my small band of survivors down the stairs and through the halls and back to a torture chamber full of supplies.

And there, I perform my final act as a leader and tell them to follow the most devious, unreliable, and untrustworthy person I know. I tip the game in Ravel's favour and back away.

He gives me one stunned glance and snatches at my sleeve. But I slip out the door before he can stop me. Before it has even closed, I hear him taking charge with that hypnotic voice of his.

Good. He's better at playing this role than I am anyway. Much joy may it bring to him. And if he fails them, may all my ghosts haunt his every step to the final breath of his miserable life.

Cadence screams at me all the way back through the underground warren and up the stairs and only stops when I place my hand on the chilly surface of an unremarkable door that leads to a place I've only seen through another's eyes.

"Don't you dare," she warns. "The mission—"

Not my mission.

I don't dare breathe the words out loud, not this close to the enemy stronghold, but I know she hears me. I can feel her fury. Her confusion. Her hurt.

She is bound to the past by our memories. I'm not. And I'm afraid she'll never understand. Never forgive me. But that doesn't change what I have to do.

Because Ravel is the one with the power to save everyone.

Which means I'm the one who's free to go after the stragglers. I'm the one who has to reach those who can't escape, or who have never dreamed of escaping.

And, because I've decided to be brave but I'm not confident it's going to work all that well for any of us, I plan to start with both the hardest and the most valuable rescue of all.

Cadence falls silent as I ease that unremarkable door open and slip from the dim and dirty stairwell into unparalleled opulence. The corridor glitters with gold and concealed lights and strategically placed mirrors. I twitch and spin, jumping at every reflection, straining to catch sight of the telltale blur of coalescing Mara before they spot me.

The mayor of the Towers of Refuge could have imprisoned Ange anywhere. She could have had her killed or sacrificed her to the Mara for the sin of her defiance. Maryam Ajera is, if not Ravel's mother in the most literal sense, at the very least the woman who caused him to exist and raised him. More or less. And I've spent time in her devious head. If she had wanted Ange dead, she would have sacrificed her to the Mara in front of her followers. If she had wanted her kept prisoner, she would have kept her with the group to show how powerless their leader really was.

No, if I'm right, she will have kept Ange alive and within reach. A hostage. Maryam's probably known about her and her little breakaway group for years—decades, even.

She doesn't want Ange. She wants what she has always wanted.

Me.

MIRRORS

I HUG THE mirrored wall and hold my breath. My feet whisper against thick carpet as I peek around the corner.

This is usually when Cadence chimes in, but she seems to be punishing me with disapproving silence. I'll have to find some way to make up with her later.

This is what we do, after all: fight, reconcile, and fight again. And, if I'm about to be caught and sacrificed to the nightmares, I'd rather she weren't around to see it anyway.

I expect to find Ange in the mayor's extravagant audience chamber, but when I reach it, all is still and silent. I creep through one glittering jewel of a room after another, marvelling at each new display and wary for the slightest sound or hint of movement.

I know this is a trap. I just don't know what kind.

A startlingly plain, off-white door catches my attention. It's the only thing that doesn't fit. I backtrack as quickly as I can without making noise, peering around the corners of spaces to either side of the corridor. But there's a distinct lack of Refuge Force uniforms lying in wait.

They're probably on the other side. The problem is, so must Ange be. I tiptoe across thick carpet. Press my ear against the smooth, cold surface of the door and hold my breath. Not a sound.

I test the lever-style doorknob, first flicking it with my nail, then tapping with the pad of my finger, before I trust my whole hand to it and press—

It's unlocked.

But, instead of some kind of torture chamber or cell, I step into a lost world.

The windows draw me first—enormous, unbroken panes taking over two walls. Beyond, brilliant sunlight winks off blue waves and the silver peaks of distant mountains.

I press my hand against the glass and stare at the wheeling gulls and scudding clouds. Traffic—both pedestrians, and strange-looking closed vehicles—churns in kaleidoscopic patterns through streets.

But then the pattern repeats. And starts over again, a third time.

It's not real. The glass doesn't show an endless vista, but a fingers-breadth recording.

It's still hard to step away.

The rest of the room is less immediately gripping—more like living quarters I've seen in Nine Peaks than anything else in Refuge, or below. It has everything you might need—a glossy but restrained kitchen along one wall, comfortable seats facing an enormous blank screen against another. Stairs climb to another room tucked high above my head behind a glassed-in railing.

There are too many closed doors for comfort, though. I ease up to each one with my breath caught in my throat and my knees bent as if I'll have a hope of darting away when a squad of enforcers lunge out at me.

But the first doors only open onto closets, and the next, into a large, glistening bathroom. I pause to longingly stroke the thick towels, wishing absurdly for time to clean up before continuing this ill-advised rescue mission. Even in fresh clothes, I reek of seaweed.

The next door leads to an enormous bedroom with yet another bathroom attached. And it's the bedroom that holds the key to what this museum of the old world is doing on the mayor's floor. Framed pictures clutter the tops of cabinets and hang on the walls: photographs of a handsome black-haired man with long, dark, laughing eyes, and a pretty but severe-looking young woman.

Her smile is a little too sharp, her hair too precise, her clothes even more so. Her eyes are a pale, almost tawny brown, the shadows underneath not fully concealed with tasteful, skin-tone makeup.

I shiver. She looks nothing like the mayor—except for in a single photograph. She's curled against the black-haired man, laughing and looking at him instead of the camera, and in that one image alone there is in her face the pale reflection, just the very slightest hint, of Maryam's impossible, inhuman beauty.

I pick the framed photo up from a low surface beside the bed and take it with me. If it comes to it, maybe I can throw it at an attacker and hope the glass cuts them or something . . .

And it's about time I came up with some kind of weapon because there is only one door left unopened. Not only that—there's a low, even sound coming from the other side. Someone's in there.

I flatten myself against the wall. My heart races. They must know I'm here. Why are they still hiding? What are they waiting for?

And why can't I just walk away?

I watch from an impossible distance, as if it's someone else's hand reaching out to the lever. But no one jumps out at me and nothing attacks. The only living thing on the other side of that door is a woman slumped in a strange chair that sits on curved rails instead of four feet, her face curtained by a fall of shining hair.

I strain to catch sight of the trap that surely lies in wait, but it is well hidden. If the mayor had set out to design the least threatening-looking space possible, she certainly hit the mark.

The walls are painted pale grey, with delicate shapes scattered across their surfaces in muted hues of green and blue and yellow—stylized clouds, rainbows, strange animals. A boxy white structure with slatted sides fills one corner, an array of tiny fabric-covered shapes in matching pastels suspended above one end. A tall cabinet with a moulded, high-edged cushion on top has pride of place on another wall. Everything is round-cornered, and plush, and gentle looking except the woman in the chair.

It is not Ange.

"I'd offer you a seat, but . . ." Maryam Ajera sweeps one elegant, manicured hand at the room, indicating the lack of chairs. Golden chains and bangles clink as she leans back, crossing her long, slim legs. Her diaphanous layers shift, showing a shapely calf and fragile, bejewelled ankles. Nothing about her belongs in this place.

But her brilliant, heavily made up eyes are pink rimmed, and her palm had been lined with weeping crescents of red when she gestured.

I should run. Instead, I inch further into the room and try for boldness. "I've come for Ange. What have you done to her?"

She laughs, a throaty purring that cuts off abruptly as she catches sight of what I carry. She tilts her head, curls tumbling, earrings chiming, the warm overhead light exposing shining tracks down her poreless, ageless skin.

The heavy-lidded golden stare she levels at me reminds me uncomfortably of her son.

"Perhaps we can dispense with the games, you and I." Her honeyed tones have vanished along with the laughter. Her posture shifts to match, upright, contained. Commanding. "Oh, come in and settle, child. I'm not the one who bites."

I step out of the doorway, but only just, putting my back to a wall so I can keep an eye on both her and the open door at the same time. "I'm good."

I give her a narrow look of my own. Her lips twist into a pale shadow of that smile I saw in the photos of the woman she used to be, still keen, now weighted with exhaustion.

"Your little friend is fine," she says, shrugging heavy locks back impatiently. "You kept refusing my summons, so I had to do something to get your attention. You will get her back as soon as we finish our chat. But first, I'll have my property back."

I check the hall one more time before edging forward just enough that the framed photo brushes her fingers, forcing her to lurch off-balance to catch it when I let go too soon.

This time, her laugh is sharp. "So. You've learned to play, have you? What else have you picked up since you left my care?"

She is hateful and dangerous, and I wish with all my being that I had never spent one moment inside her head. If I hadn't seen her ghosts back then, watched from behind her eyes as the Mara taunted her with their deaths, I wouldn't be able to guess that this place is not a museum but a memorial. That smaller-than-child-sized, so carefully fenced-in bed never held Ravel's infant form. She never rocked him in that chair, never put him to sleep in this gentle, soft room. Not him, no, but the child before him. The one that broke her, I suspect— and through her, generations.

She is the monster behind my parents' death, and so many others' beside. Her actions broke me in two, and stole my past, and made me believe I was broken. Maryam is at the heart of everything bad that has ever happened to me and those I care about, and it shouldn't matter that she is also the one who has kept the Mara at bay all these years, if only barely, no more than it should matter that she lunges for that photo when I let it drop; that her eyes fill when she glances at it; that when she tucks it quickly away with its face to her chest, it joins the threadbare, tearstained toy already clutched there.

It shouldn't matter, but it does. It's enough to keep me standing here, waiting to see what this woman made monstrous wants with me.

"Good. Silence is good," she nods approvingly, sending a chill up my spine. "You might just do after all. Let's begin."

GETAWAY

THE AUDIENCE CHAMBER swims into view, all golden and glittering. I don't know how I got here, but I'm not alone—someone's breathing. Behind me.

I pick myself up off the floor warily twist, and lunge to attack. Bad idea—my head spins and the contents of my stomach try to sear their way back up my throat. I stagger a couple steps, bouncing shoulder-first off a mirror. The spiderwebbing cracks are shatteringly loud.

I cringe, but no one comes running. And the only other person in the room is Ange.

Her ankles are bound to the legs of a gilt chair, her wrists wrapped in thick gold cord. She must have been drugged; such restraints seem as if they could hardly hold her long. Still, I wait several long moments before moving to free her. This has to be part of Maryam's plan, somehow. But, since no one seems to be attacking us right this minute, all I can think to do is free my friend.

The knots fall apart in my hands. I shake Ange's shoulder. She shifts, muttering in her sleep, but doesn't wake.

I waste another few minutes examining the corners of the room for any hints of the trap I must be springing before hauling her up. She's slight and I've grown stronger, between Susan's chores and Steph's training. It's still an effort to drag her across the room.

My steps falter at the thought of the long, dark stairwell ahead of us. The hair on the back of my neck stands on end. My shoulders hunch not only against Ange's weight but the threat of attack at any moment.

I can make out just a hint of distant murmuring as if from a conversation a couple rooms away. And yet, I stumble from the mayor's shining domain into the darkened stairwell without encountering the slightest resistance.

No squad of enforcers steps from the shadows. No monsters coalesce from the air.

I reposition my grip and start down the stairs. Something is sure to go wrong any moment now—but I might as well gain as much distance as possible before then.

I have to stop and rest several times. Every time I let Ange slide to the floor, I think it will be the last. I imagine distant rustling, muffled boots, hushed breaths. I sense the immanent tug of fingers in my hair, or the shove of a hand at my back, pitching us down the sharp steps.

Near the bottom, Ange squirms and mutters, the drugs evidently starting to wear off. Her tears wet my shoulder, scaring me more than anything so far. But she only weeps silently, refusing to respond to questions. By the time we take our first steps into the empty halls that once housed Freedom, she's at least bearing some of her own weight. I feel suddenly lighter, inside and out.

I did it—saved her—all by myself? I can't quite believe it yet.

I stagger around one last corner, Ange moaning in my ear, but it doesn't dampen my eagerness to celebrate her rescue with everyone. Except, when I peer down the corridor leading to the once-torture-chamber-now-storage-room where I left Ravel in charge of the ragtag band of refugees, the door hangs open. The room beyond is dark and silent.

We took too long. They've gone on ahead without us.
Good.

Horror at being left behind wars with a quiet glow of satisfaction. By now, they must all be across the barrier and free—and so shall we be. Soon.

I stagger onward, propping up Ange's faltering steps. We'll make it. Just a little further, and we'll find Ravel, waiting for us. Maybe he'll even backtrack, meet us part way.

I could use the help—I pant with the effort to keep Ange upright and moving forward, blinking away the sting of sweat. Any minute now, he'll turn a corner with that cocky grin and those dangerous, brilliant eyes. He'll help get Ange and me across, the last of many. We'll settle the refugees a safe distance from the monster-haunted shoreline with their supplies. Maybe put our pursuers to good use minding them, or even guiding them back to Nine Peaks.

I smirk at the thought. The elders said it wasn't worth coming back here. They thought no one could be saved. They thought wrong—and I can't wait to show them just how wrong.

Of course, I'll have to wait just a bit longer for that particular pleasure, because once Ange is safe and the refugees are secured on the other side, Ravel and I will return.

This part of the plan I never discussed with him, or Cadence. I am neither burdened by her memories nor driven by her need to complete the mission our parents sacrificed themselves—and us—for.

Which is just as well because I'm not the child they brought into danger and abandoned. I am not bound by their purpose, or path, or powers like she is.

I'll use whatever and whomever it takes to save my home and the people like me, abandoned in a place they never had the option not to choose, deprived of even the idea of choosing anything else.

I'll steal the Mara's prey out from under them and starve those nightmares for lack of dreamers to devour.

There's more than one way to kill a monster.

Cadence keeps her silence, stunned, perhaps, at my brilliance. Or maybe just absent and sulking. Doesn't matter either way—because Ange and I stagger around that one last bend to find more than just Ravel waiting for us.

And every one of my self-satisfied, oh-so-clever plans shatters and joins the shards of the tunnel at my feet.

MASSACRE

BLOOD POOLS AT my feet. Screams echo against the walls. I don't know how I didn't hear them sooner. And then I do.

"How dare you," Cadence says. "You know nothing. You're powerless. Your plans are worthless."

Her unexpected attack heightens the unreality of the scene. At the far end of the chaos-filled pipe, Ravel splashes through the barrier with a ragged gasp and seizes the nearest warm body. His golden eyes are wide, teeth bared. He catches my gaze for a single desperate heartbeat. Then he throws himself backward, vanishing with his human cargo.

My gaze stutters from one horror to the next, unable to take it all in. There's a crush of people massed from one side of the oversized pipe to the other—people who should've crossed over by now. Churning in their midst are dark whirlwinds of destruction, the Mara, gleeful in unobstructed carnage.

How are they here? I thought—they weren't supposed to be able to come down this far . . .

A double-thick line of enforcers stands between us, arms locked. A human fence. One peers over his shoulder at me, mask askew, goggles missing, his strikingly familiar face sick with desperation. It's Haynfyv—Refuge Force inspector and the younger brother of Ange's lost lover.

She cries out and reaches for him—seeing, as I did at first, his brother in his face—only to be shouldered aside when he turns back to his duty. I settle her against a wall, alarmed at the feebleness of her protests.

Then I hurl myself at the enforcers. If I can just break their line—

"You can do nothing. You are nothing," Cadence's voice is biting. "This is all your fault."

The uniforms are tough, armoured against my efforts. Without a weapon, I can do little more than annoy them. An elbow whips back, doubling me over. A blow to my head knocks me to the floor. The enforcer who delivered it breaks ranks to follow up with a kick to my midsection.

I lift with it to deflect the force and snag him behind the knee with one hand. His arms windmill. He takes his neighbour down with him, distracting the rest of the squad enough for the line to waver.

But when I renew my attack, they are prepared. Ravel splashes through the barrier and shouts, drawing their attention—and that of the Mara—long enough for me to wrestle free of their grasp. But there is a minefield of monsters and helpless refugees between us, and I'm more relieved than hurt when he grabs the nearest upright body instead of trying to free me. Ravel drags the lucky refugee away to the other side, and whatever measure of safety can be found outside of this hellhole, without a backward glance.

Cadence snorts. "He can't save them all. You do realize all you've done is herded all Refuge's troublemakers into a convenient killing ground, right?"

My knees sag at the thought. I glare at the enforcers' backs to keep myself from looking past them. I can't stand to see their faces—strangers, children, friends—as they fall to the Mara. I'm desperate to block out the fangs and talons and the flash of hungry, victorious eyes as the monsters glory in destruction and gloat over my failure.

And it is my failure. I saved the innocents once before. I should have been the one to do it again.

I came back to lead them without any magic to draw on at all. I can't even help Ravel transport them across the barrier—the one they followed him to, trusting we had a plan.

Something inside me twists, wrenching the strands that hold me together until I feel like I'm tearing in two. I'm meant to save them—

"You can't," sneers Cadence.

I have to save them. More than that, I want to. In this moment, it is all I want. It's all that matters.

I dive against the line of uniforms with every ounce of skill, and energy, and determination I have. The faces of the refugees trapped on the other side turn to me, hope dawning amidst their terror and anguish. I tear at the human barrier in a frenzy that rivals the Mara, biting and scratching when all else fails to break through. It stretches to the breaking point—

"It won't be enough," she croons, soft and cruel. "You know you're not powerful enough. You can't do this on your own."

Still, I wrestle against the enforcers, lashing out when I can, letting my weight drag against their strength when I can't. There is a sudden rush, a wheeling spin as the uniforms give way. I stumble into the midst of the desperate crowd they've been holding back.

But it's a feint. I'm seized and yanked backward only moments after breaking through.

The pitch of the screaming heightens. The refugees batter with renewed energy at the human barrier, seeing what little hope they had snatched away. I call out, warn them back. They're better off fighting through that monstrous minefield toward the barrier and the slim chance of Ravel's rescue.

A blow to my head blurs my vision. When I shake off the stars and look out over the crowd again, everything has gone still.

Even the Mara have paused their destruction, whirling in place as the few victims who can still move stagger or crawl out of their path. The air is heavy with whimpers and moans, and the soft plash of blood and seawater.

Ravel's footsteps squelch as he makes his way through the crowd.

I risk another blow to shout him away, but he doesn't even glance at me as he bargains with the enforcers for my freedom—and when that fails, my life. The crowd behind him shifts and wails, aware that, whatever happens, their doom is all but assured.

"He could have saved more if you weren't here," Cadence whispers. "Even a reject like him could have managed to make a difference if it weren't for you."

I turn my head to shut out her cold tones and catch sight of Ange, limp in the arms of her captors. She's not fighting back. I'm not sure she's even conscious.

I close my eyes, muting Ravel's traitorous negotiations, and Cadence's loathing, and my own misery. Then, finally, I force myself to examine the carnage for familiar faces. Ange is, if not all right, at least alive. But Lily, Sam, Amy, the not-quite strangers I'd met in Under—how many had Ravel managed to save before the Mara descended?

Not all the bodies—or parts of bodies—strewn across the floors were full-grown. He hadn't even managed to get all the children out safely.

But neither do I recognize all the faces. I don't spot Lily or her mother amongst the living or the dead. That has to count for something.

At least on the other side they have a chance. Maybe the dreamwalkers from Nine Peaks will find them and get them safely through the mountains. Maybe Lily will grow up safe and strong, and some good will come of all this.

"They'll just be eaten by different monsters," Cadence says. "They're worse off, stuck out there with no protection and no idea of how to survive. You only ever break things."

I don't argue with her. Ravel is walking away, defeated in his negotiations. He's giving up.

But not on me. I scream at him to stop. Some few, brave refugees move to block his way, before the Mara take them. He trudges on through the carnage, head down, shoulders set.

"All your fault," Cadence singsongs.

He goes slowly into the barrier, giving his limbs to it with the same reluctance I'd feed my own to acid.

And then he's gone—and I pray he won't return.

Because the price he has just agreed to pay for my release is the return of every soul he's taken across that barrier. And I am under no illusion what will happen to every last one of us when he finishes returning those we have stolen.

37
FAILURE

THE INNOCENT DIE screaming, and all I can do is watch.

Inspector Haynfyv blanches, staggering out of rank. He gives me one white-eyed, slack-jawed look of horror and lurches away, a gloved hand clapped over his masked mouth.

Cadence is silent for the moment. She doesn't need to say a word; I know full well this is all my fault.

The Mara have always killed in Refuge, and under it. But there was a time when I could have stopped this carnage.

Even if I had just stayed away, maybe the horror and the pain would have been less. Maybe these lives would have lasted just that much longer. And if I'd managed to regain my abilities, if I'd only found the secret, or stuck it out longer, or tried harder, or worked out what I needed to say or do to make the elders want to help me instead of resisting and struggling and forcing my own way—if I'd even just left Ange behind, as she'd surely have wanted, to keep her people safe . . .

It shouldn't be like this. This was never what I wanted. I shouldn't even be here.

One small hope remains: maybe Ravel won't return. Maybe we will all die, all of us left behind—but he'll get away with those few he has managed to save, and our sacrifice will be worth something.

Maybe.

Something like a plan untangles itself from the knot of misery inside me: what if I weren't here? If I were already dead by the time Ravel returns, he could escape this death trap and lead what survivors remain to safety. He knows the way back more or less. It would be better than nothing.

"You're giving up?" The loathing in Cadence's voice has shifted into something new. "The only thing you want is death?"

I want to stop the dying. If my death is all I have to offer—

"But not all I have to offer," she says eagerly.

Before I can find out what that's supposed to mean, we're both distracted by a disturbance in the barrier. It ripples as a form steps through—alone.

I suck in a relieved breath. Though my death is all but assured either way, I wasn't looking forward to having to accomplish it personally. Ravel's return means none of us left here go free—but at least those he has already saved get to keep their freedom.

Except, the figure that emerges from the barrier isn't Ravel.

Ash's face is set in grim lines, his gaze inscrutable as it finds mine across the crowd.

He is the last person I expect to see. It hadn't even occurred to me to hope for rescue from that quarter—but now that he's here, now that a real dreamwalker is here—

He lurches, nearly falls, and I go cold. He's not okay—injured, or sick. Still, he works his way through the crowd, slipping between the whirling death-fogs of the Mara and the desperate, reaching hands of refugees alike.

The uniforms square up against him, shouldering me from view. There are so many enforcers and Ash is entirely alone. Even if he could fight through a full squad all by himself, there is still the Mara to contend with.

I shouldn't get my hopes up.

So I don't, not until rough hands pull me to my feet. I stare at Ash's back as he tows me across the parted line of enforcers and against the tide of surging, pleading refugees. I dig in my feet and yank, forcing him to stop and face me.

But when he does, I hardly know where to start. The Mara continue to ravage the living and rend the dead. But they seem content to ignore us as long as we return the favour. The enforcers stand aside and watch in silence and I can't think *why*, what power he could possibly have over them to just make them let me go without a fight—and why he isn't turning to fight the monsters.

"We need to go." His expressive face has gone dull, blank. "Your friend is waiting."

"What about them?" I don't have to point. The death that surrounds us provides an inescapable reminder of what lies in store for the remainder who have yet to be devoured.

Ash's gaze doesn't waver, though there's a brief crack in his stone-like facade. He plasters over it before I can read him. "I came for you."

He continues trying to drag me toward the barrier. I argue, resisting with each step. When he won't slow, I fight.

I don't want to hurt him—I need him strong to be of any use—but I can't let him rescue me alone.

I should have fought harder. He turns on me with merciless speed. The world churns—airless-cold-crushing—and then we're through to the other side.

The tide must be lower this time. It only takes a few moments of splashing for my feet to find purchase. I swipe stinging salt water from my face and look for survivors.

They're huddled at the edge of the waves. Ravel is the last to look up, apologetic. Resigned. He has managed to save more of them than I thought—except, not all of these faces are ones I know from Refuge.

Grace gives me a cautious smile. Steph glares. I recognize several others from her class of trainees. And they're not the only ones from Nine Peaks, though Grace is by far the youngest. Ash's squad is here too, and more besides. For an army, it's small, and its soldiers are young.

But it's still an army.

I whirl to smack Ash in the chest. "Why didn't you tell me they were here? I wasted so much time fighting you!"

He slumps to his knees, panting, blood dripping from his nose, and then, horribly, his ears and the corners of his eyes. I stagger, trying to keep him from falling facedown in the sea. But no one comes to help us. I scan their faces, frantic, but each one of them avoids my searching gaze, finding reason to examine their shoes, or the darkening sky, or to bustle over to check on a huddled, shivering refugee.

All except Grace, whose eyes are welling with tears.

She's not the only one who shows no trace of the silvering that marks a dreamwalker's magic. I scan the ranks of Nine Peaks' rescuers. One pair of dull eyes after another whispers that they're not dreamwalkers, not most of them. Far too many are just like her. Like me.

Powerless.

"Steph," I plead, refusing to give up hope. She can fight, at least. Her squad, and Ash's. I push away the thought of how young she is, how unlikely it is that she could be anywhere near prepared for what awaits on the other side, how I made up my mind back in Nine Peaks that I would not sacrifice their children to save my own people. "Go with Ravel. Get as many out as you can, before—"

She moves in front of Ravel, blocking my view. Ash reaches up, his grip on my arm frighteningly weak.

"We can't save them all," he says. The words are cold, but faint, and his face is anguished. "You never should have come back here."

"You can save some," I look to the shore again in an effort to include Steph and her squad mates in the conversation, though I know—I *know*—it's not right. I shouldn't ask them to risk their lives for this. But I can't stop myself from trying to convince them anyway. "Those of you who can fight back—you can cross the barrier. Save as many as you can. Save—Ange is still over there. At least her—"

My voice rises, wavers, and cracks. My throat is tight, eyes burning. I can see it in his face—they won't go back. They won't even try. He won't let them.

"They only let you go because I promised we would cede the city to them," Ash whispers, his voice barely stronger than the wash of the surf, though he manages to stagger to his feet. "We can't return. Even if we could cross the barrier as easily as Ravel, there are too many of them lying in wait."

I pull away, leaving him swaying in the waves. "Ravel. Steph. Please."

I go to each one in turn. "Grace, tell them——"

She moves toward me, looking worn. The journey down hasn't been easy on her. I know she has never been more than a couple hours' ride from the walls of Nine Peaks before, and this has to be tragically far from the kind of adventure she'd dreamed of.

"You don't understand," she says. "We're not what you think. We only learn to protect ourselves on missions, to defend one another while we gather data and collect resources. Not to fight in a war that was lost lifetimes ago."

"No. No—you were going to help me, you, and Steph. You had a plan to help me escape Nine Peaks. You led your people here to join our mission. And Ash, he said he'd help me save——"

"We were wrong. We forgot our purpose. Ash reminded us of who we are and of what we can and cannot do."

I stumble back, scuffing through pebbly sand, splashing into icy waves. No one follows. Shapes rise in the growing darkness, sea monsters rearing from the waves to watch with glittering eyes. They make no move to attack.

I stand at the edge of the ocean and look back to those waiting on higher ground. "You can save some."

They just watch, silent. Tears run freely down Grace's face, and the cheeks of more than a few of the others from Nine Peaks glisten in the low light.

They won't help. Cowards. Traitors.

I'm not being fair. I know that. Though I tried so hard to block it out, I heard Ash bargain for my life, promising never to return to the city nor to allow any dreamwalker to fight against Refuge if they would only allow him to take me away.

Even if that weren't the case, I can't spend their lives to save others. I *know* the risk is too great, with both the Mara and enforcers lying in wait on the other side.

But I can't just give up and walk away, either.

I turn my back and wade deeper into the waves. I have no idea how I'm going to fight the monsters, or even get across the barrier, never mind stop the Mara and save all those left behind.

But I won't leave them. I won't let them die alone.

The water deepens, lifting my feet from the sludge underfoot. How can it have risen so much in such a short time?

I thrash, gulping first air, then brine. The sea closes over my head, and I kick harder, for the surface or for the barrier, I hope. But the darkness around me is unbroken, pressure crushing my lungs.

I gasp, mouth filling with nothing but water—

"Shame to drown for no reason," Cadence says. "Why don't you let me help?"

DEALMAKING

A GIRL COMES back from the dead, salt water sluicing from her clothes.

She slogs out of the ocean and sea monsters watch her go. She staggers up the beach and past the knot of watchers, ignoring friends and strangers alike. They follow her, heartbroken but relieved she has finally seen sense.

That girl is not me.

I refused to turn my back on those who needed me. I would not abandon my city and my people to escape to safety and comfort. I promised myself I would fight until my last breath to save the ones no one else would.

And so, in the dark of the night, a girl creeps from the midst of the sleeping camp and races back to the shoreline. She enters the water once more, unbothered by monsters and unrestrained by friends or the needs of the few survivors on this far shore, now a safe distance inland and untroubled by her fate.

She swims with purpose and skill, cutting a clean line across the inlet to the malevolent shell of the barrier. And then she dives, deep into the dark and the cold.

She crosses that barrier like stepping through a whisper, striding with confidence into a wasteland of death.

That girl is still not me.

Because the moment I made my deal with Cadence, the world slipped away.

I AM ELEVEN and strong. Strong enough my parents are willing to take me along on their mission. Few dreamwalker children are allowed out so young, much less our rare and precious dreamweavers.

But my skills are exceptional, and my family is both influential and legendarily strong.

The journey starts out exciting—and gets boring fast. There is a lot of sitting and way too many chores and not nearly enough fighting for my taste. Dad wants to teach me about the land every time he lets me off the back of his quad, but after a while, it's just a blur of stinky old plants and dusty ridges that all look the same.

Mom wants me to train, but I'm too distracted and worn out by the end of each day. I can tell she is too by the way she lets it go more days than not. That would never have happened at home. Even in the rain, she used to take me out into the forest to build my skills.

And that was before and after regular sparring sessions with my squad. Ash and I even get to train with the older kids sometimes. We're that good—that close to being ready to go out on our own. But when the older squads get sent out on training missions, we have always had to stay behind. Until now.

I can't wait to take down my first monster on my own— and tell him all about it.

But I don't get to fight for days, not until we're out of the mountains and picking our way across the crumbling, fog-shrouded flats toward the target. And even when we run across monsters, mom and dad won't let me take one alone. They expect me to stay back and observe while they clear our way together.

Just watching is a lesson in grace and power. Dad is a master with all kinds of bladed weapons—though he's a dreamspeaker at heart—and mom's shimmering threadwork is brilliant and a little intimidating at the same time. But even these lowland monsters aren't much of a challenge, and it always ends all too soon. Only once do I get to throw a blade and, worse luck, it almost hits mom. My own threads can barely reach the monsters, they make me stay so far back.

Dad consoles me by saying these monsters are weak and starved anyway. He says they'll definitely need my help once we reach the target, but I know he's really just teasing. They probably wouldn't actually have brought me along if it were that dangerous.

And, as everyone loves to keep reminding me, dreamwalkers aren't trained to fight monsters, we're just taught how to defend ourselves so we can get on with our real work. The world won't fix itself—or maybe it will.

That's what all our measurements and samples and missions are about. We're ecologists. Scientists with a little extra magic to spend trying to bring the world back to balance, or magicians with the benefit of the scientific method trying to perform the greatest working of all time, take your pick.

I do wish mom and dad would at least give me a chance to get some proper combat practice in, though. I mean, I'll definitely need to be able to fight a monster on my own one day, so why not let me start now?

The fog is thicker than ever when we finally reach the ocean, but even the infested water can't dampen the way I fall in love with it. I've only visited the ocean in the dreamscape, when Ash and I play there. But it's not the same.

The sea monsters scatter so fast we don't even have to fight, and for once, I don't mind. I'm a little in awe of the barrier around the city, too. Mom keeps her arm around me as we approach and cross, sheltering me from its greasy chill.

It's not an easy crossing—not for any of us. The barrier does something to us, making us sick and weakening our magic at the same time.

Even aside from that, I didn't expect to hate the city this much. It feels heavy and wrong. The fog-filled air is so thick and sour I walk around with my mouth screwed up, trying not to spit.

The few people we encounter are either cringing with fear or hostile to the point I think dad will have to draw his blades. If it comes to that, I'll help keep mom safe with the one he lent me. We're not allowed to use our threads against humans.

There are a few scattered fights against the monsters here and there. Mom even lets me join in a few times, but we defeat them pretty quick. It's weird, though, because even though these monsters seem weak and we win every battle super fast, mom and dad grow more and more tense. They bicker with each other and snap at me as we move through the crumbling streets, and its nowhere near as fun as I'd thought it would be.

It's probably the fog and the damp at fault. We all develop a cough. The city is more than half-flooded. We have to improvise bridges from the crumbling bits of buildings, or find floating bits of rubble to make rafts, and even swim while fending off monsters in some spots.

But it's not until a bout of coughing wakes me to their whispered argument that I find out what mom and dad are really worried about. There is more to this mission than I had realized. It's not just about collecting data and maybe rescuing a few survivors—if they'd even follow us out.

It's way bigger than that: the Council of Nine sent us to take down the barrier.

Only, it's not that easy. They figured it had something to do with the monsters being different here, a little more dangerous, maybe, but the monsters they've fought so far seem too weak. And fighting them doesn't seem to have any impact on the barrier so far.

Mom wants to stay and investigate a rumour about a hidden settlement somewhere among the crumbling towers. Dad agrees it's worth checking out—but wants to send her back home with me and go on alone. The air is poisoned. I'm too young to withstand it much longer. They shouldn't risk my health. They argue, mom wanting us to stay together, more afraid of us splitting up than I've ever heard her, dad reluctant to give up on the mission.

I muffle my coughs and strain my ears for every word, miserable at the thought of being the reason our mission fails. Miserable at being sent home before doing anything.

I'll barely even have anything to brag to Ash about when I get home.

Mom and dad fall silent, finally asleep, but I lie awake scheming. They underestimate me. Sure, I might have a bit of a cough, but it's not like I'm helpless. And I'm not scared.

I pull on my jacket and boots and sneak out of bed, careful not to splash as I wade into the foggy gloom. I'll find that hidden settlement and be the reason our mission succeeds.

It almost works. I'm good at sneaking up and listening without people noticing. I find that one special tower in the midst of the crumbling forest of towers. Only, the closer I get, the sicker I become.

I stagger across the rubble until the coughing sends me to my knees—and brings a coarse-voiced cluster of white uniforms to investigate.

Their faces are covered by smooth masks and bulging goggles, their hands gloved. At first, I'm relieved to be found by people and not monsters. Then they start to drag me toward the tower.

My energy gutters, eyelids fluttering with the effort to stay conscious. I've screwed up—bad. Mom and dad won't know what happened to me. I could end up in trouble for getting captured, instead of getting credit for saving the mission—But then I hear them shouting in the distance.

The uniformed strangers put me down and turn to watch my parents approach.

I'm exhausted and ill, but the sight still makes me smile. They are fierce and strong and beautiful, and when they're with me, everything is good.

Only, their steps slow well before they reach me, feet dragging, legs straining as if running through syrup. Their faces redden, the silver mist of a dreamwalker's magic thin and patchy over their skin. Dad drops into an offensive stance. I can't catch my breath enough to tell him it's fine— the strangers aren't hurting me. Mom places one hand on his back, but it doesn't look like she's trying to calm him as much as brace herself.

Threads coalesce around her fingers—and slip through her grasp.

I try to get up and go to them instead, but start coughing harder, lungs seizing, throat burning. Tears roll down my cheeks with the force of it. What happens next comes in the snapshots between blinks, fuzzy-edged and smeary.

The uniformed strangers leave me where I am and approach my parents. Only, something goes wrong. They start fighting. Whatever is affecting me seems to be hurting mom and dad too. They're too slow, too weak. Their connection to the dreamscape is the slightest sheen on their skin instead of the glittering cloud it should be, and they can barely hold on to their weapons.

I can't see what the strangers hold, but it knocks dad down first. And then mom is screaming. I would too, if I could just catch my breath.

Dad's just lying there on the ground, not moving. The strangers seem to be arguing, but I can't hear between the coughing and the screaming and the rushing and—then it's later. I'm being carried through a strange building.

Then it's later still, and the walls and ceiling have gone from dusty and grey to shiny and gold. Mom is there, but she's hurt. The uniformed strangers are there, too, and a really fancy dressed up lady with eyes the same shade of gold as the walls.

I can't hear her over the roaring, but she seems angry. My attention snags on a gold-eyed, black-haired boy staring at me from around the edge of a curtain.

This isn't right. We have to break the barrier. We're here to save the city

They should be welcoming us, helping us. Why are they angry? Why did they hurt mom? And—and dad. Where's dad?

Mom lies on the floor, not moving. Her power swirls, a dry, brittle-looking silver.

Then it drifts away.

I SURFACE FROM the memory, reeling. It wasn't the Mara's or even the mayor's fault my parents died, at least not entirely.

It was mine—Cadence's, I correct immediately.

We're the same, idiot, she thinks, chewing one ragged nail. *You're as much to blame for their deaths as I am.*

How could she keep this from me? Had she known the truth all along?

She shrugs. *I needed you to want to come back. I couldn't finish our mission without you.*

Our mission—I look around, disoriented at the way the world is visible in every direction all at once. The dimensions are all wrong. Flat yet somehow tilted and—when I focus—it's like I can see *through* things that definitely should be solid. The colours are wrong too—kind of faded and off-balance.

Her lips curl. *You'll get used to it. I did.*

Where are they? Did no one come back with us? For that matter, where are we?

There's been a change of plans.

Now I'm panicking—I think. It's harder to tell without all the usual signals. The itchy prickle of cold sweat, the dry mouth, the speeding pulse . . .

She sighs. *Bodies do have their inconveniences. I'd almost forgotten how gross dirt feels. You suck at basic hygiene, by the way.*

Did Ange make it? And the others—Did we save them? What happened?

She walks around a corner, and I realize what's been bothering me ever since I surfaced from her memories.

We're not surrounded by grit and grey concrete. Instead, we move through a landscape almost identical to the one I just left behind: all gilt and shimmer, polished mirrors reflecting golden light and opulent furnishings. We're in Maryam's domain.

What did you do?

She laughs, a low and bitter rasp. *Just completing the mission.*

If I had skin, I would have shivered at that laugh.

Our mission was to get back to Refuge and save as many as possible—first the refugees, and then everyone else we could reach, taking them across the barrier in any way we could manage.

There are only two reasons I can think of for her to be on this floor, and that's because she's saved everyone else while I was unconscious and come back to rescue Maryam as well— or there's no one else to left to save, and she's here to check one last room for survivors. Or, I suppose, to take revenge.

Wrong mission, Cadence thinks in an eerie singsong.

Then she swans into the glittering throne room of an audience chamber and takes the hand of the exquisite mayor of Refuge, who guides her into a chair at her side.

39

SCHEMES

Y SCREAMS GO unheard.

My screams go unheard.

Cadence sits upon a gleaming throne at the side of the woman who oversaw the murder of our parents and bestows a sharp-edged smile upon the visiting Mara. Silver frosts her skin and shines from her eyes.

She has the ability to *make* them bow—not in mocking deference, but in desperation for their very existence—and yet she does nothing.

The only revenge I can take is to torment her, and so I vow to devote every possible moment to doing so. I screech and babble and sing and howl until I'm sure she has a raging headache. But when the Mara go and Maryam leans in close to whisper in Cadence's ear, I'm too curious not to fall silent and listen in.

Cadence, it turns out, really is just as devoted to the mission as ever.

Only her mission dates back further than mine, to when she first came to this broken city—back to a child's understanding and a foolish plan with a tragic ending. Back to the memory that she had been hiding from me, from everyone—until now.

She didn't come back to Refuge to save anyone. She came back to destroy it.

That's not how she understands her mission, of course. Even now, she splits her focus arguing against me while simultaneously scheming with the devious mayor. She is who Maryam really wanted, all along—the one with the ability to end it. She's the one Maryam meant to summon, and the one who struck a deal behind my back in that mausoleum of a nursery.

Cadence decided then to use her memories and our powers to take control of our body. Maybe she even stole our magic from my control in the first place to make all of this possible.

I don't know how long she has been planning this. But her confidence in being the holder of all knowledge and power means she has underestimated me.

I know things too, now. I know she betrayed me, not just once, but over and over again. I know it was her fault our parents died. I know Maryam only ordered her enforcers to let me leave with Ash in the first place to isolate us and give Cadence the chance to seize the upper hand.

I know how guilt drives her to ever-greater destruction.

And now, I'm the ghost of our past who clings to existence only in the dreamscape. Unlike her, I am no longer limited by a clumsy, weak, needy, growing body. I don't need to sleep. And I'm nowhere near as alone as she thinks.

Cadence learned how to wield her abilities as a child. But I've been learning too, through pain and struggle and loss. And, because I've also been learning to listen, and to see, I know something else she doesn't.

Cadence and Maryam scheme to destroy the barrier around the city once and for all. They believe its destruction will obliterate the Mara and set us all free.

They're wrong. The Mara's hunger is only fenced in. It grows as they feed—but soon they will reach the end of their reserves of prey.

Which brings me to why Ash refused to deliver the help he'd promised—which he since apologized for. The forest's gift isn't easily dismissed. It followed me to the city on its own, mostly unaided by Ravel despite my suspicions, and it followed right me into the dreamscape, too, bringing the forest with it.

Unlike Cadence, my access to the dreamscape doesn't appear to be limited to our city alone. Thanks to that persistent bit of wood, I can talk to dreamwalkers beyond the city borders—well beyond. And they're eager to offer all the help they can.

But though he's now aware the full extent of Cadence's betrayal, Ash isn't coming to save us. Not because of the bargain he was forced into making to "save" my life, but for the same reason he wouldn't let the other dreamwalkers come to rescue me in the first place.

Though they could have made it across the barrier, they would have been too weak to protect themselves from both the Mara and Refuge Force lying in wait on the other side. If the Mara were to devour the strength of Nine Peaks' young, the monsters' power would be unstoppable.

And if the barrier is removed, they'll be unleashed onto the entire world.

I won't let that happen.

THE STORY CONTINUES in book three of the THREADS OF DREAMS trilogy, coming in 2021.

In the meantime, sign up at kaie.space/newsletter for biweekly updates and exclusive content including a free ebook of series prequel novella UNDER.

ACKNOWLEDGEMENTS

T O THE READERS who embrace the confused, overwhelmed, unmotivated characters *who just want to be left alone, thanks*—as well as the fun chaos-causing ones. Special thanks to Ashley of @adventurenlit for the unflagging enthusiasm!

To my parents, who continually amaze me with how supportive they are of my insane dreams.

To siblings, family, friends, and total strangers who graciously read the messy early drafts and slightly less messy later drafts and keep asking for more. Special thanks to Nancy for the enthusiasm and cheerleading, Kevin and Emily for the research notes, and Līssí for relentlessly pushing those 'ships.

To Lisa Poisso for guidance through the dark and twisty plotting woods, Catherine Milos for the diligent edit notes (as always, any and all errors are stubbornly my own) and Christian Bentulan for the tentacular designs amidst the pressures of a global pandemic.

To the one to whom I am always enough. I can't imagine life without you. I'm so grateful I've never had to.

And finally, to all the awkward, prickly kids out there who are afraid to try, who try too hard, who try and fail, who try and keep on trying. You're enough. You're not done yet. You never will be. But you're enough.

Keep fighting on.

ABOUT THE AUTHOR

K.A. WIGGINS IS a Vancouver-born Canadian speculative fiction writer, speaker, and creative writing coach.

Known for the 'climate change + monsters' YA dystopian dark fantasy series Threads of Dreams, her fiction has also been published in Enchanted Conversation Magazine, Frozen Wavelets by The Earthian Hivemind, and the Fiction-Atlas Press anthology *Unknown Worlds*.

Find her at kawiggins.com or @kaiespace on social.